# About The Author

Miller Caldwell is a Scottish-based novelist. He graduated from London University having studied African industrial development, traditional African religions and the colonial history of West Africa. He has had articles published in health magazines and The Scottish Review.

In a life of humanitarian work in Ghana, Pakistan and Scotland, he has gained remarkable insights into human nature. He brought an African President to tears in West Africa in 2000 and he confronted Osama bin Laden in Abbottabad in 2006. He retired from being the Regional reporter to the children's hearings as he had mild cognitive impairment. He was, for twelve years, the local chair of the Scottish Association for The Study of Offending. He also served on the committee of the Society of Authors in Scotland, as its events manager

Miller plays a variety of brass, woodwind and keyboard instruments. This is mentioned because they provide a break from writing. Married, he has two daughters and lives in Dumfries.

# The Trials of Sally Dunning
## and
# A
# Clerical Murder

Miller Caldwell

Matador
9 Priory Business Park,
Wistow Road, Kibworth Beauchamp,
Leicestershire. LE8 0RX
Tel: 0116 279 2299
Email: books@troubador.co.uk
Web: www.troubador.co.uk/matador
Twitter: @matadorbooks

ISBN 978 1788038 126

British Library Cataloguing in Publication Data.
A catalogue record for this book is available from the British Library.

Printed and bound by CPI Group (UK) Ltd, Croydon, CR0 4YY
Typeset in 12pt Adobe Jenson Pro by Troubador Publishing Ltd, Leicester, UK

Matador is an imprint of Troubador Publishing Ltd

*Dedicated To Robert and Eunice*

# Acknowledgements

Special thanks are due to David Watt, formerly of AFNOR (Association Française de Normalisation) - the equivalent of the BSI (British Standards Institute) in the UK. He is a translator, reviser and proof reader, who came to my aid and sorted out my muddling sentences. What a new friend he is indeed. To my dear friends Robert and Eunice without their support this book would not have seen the light of day. To my agent Mathilde Vuillermoz who keeps faith with me while answering all my demanding questions. And to Jocelyn who leaves me to daydream, walk the dog, garden, shop, and cook. In the process of these chores, I work out my next line.

# Contents

**The Trials of Sally Dunning**

# The Trials of Sally Dunning

A crime story about an autistic victim

# Introduction

In society the prevalence of mental disability has been much neglected in recent years. There are a plethora of ailments of the mind. I retired from work at the age of 53 on account of MCI. What? That's mild cognitive impairment. Within my own family there are relations with Bi-polar and dementia conditions. In fact, before we die we are almost certain to have some form of mental illness, or a developmental disability, even if it is just a peg or two along from the neutral position of the wellness continuum.

The protagonist in this tale, Sally, is a fifty-three year old woman. She is a very pleasant individual with a good sense of dress. She polishes her shoes with vigour each day. She shows a shy smile to all and sundry and those who see her delicate sweet face must assume there is a lucky man sharing her life.

Sally shares her life with her mother in their rambling Victorian mansion on the outskirts of Wigan in Lancashire. She helps her tidy her garden. She polishes her mother's car meticulously for her weekly outings to play Bridge and her daily shopping. To all intents and purposes, Sally and her mother are good neighbours even although the nearest house is five hundred yards away.

However when Sally was born she received too much oxygen. This meant her brain was affected and now she has the learning age and personality of a ten year old. She also suffers from an Autism Syndrome Disorder (ASD). This definition encompasses cases of Autism and Asperger's syndrome. It is the term for the learning disabilities which affect 2.8 million people in the UK.

This protagonist's character is based on two people. Firstly there is my 65 year old cousin, Brian, who was blinded at birth. He has a mental age and ability of a ten year old. That personality is added to the autistic friend I have recently acquired as a friendly neighbour.

# 1

# Lost

She was lost. She wasn't used to this situation. She was a methodical woman whose daily chores did not deviate much from day to day. Yet she could not explain where or why she was there that night. Devotion to an ailing mother was her only concern and her current predicament could not help her.

She was in Wigan, of that she was sure. It was after all, the town she was born in fifty three years ago, yet she was sure she was lost. Dark shadows followed her that night. The suspicious trees whispered but gave no valuable information. It was eerie. She stood still. She looked around.

She tried to remember where she had been. It was simply an evening walk that had gone so terribly wrong she recalled. She did not wander late at night normally. What she realised now was everything took on a different perspective in the dark. When she saw the entrance to the Plantations something attracted her to its path. Maybe it was the bark of a friendly dog or a whistle. She could not remember. Perhaps the silent flight of an owl caught her attention. Whatever it was had led her to her present distress.

There was no shortcut home she realised and she was now deep into the park. She was unsure how to retrace her steps. Then she saw clouds part and the half-moon appeared, lighting up a passing veil of a cloud. It gave sufficient light for her to realise she was close to the Douglas River in Wigan's Plantations but the stream's course wound round and round again, giving no direction to solve her predicament.

'Y'll right, luv? Ye lost?' a voice approaching from behind said in a curt manner. The girl wore black. Trousers, jacket and peaked skip, all were black. Her trainers were lighter, with splashed mud on both shoes. Her peaked cap was back to front. The girl, probably around her mid-twenties, stood close to Sally. She repeated herself. Then her eyes flirted from side to side.

'Yes, lost,' said Sally standing slightly bent, shaking her arms and focussing her eyes somewhere beyond the girl.

'You mean you are lost or have you lost your dog?' she asked looking around.

'No. No dog. I don't have a dog. I had a cat. It died. I'm lost.'

The woman realised this was not a usual conversation. Perhaps she was just gullible, soft, an easy touch, perhaps even an easy target. The sort of person she could find useful or ...maybe....perhaps she was, just lost.

'So where do you live?' she asked raising her eyebrows at this enigmatic individual.

Sally hesitated. She took a moment to reply to this stranger. She gazed at her with the eye of the cautious. No, she had never seen her before.

'Leyland Mill Lane,' she eventually said tugging at her jerkin sleeve.

'Okay, follow me, luv,' the girl said turning round and flipping her cap once more to the front.

Sally was pleased to have been found and more than happy to be on her way home with her rescuer.

'What's your name?' Sally asked in a very direct manner.

The young woman looked at Sally for a moment.

'My name's Donkey,' she said with a tease of a smile.

'Donkey?' Sally's lips widened a little. Perhaps a joke was about to hit her. Would she understand it?

'Yeah Donkey, it's my nickname. Have you got one?'

Sally had had nicknames in the distant past; Stupid, Dafty, Dreamy, Spaceman but these did not last long once the joke was out. The teachers made sure of that. Nor were they names she wanted to keep.

'Nicknames? No, I've no nickname. I'm Sally.'

They continued in silence until the gates of the park were behind them. Traffic flowed both ways; many cars had recently left the hospital car park just out of sight to the left, and were now joining the busy night traffic. Taxis, buses and cars mingled. The Panda crossing gave a quiet buzz on its night duty as a man crossed with his poodle, on his late night walk.

'I know where I am now,' said Sally with the excitement of a child playing hide-and-seek.

Donkey looked around, lowering the peak of her cap closer to her eyes.

'Best make sure I get you home safely.'

'Yes, home safely, to mum,' she replied shaking her hands once again.

7

They crossed the road. Donkey took out a cigarette from her jacket pocket and lit it.

'Want one?' she said offering a cigarette protruding from its packet.

'No, I don't want one.'

'You mean, you don't want one now?' she asked with a slightly threatening voice.

'No, not one now.'

'Have you ever smoked?' Donkey asked drawing in the cigarette's smoke.

'No, I've never smoked,' she replied looking straight ahead holding her breath.

Donkey replaced the rejected cigarette back into her Regal packet of twenty and from her torn pocket brought out another. It was not white; it was a hand rolled brown reefer. She lit it.

'Here, try this. If you've never had one you won't know if you like it.'

Sally's shoulders were tense but her hand reached out. She did not want to displease her rescuer. She took her first puff. She did not inhale; she just puffed and spluttered out the weed's smoke.

Donkey smiled. 'That's ma girl. Good isn't it?'

Sally smiled back, still anxious to please her rescuer. She was reluctant to return the joint to her lips again but she did so, a couple of minutes later, as its length decreased.

Donkey put her hand into her other inside jerkin pocket. Her fingers fumbled around. 'Like the cinema?' she asked.

'Cinema, the pictures? I've not gone for a long time.'

'You'd really enjoy A Man called Ove. It's a comedy. It will make you laugh. Okay, here's the ticket, luv,' she said thrusting it into Sally's midriff.

The ticket was now in her hand. She looked at it with confusion. 'I can't pay now.'

'You don't have to pay. Hey, we're friends. I've an extra ticket anyway. A friend couldn't come. Donkey keeps her friends,' she said thumping her back.

Sally was initially unsure how to react. Her social skills were restricted. But in time she saw the sentiment as sincere and so nodded profusely, smiled her agreement to this new relationship and said so formally.

'Thank you very much,' she said at last, placing her cinema ticket in her gloved hand.

Eight minutes later, they were on the outskirts of town, it was now a 40 mph zone. Sally pointed down the road.

'I live along here.'

Donkey's eyes closed in concentration. She saw no house lights ahead.

'I'll see you home, best that way. There's not much lighting around here.'

'No, not good lighting.'

They proceeded until they reached Sally's drive. It was a long snaking path with a large Victorian house situated at the top of the incline.

'You live here, luv?' asked Donkey in disbelief.

'Yes, with my mother.'

Donkey looked at the dark foliage as they progressed up the drive. She noticed good cover if needed.

She saw the detached stone-built three story dwelling. Ivy gripped its front wall. Her eyes lingered on the white painted bay windows at the front, and then they drifted upwards to the attic in the red tiled roof. Moonlight seemed to shed light through the window onto a low light canopy. Possibly a snooker table was up there, Donkey concluded with a tight grin. A double garage joined the building with a modest five-seater Vauxhall Meriva under its roof. Sally's house seemed palatial to her.

'Bet your house is worth a million.'

'Yes, I think so.'

Donkey held her breath 'So you are a wealthy woman?' she said shaking her head in disbelief.

'Yes. My dad died and left me a lot of money.'

Donkey could hardly hide the smile breaking out over her face. Sally's words were like music to her ears. She was onto a winner. Sally was not a potential drug courier after all. Instead Donkey sensed a golden goose.

'Okay Sally. 7.30 p.m. on Saturday night. We'll meet you at the Empire Cinema centre. Anjou Boulevard. Know where I mean?'

'Yes, at Robin Park.'

'That's it. Oh, by the way, I'll be with my partner, okay?' Donkey said hoping Sally could accept this arrangement.

'Your partner?' enquired Sally.

'Yes, I've lots of friends,' smiled Donkey patting her shoulder.

Sally wondered who her friend might be. Would she know him? She asked anyway.

'Bones is what he's called.'

Sally smiled. 'Nickname?'

'Yeah, it's his nickname. He's my partner.'

Before Sally went to bed that night, she told her mother she had made a new friend. She had found her when she was lost and had brought her home and what's more she had given her a cinema ticket. Her eyebrows were arched and her smile extended from ear to ear at the prospect of the film. Her fingers shook in excitement. Then she waved the ticket before her mother's eyes.

'It's for Saturday. She's going with me, Mum. We'll meet at the Empire cinema.'

Her mother Elsie smiled. She approached her daughter and gave her a hug. 'That was very kind of her,' she said. A glow of happiness came over her on hearing the news of a thoughtful new friend for her autistic daughter.

'Yes, mum. Donkey is very kind.'

'Donkey?' she asked with a tortured look.

'Yes, mum. She has a nickname.'

'Oh, I see,' she said with a degree of relief. 'That's unusual,' she concluded.

Elsie walked through to the wall calendar behind the kitchen door and made a note of Sally's outing to the cinema on Saturday. Beside it she wrote: Prepare sandwiches for Sally and her new friend.

# 2

# Nicknames

Sally's bedroom was almost stark. Her walls were white and clean. Her bed had a conservative grey and blue diagonal stripe and matching pillow. Her bedside desk offered the only other insight into her life for she had harmonicas in every major key laid out in size-ranking order on the wooden surface. Speakers were inserted into the wall and a stack of CDs towered up past the end of the orange and blue floating balloon curtains. Sally spent hours playing her harmonicas. She played classical, folk, traditional and marching tunes. She played by ear and she was attuned to any song which Chris Evans or Ken Bruce played on BBC Radio 2 in the morning, as well as all the programmes Classic FM had to offer, both in the afternoon and at night.

Sally's siblings were not at home. Her older sister Becky treated skin conditions as a NHS consultant dermatologist in Manchester and her brother, Alec, was professor of Chemical Engineering at Bristol University. Sally had little idea what that entailed but she knew her brother had travelled all over the Far East sorting old and failing chemical installations. But now she knew he taught at the university. The Dunnings met at the family home at the usual Christmas and Easter seasonal events.

Thanks to her dark blue Opel, Becky was able to visit more regularly calling round to see her mother and to lavish love on her sister Sally. She always had a cuddle for her.

On Saturday after tea Sally set off to the cinema, with a bag of mixed sandwiches. She walked down Spencer Road as cars passed her by. She wondered how many of them would be going to the comedy film.

After twenty minutes walking she was in Robin Park approaching the Regal Multi Film centre where she would be meeting Donkey and her partner Bones. Donkey and Bones, Donkey and Bones, she was sure to remember their names.

She reached Anjou Boulevard and stood at the steps leading to the cinema. Her stance was straight and motionless, her sight focussed in the distance, not wavering. Like a boulder in a river, she stood against the human flow. This posture attracted comments.

'This way to the films dear,' said one passer-by pointing up the steps.

'Turn round and go with the flow,' said a laughing couple of young lads in torn jeans.

'Fancy a snog with me in the back row?' a spot flecked youth challenged. Sally ignored him as she ignored any remark which she thought was not directed specifically towards her.

Others showed some pity with head slanted gentle smiles, but Sally only scanned the faces to find her two new friends. She began to bite her left sleeve. It was now 7.25 p.m. She turned to look the other way. She studied her cinema ticket and her heart began to race.

Her choices were stark. She could make for the stairs and find her seat. Surely her new friends would join her. But they might be angry at her for not waiting and that caused her to clench her teeth and hands. Decisions were not Sally's strength. Her feet began to march on the spot.

The stream of film goers dwindled. There was still no sight of Donkey and Bones. Her vision remained piercing, like a needle through a button's hole. She remained fixed looking right. So it was a shivering shock when her shoulder was thumped by a solid solitary hand. She turned round and smiled.

'Hi Sally. This is Bones.'

Sally nodded. 'Hello Bones. I like your nickname.'

Bones remained silent. He smiled gingerly at Sally.

Donkey winked at Bones. It was the signal that Donkey was right about her new friend acting gullible. Bones' smile enlarged, creasing his eyes in the process.

'Okay, let's go, the ads will be finished soon,' he said.

Sally sat with Donkey on her left and Bones further away. Every now and then a joke or a humorous act got the audience shrieking. Sally looked round about her each time.

Donkey nudged her. 'Enjoying it?' she asked.

Without her eyes leaving the screen, Sally replied.

'Yes, I like it.'

After twenty minutes had elapsed, Sally remembered the knapsack she had in her hand.

She opened it and produced a Tupperware box of sandwiches. They were egg and chives, tuna and cucumber, ham and mustard. Donkey grabbed a couple of ham sandwiches and Bones took both tuna leaving egg and chives for Sally. Was this her mother's intention? Sally had hoped they would share the sandwiches. Her face screwed up. She then handed out three chocolate digestives which were gratefully received, but only Sally ate fruit. She gathered grapes in her hand. She offered them to her friends.

'Grapes are for monkeys,' said Donkey and Bones agreed. Sally wondered if that was a joke as she popped them in her mouth.

An hour and a half later the credits began to roll. Donkey and Bones rose from their seats and turned right. When they got to the end of the row and turned to join the advancing column of people, they noticed Sally was still watching the credits, her stare as fixed as the seat she sat on.

'Sally, c'mon,' said Donkey motioning with her hand.

Sally heard her name and diverted her eyes from the screen.

'I want to see the end of the film,' she declared.

She saw Donkey looking embarrassed, making the advancing picture goers crush like the neck of a bottle. Bones took a deep breath ready to enforce Donkey's command but Donkey put her finger to her pursed lips.

'Bones, it's alright, luv. You wait outside. I'll bring her.'

Bones nodded, remembering the need to keep Sally on their side. He smiled at her then proceeded to mount the stairs and he then disappeared into the foyer.

Donkey returned to her seat beside Sally. She

15

waited watching the best-boy and the grip employees being named in the credits. Then the companies which made the film possible appeared as the music came to a crescendo and ended.

Only when the curtains advanced to hide the screen did Sally accept the film was over. She got up briskly motioning to Donkey to move. It took her by surprise but she was equally surprised to see more than a handful of the audience had stayed to the curtain call and they were now, like them, on their way out of the cinema, without a crush.

The trio met outside in a shower of rain.

'C'mon, let's go the Tuning Fork cafe in the Wallgate. It's not far, not far at all.'

They entered the cafe and ruffled dry their hair. They sat at the rear of the shop.

'What do you want, Sally?'

'I want a coke.'

'I'll have a coffee and bacon roll,' said Donkey and Bones nodded to confirm he'd have the same. The waitress came and took their orders and as she turned to go, Donkey looked at Sally.

'You got enough to pay for this?'

'Yes, I've got my wallet. I can pay.'

Donkey turned to Bones and gazed at him. Bones gave a gentle but devious lip curving smile.

'Did I tell you Bones is an accountant?'

'An accountant? No, you did not tell me. You mean is that a banker?' asked Sally turning to stare at her partner Bones.

'I'm not a banker. I said I'm an accountant. I deal

in gilts and foreign currencies; those sorts of things you know?'

'I see. Do you work in London?' asked an impressed Sally, shaking with delight.

'London? No, I save a lot of money not working in London. I work from home, by computer. No rented offices involved. You see?'

A nod of agreement could have sufficed but it never arrived. Sally's mind was elsewhere. 'I don't work, I look after Mum.'

Bones drew his chair nearer and lowered his voice.

'Wouldn't it be good if you could have a lot of money to make life comfortable? You know, after your mother is no longer there, Yeah?'

'I've got some money for that.'

Bones' eyes looked up at Donkey and she nodded her approval. It was the queue to go for the jugular.

'You see Sally,' said Bones lowering his voice to a mere whisper, 'You can never have enough money. I guess your money would run out after a few years. You just can't assume you have enough. I can make £500 double in six months by playing the market.' He sat back with a broad smile for a brief moment. Then he bent forward again with his elbows on the table and in a normal voice told her, 'all legal of course.'

The waitress returned with a tray and deposited its contents before them. Donkey and Bones remained quiet while Sally digested the figures she had just heard.

'That's a lot of money to make in a short time,' she said.

Bones and Donkey nodded at the same time. The

waitress deposited the bill on a saucer and placed it on the table.

'Just think what interest the bank gives. Very little. I can beat that any day,' resumed Bones when the coast was clear.

'How?' asked Sally.

'I speculate on the market. I never make a mistake, do I Donkey, luv?'

'He's made us wealthy. We invested £2,000 and it got us £3,500 in a year, easy money. And if you are not working Sally, then this is your lucky day. Isn't it?' asked Donkey.

Sally felt lucky. She knew some people had lots of money and they always had financial people behind them. With no feelings of doubt in her mind, she made her mind up. 'Yes, my lucky day,' she repeated smiling at the cafe ceiling.

'So listen Sally, you give me..... let's say £500 and in six months you get it back twice as much. Now that makes sense, doesn't it?' asked Bones.

Sally resumed her stare at him. She nodded with her mouth wide open. 'So, I send you a cheque in the post. You give me your address and I'll send the cheque in the post,' she repeated.

Donkey held onto Sally's sleeve as it reached for her cup. She lowered her voice once more. 'Cheques are not good. They can get lost in the post. Take longer to clear through the bank, longer to make money. Cash is best.'

She let go of Sally's arm. Sally took a sip then replaced her cup on the saucer. She had to agree with her. 'Cash is best, yes isn't it?'

Bones took the bill-bearing saucer and slid it towards Sally's plate. 'Yup I always deal in cash. Ready cash talks, Sally. Ready cash brings in the profits you understand?'

Sally nodded pleased with her accountant friend's advice.

'So Sally, let's do it. You bring me £500 and let's make it grow,' said Bones whose encouraging smile comforted Donkey.

'Where will I bring the money?'

'What about the top of Spencer Road by the letter box 7.30 p.m. on Monday night? That will give you time to get the money.'

A visit to the bank on Monday morning, Sally concluded, yes that was okay. But another night out might get her lost again. She gave it some thought. 'You could come to my house. My Mum would like to meet you I am sure,' suggested a contented Sally.

Bones was quick to respond with a slight frown on his brow.

'Listen Sally, you are a mature woman. You don't want your mother to know what you are doing with your own money, do you? This is your money we're talking about not hers. Keep it a secret. Then when we've made you your first million, you can tell her. Now, how does that sound?'

Sally felt she was being treated properly. She processed the making money in her mind. A million pounds, she had heard Bones say. An image of a car full of notes came to her mind. 'Top of Spencer road 7.30 p.m.' she said nodding and shaking her hands robustly with Bones at the same time.

Bones and Donkey raised their collars as they parted from the cafe. 'Don't forget, to pay the waitress, Sally,' said Donkey.

'Okay I'll pay her now,' she replied as she got up and approached the counter. Her friends kept the door open, waiting for her.

'Bit chilly,' said Donkey ramming her hands into her well-worn jacket pockets. Sally mimicked their collar-raising on the pavement as they made their separate ways home.

Sally related the film as best she remembered to her mother and she showed polite interest, not having understood the storyline. When Sally mentioned her new friend, Donkey's partner, was an accountant, her mother smiled and gave Sally a cuddle.

'Your new friend's an accountant? That's wonderful. I hope you will stay pals with them for a very long time,' she said. 'They have been very kind to you,' she continued as her face creased in a broad smile.

'Yes Mum, they are.'

# 3

# Codes and Numbers

Inspector Mark Rawlings was the lead officer in the Drugs Squad at Wigan. His name was emblazoned on his door in highly polished brass. His dark blue suit and gleaming black shoes gave the impression that he was a graduate heading ever upwards. The truth was, until earlier this year, Sergeant Rawlings was the lead raid man dressed more like a road sweeper as he barged through front doors and leapt up stairs to make drug arrests. He had earned his promotion.

He removed his glasses and wiped them with his tie. 'Gentlemen, I'm pleased to report in this past month there has been a dip in housebreaking, fewer violent crimes and crimes of a sexual nature. However credit card frauds and the black market are still on the rise - the new cash for drugs. But not all are onto it yet. What's the talk of the streets, Jim?'

Sergeant Jim Boyd stretched his neck upwards. Thirty years service meant he could consider retiring but he loved his job. He was the quintessential street Bobby known to all the kids, their parents and their parents too for that matter; such were the restricted breeding habits of his patch, a deprived area of town.

'The Brownlees are quiet and so too are Eck and Tam Barker. No real news of 'Donkey' Riley or 'Bones' Ritchie.'

'Sounds good but maybe Bones and Donkey are inside still,' queried Officer Paul Rice.

The inspector grinned and shook his head. 'No such luck, they have been out for six weeks already. In fact, I saw them at the Regal cinema the other night. More suitable recreation at last perhaps,' commented Inspector Rawlings. Then the officer gave a thoughtful stare and caressed his chin. 'Or the lull before the storm might be more likely,' he concluded. His remark caused head nodding agreement.

Sally had gone to her bank earlier in the day. Her request was clearly stated. The teller made her enquiry. 'Is this you having a party then, Sally?'

Sally smiled at the thought of a party. Maybe she'd have a party when her next birthday fell. 'No, it's not for a party,' she said. 'The bank does not give a good return,' she said recalling what Bones had told her. The teller raised her eyebrows and agreed. '£500 is quite a sum, though.'

Sally's knuckles began to tap the counter.

'I have to give it to my accountant. He will make the money grow.'

'I see,' said the teller. 'I don't blame you. Some of our other customers are doing that too,' she said collecting the money and flicking through the notes like a threshing harvester ensuring the right amount was handed over.

Her business at the bank was over from the moment she received the money. With no other town interests she returned home satisfied she had obtained the right amount of money.

On Monday night Sally made her way at 7.20 p.m. to the red pillar box. True to their word Bones and Donkey arrived on time with welcoming smiles fixed on their faces. They greeted Sally warmly patting her back. Bones gave Sally a kiss on her cheek. She smiled at him feeling he had made her feel very special. However no preamble was forthcoming. Such was their way. They came directly to the point.

'Have you got the money, Sally, luv?'

Sally did not answer. Rather she put her hand into her blue jerkin and pulled out a letter.

'It's for you,' she smiled, 'from my mother.'

Bones' face went white. Donkey snatched the letter in disbelief. To her this meant their golden egg was cracked. The fortune was slipping from their grasp. She tore the envelope open and pulled out a card.

'What does it say?' asked a worried Bones.

A smile came over Donkey's face.

'Aww, how nice of her. Do thank her from us both,' she said, handing the card over to Bones.

Bones was more relaxed as he read her mother's appreciation for finding her daughter when she was lost and taking her to see the film. 'That was very kind of her indeed,' said Bones. 'I'll put it up on our mantelpiece when we get home,' he said stuffing the card into the back pocket of his jeans.

'So the money Sally, you got it?'

'Yes, here it is.'

'Is it £500?' asked Bones impatiently.

'Yes, £500,' she replied in a loud voice, upset to think she could have short-changed him.

Nevertheless Bones took hold of the bundle of notes and opened out the money. He counted it himself.

'You won't regret this Sally,' said Bones still flipping his dirty fingers through five hundred pounds.

'I can't do this every week,' said Sally.

'No, no, of course not. We don't want to make you poor while your money is growing every day. We won't let that happen, honest, Sally,' said Donkey in an actor's caring voice.

'No, no you don't understand. I am going on holiday with my Mum soon.' Sally's announcement ignited her tic as her hands started to tremble and her rocking stance took off.

Donkey and Bones looked at one another. They saw a necessary break in their illicit gold pot income. But two weeks away was not the end of their business with Sally. It was only a time to cool off.

'So where are you going?'

'We are going to Malta,' she said continuing with her rocking back and forward on her toes and heels with her eyes fixed on Donkey who had asked the question.

'Malta, that's in the Mediterranean Sea, isn't it?' questioned Donkey.

'Yes. It will be warm,' Sally said with a look into the sky to a warm place, far from Wigan.

'Oh yes, very warm. You will enjoy it,' said Bones.

Donkey was oddly animated. Her face was flushed

and she had a strange glow in her eyes. 'So,' she said turning to Sally. 'Will there be anyone looking after the house while you are away?'

'No, no one.'

'I see. Well, you had better put your burglar alarm on then luv,' suggested Bones looking thoughtful and catching his co-conspirator's eye.

'Yes, we will.'

Bones looked up to the sky. 'We often play a game. Usually at home when there's nothing on the telly, you know, something to do.'

'Oh, which game? I love games,' said Sally.

'Let me give you an example,' said Donkey looking up at the star flecked sky. 'So we were talking about security codes. So Sally, I try to guess yours. Is it 9876?'

'No it's not,' she replied clenching her fists in excitement.

'I know what it is,' said Donkey, obviously familiar with this game. 'It's 1234, isn't it?'

Sally laughed quietly. 'No, it isn't.'

'Don't be silly Donkey, that's our house code,' said Bones.

'So it is,' said Donkey punching her fist into the palm of her hand.

'I give up.'

'Both wrong, cos it's 3629,' said Sally triumphantly. 'It's my Mum's birthday. Third of June 1929.'

'Got that Donkey? 3629, Sally's Mum's birthday. That's a good one Sally,' said Bones, trying to hide his excitement. 'We'll get her a card on her next birthday. But don't tell her, like. Keep it a surprise, luv.'

Sally smiled at their thoughtfulness. 'Can we play again?' asked Sally.

Donkey shook her head but Bones raised his hand and nodded gently. 'Okay Sally, let's guess what month you were born. Okay?'

'Yes, that will be good.'

'Is it March?

'No.'

Bones placed his index finger on the point of his chin. 'Then it is July?'

Sally laughed. 'No.'

'I know, said Donkey. It is December.'

Sally laughed almost uncontrollably. 'No, not December.'

Bones sucked in a breath of tobacco. As he exhaled he said June.

'Yes, 5th June,' she said. 'You got it.'

Bones and Donkey laughed as if this was the best game ever invented.

'Can we play again asked, Sally?'

'I think we've had enough of that game now. I'm still thinking about you swimming in the Mediterranean Sea, Sally.' It was time to delve deeper into this holiday.

'So when are you going to Malta?'

Sally's hands started to flap by her side involuntarily.

'12th April....quite soon.'

'That's only three weeks away,' said Bones.

'Yes, I think so.'

'Got your swimming costume packed then, Sally?' asked Donkey laughing.

'No, not yet, but I will.'

They walked further along the road. Donkey lit up a cigarette from Bones' fag embers. She offered one to Sally who refused. Donkey stared at Sally for a long hard moment.

'Not been getting lost recently, I hope, luv?' he asked.

'No, not recently.'

The memory of their first meeting brought a smile to Sally's face.

'Think, had you not been lost, we would not have met and now you are going to be rich. That's what friends are for, not so?'

'Yes, ......I don't have many friends.'

'That's all right,' said Bones. 'You don't need many friends but you do need good friends, like Donkey and me.'

Sally's smile was cat-like seeing a bowl of milk. As she walked along with them her head began to nod. She appeared to be in a world of her own. She was.

Donkey took out her phone. 'Let's keep in touch. What's your phone number Sally?'

Sally poked around her pockets for her phone. 'I don't use my phone much.'

Donkey looked up from hers. 'But you've got a phone haven't you?' she asked with concern.

Sally produced her mobile phone. Donkey took it. She looked at it in disgust.

'Very basic. No camera? Let's see,' she said scrolling down the contact list.

'You've not got many contacts, Sally.'

'No, not many contacts.'

'Is Becky your girlfriend?' Donkey enquired with a mischievous grin.

Sally laughed nervously. 'No, Becky is my sister.'

'Okay, I see. Then you have a brother too?'

'Yes, I have a brother.'

Bones took note. 'Alec, that right?'

'Alec is my brother.'

'So that's your family; mother, brother and sister, yeah?' he said handing the phone back to Sally.

'And Boris?' said Sally.

'Boris? Who is that?' asked a bewildered Bones.

'That's my sister's dog. Boris is a Great Dane.'

Bones looked up at Sally and smiled but kept silent. There was no need to ask why Boris was on the contact list. Donkey laughed and Sally looked empty.

'Don't phone many folk then?'

'No, but they phone me lots of times.'

'So why don't you use your contacts list?'

'I don't need to,' she said indignantly.

Donkey's puzzled face challenged Sally's assertion. 'It makes life easier if you use a list of contact numbers, you know.'

'Don't need a list. I told you. I know them all.'

'What?' asked an astounded Bones as Sally instantly began to fire out the mobile numbers and names of her nieces and nephews, one after the other. Then came the butcher's number and finally the milkman's. Donkey smiled at Sally's ability on show.

'That's amazing. You've got a great memory Sally,' said Bones.

'Yes, I've a good memory.'

Donkey's mind was racing ahead. 'So what's your phone number then?'

'It's 07194286791.'

Three days later Sally's phone rang as she was playing her harmonica in the key of D. She came to the end of the tune before picking up her phone and just before Bones switched his off after a two minute wait.

'Sally?'

'Yes, is that Bones?'

'Yes, were you, on the loo?'

'No, not on the loo.'

'Hmmm...so, why the long wait? I nearly switched off.'

'I was playing music.'

Bones' mouth was ajar in disbelief. 'You could have put the sound down or off.'

There was a brief hesitation. 'No, I was playing real music.'

'What? You mean you were playing something?'

'Yes my harmonica. I was playing Are You Going to Scarborough Fair.'

'Okay, never mind. I'm phoning you to let you know your money is making great progress. And...wait for it....I can even make you much more. Interested?'

'Much more?'

'Can't say exactly but we are sure to be talking at least double.'

'Then yes, I'm interested,' she said clutching her harmonica.

'Okay let's meet again before you go on holiday. Same place on Spencer Road, same time and bring another £500. That way your £1,000 will go much further, I promise you, luv.'

'Okay, same time and place with £500.'

'Yep, tomorrow evening. You can get the cash tomorrow morning. You won't regret it, Sally. I'm your friend, the accountant and we're making you rich, ain't we?'

'Yes, making me rich.'

'So that piece of music, can you play it again. I'll listen in.'

'Yes, I'll play it beside my phone so you hear it.'

'Great.'

Sally began to play note perfect as usual but before she had got to the seventh bar, Bones had switched off his phone. His latest deal had been achieved. Simon and Garfunkel was not his scene.

The following morning Sally returned to the bank. The same bank teller was in front of her.

'Another £500? Seems your accountant is onto a good investment,' she said. 'Perhaps I should be using him too.'

'Yes, he's very good,' said Sally gathering the money bag and leaving with it stuffed in her jeans pocket.

The next night Sally returned to the post box on Spencer Road. It was a collar raised, slouching, stare-at your-shoes drizzly night. Her two friends arrived without any meaningful waterproofs and looked miserable as the rain dripped from their noses.

'Hi, what a night, luv,' said Donkey.

'Yes, not nice,' said Sally.

'Anyway I've got a surprise for you. Here's fifty

pounds, a good will gesture for your holiday, just to show we are serious about making you money'.

'Yes, making me money. Thank you,' she said putting the money in her purse.

Sally then took from her inside jacket pocket another plastic bag of notes.

'Thanks Sally, it will be making money tomorrow morning,' Bones said, squeezing the notes to gauge the £500 content. Counting days were over with Sally. She was ever so obliging.

'That's good,' said Sally raising a smile as her hair dripped rain.

'Just one thing on my mind, Sally,' began Donkey carefully choosing her words. 'About you going away, best put an extra key somewhere. I put mine under a flowerpot in my greenhouse when I am away. That way I can't possibly lose my keys when I return. So that's what I do when we go to our cottage, you see.'

'What cottage?'

'The cottage. It's in the Highlands of Scotland, near Oban. We've got a holiday home there. Overlooks the sea, so it does.'

'That's nice.'

'Yes, it is. All from our profits. The ones you are starting to make right now, as I breathe. We can take you there someday when we have time. Can't we Bones?' she asked nodding her head to encourage agreement. Bones reciprocated with a teeth clenched, closed mouth smile and many nods, without a word. His thoughts were elsewhere in the real world.

Sally was relaxed. She showed no signs of her

twitching or shaking episodes. It seemed the right time for Bones to home in on their next plan.

'So Sally, what do you do with your keys when you are away?' asked Bones, looking nonchalant and away from her.

'It's only the back door key we hide,' said Sally rocking to and fro ever so slightly. Was this a sign of anxiety thought Bones?

'Yeah, no need to hide both front and back,' agreed Donkey. 'So, where do you hide the back door key?' she persisted.

Sally had a little hesitation in replying. Her thoughts were not entirely clear but her mother had shown her where the key was hidden and it was their secret key. But Sally thought the game they had played the other day was the same as this game and so she made the fatal mistake. 'It's a secret key. It's under a slate stone by the pansy bed.'

'Good place Sally. No one could find it there,' said Bones glancing at Donkey.

Donkey's face cracked into an all-too-familiar smile.

The rain slackened off. The air was cool.

'Warmer air in Malta, Sally,' said Bones.

'Yes,' said Sally looking contented. 'I am going to Malta. Quite soon now.'

On that note, they parted. As soon as Sally was out of sight Donkey punched the air. 'Yes, yes,' she said.

Bones offered a high five and Donkey crashed her palm into his.

'God, she's gullible,' said Bones.

'Yeah, this could run for a very long time,' Donkey said kicking a stone from the pavement onto the road.

Bones tapped the notes, now in his side pocket. 'There's no telling how much we can make. Perhaps we should have a sunny holiday while she's away.'

'Yeah, but I've no passport.'

'Passport? You need a passport to go on holiday?'

# 4

# When the Cat is Away

Bones and Donkey were now flush with drugs. They would last them some considerable time. And when Sally came back, the golden goose would continue to feed their drug needs. It was a good time for them. It was time to sell what they could.

They were well known in their community. In fact so many took drugs because their parents took drugs and that older generation knew how to keep 'mum' when the police were trying to clean up the town of its drug problem. To the couple of crooks, drugs were not a problem. They were the source of income which supplemented their unemployment benefit. But their activities hardly made them unemployed.

Visits to the Charnock Richard motorway services were one drug pick-up point used frequently. Their courier was from Southport where he was the distributor for the north west of England. His name was of course a nickname too. He was called Vivaldi because this courier played the violin. In reality he was sacked from being the violinist of the Parbold String Quartet as he defrauded the quartet of £2,750 this sum being the lottery funding for their tour expenditure. He was given a six month prison sentence and was dropped from the musical group immediately on his release. He found it difficult to be employed again as a convicted fraudster and so he slipped into the world of drugs. He did not take drugs himself. Indeed he had a very healthy lifestyle but as needs must, he had heard that a driver was required and the advert led him to Donkey. He was a dark suited gentleman, diligent and keen to service the drug couple's needs. They paid him well. He presented as a man who knew nothing about drugs and that was a bonus for Donkey. He did however know what his cargo was. He devised his cover too.

Apart from playing the violin, he also had a cello in the rear of his car and that was where the drugs were hidden. His cover was that of a violinist. If challenged by an inquisitive policeman he would render an impromptu piece of classical music. Few would doubt at that point he was not a member of the Harborne Strings of Birmingham which would be a further ruse he could offer.

Distribution in Wigan was easy for Donkey and Bones. They had a contact at the Wigan and Leigh NHS hospital where a regular supply of cocaine was appreciated by weekend members of the medical profession. They paid well, not just for the drugs but to ensure they kept the service secret and would never be compromised. That was their most lucrative source. There was also a duty to provide the local drug dependent community's requirements and time passed as they performed this community service. Hash, cocaine and amphetamines always had a ready market as did K2 Spice. Bones and Donkey were seen as the drug dukes of their community and lips were sealed when the authorities probed. Social workers, advice centres and police were seen as the enemy. It was a highly structured community, dependent on each other yet one in a deprived area of town enduring ever increasing levels of deprivation and poor health.

Elsie and Sally were conveyed to Manchester airport by Becky. Ten days relaxing in the sun with meals at the hotel, poolside coffees and drinks. It was to be a leisurely holiday where relaxation and sun would be the sources of contentment. And not a worry or concern filled their minds as the plane's wheels left the tarmac and soared into the white Cheshire clouds.

Their departure date had been noted by Bones and Donkey. On the first Tuesday evening as dusk began to fall, Bones and her co-conspirator made their way to Leyland Mill Lane. No one was around. They made their way up the bushy drive to find the Victorian home in darkness, as expected.

The men went round the rear of the house and were horrified to see a light in a house much nearer than they expected. It stood at right angles to Sally's home down on the other side of the hill. It would be risky if lighting in the house was used. Perhaps their neighbours knew they were away. They took out their torches and covered their beams with dark socks. They approached the pansy flower bed on tip toes making sure they implanted no shoe prints. Sure enough a back door key was there waiting for them under the slate. They smiled at each other. Sally was true to her word. Each gave the other a thumbs-up fist-knocking moment.

They looked through the dining room window. The door was closed. No sign of the alarm box. They went round the house looking in each ground floor window but the alarm was still not in sight.

'We've got to get in and listen to where the alarm is counting down. You got the number in your head?'

'Sure have, Donkey. 3629. You got it, is more to the point?'

'Cheeky.' Donkey lifted her wrist to show that she had written the code on her bare arm.

'Hope that washes off, you nutter.'

'Course it will. I'm not stupid,' said Donkey frowning at him. For a moment they stood still to listen for any distraction. A dog barked to disturb the peace but seemed to be far away. They were content that they were now safe to enter Aladdin's cave.

The key fitted and it turned. 'Ready?'

'Okay,' said Bones.

The door opened and the alarm started to count immediately. It was not easy to locate. The alarm sounded louder somewhere in the hallway. Donkey entered the entrance hall and found a cloakroom door. Her dimmed torch led her to the source of the alarm. She held her wrist to the pad. Her shaking fingers pressed 3629 accurately and the count ceased as it reached a high pitch.

'Bingo,' said Donkey.

'Shut up, ya bugger. Take no risks,' Bones said placing a finger on his lips.

'Locked the back door?' asked Donkey.

'The back door? I'll do that now,' said Bones.

'You twat. First thing to do after the alarm was off. We don't need any visitors.'

Bones made a cursory look around the kitchen area. Then Donkey returned. 'So where do we start?'

'Okay, let's do upstairs first,' Donkey whispered regaining her composure.

'Hey, bet that Grandfather clock is worth a few bob,' said Bones.

'Don't be daft, too big. We'd need a removal van so that's out. Keep the finds small and valuable.'

They entered the first room at the top of the stairs. It was clearly Sally's room. It was stark. They saw the row of harmonicas but thought them worthless and a missing one would soon be spotted. They rifled through her oak drawers making sure everything was put back in place. At the back of one drawer was a cardboard box. Donkey opened it. Inside was a gold watch, a family treasure. Donkey picked it up in her gloved hand.

'Better take the box, fetches more that way.'

'If we leave the box Sally might think she had misplaced it instead of being stolen.'

The two thought about each other's suggestion for a quiet moment. It seemed neither could decide. Then a human tuneless whistle was heard outside. They froze. The whistling died down and the front door letter box flapped.

Bones stood behind the bedroom curtains and peaked out. He saw a young lad freewheel his bike down the drive. It wasn't the paper boy. In his hand were some coloured flyers. They relaxed.

'With the box or without?' asked Bones. 'Your call.'

Donkey's eyes seemed closer together as she tried to make a decision. It seemed to work. 'Take the box. It will get us more.' They silently but thoroughly turned over every drawer. They looked behind the curtain and pulled the bed out to ensure nothing of value was missed. They correctly concluded her interests were few, beyond her treasured harmonicas.

It would have surprised Donkey and Bones that Sally could find a new interest in life and indeed she had. Elsie had been approached by a couple also on holiday with their son. Eric and Beth were, like her, in their late seventies or early eighties and their son Tom was fifty-one. He was an Asperger sufferer and that was one bond which sealed this holiday friendship. All five met for dinner that night and Elsie noticed her daughter could not keep her eyes off Tom. He was not fazed by the attention. He stared back at her. When she smiled, he smiled. When she ate, he ate. It was like a mirror image of activity but one that both Elsie and Tom's parents were aware of and ignored. Both sets of parents quietly encouraged their early platonic interest. It only seemed natural.

A veil of doubt and misunderstanding had been pulled from Sally's eyes. She felt for almost the first time for many, many years, she had feelings for someone other than her mother. She showed no reticence. It seemed she was less confused for the time being. Her autism had dictated her perception of herself. Her differences defined her. Now she felt being herself was not such a bad thing.

The journey, her journey, to find herself, to find out what was wrong had not come to an end. But having met Tom, it seemed to have come to a new beginning.

That evening before the sun had set Sally and Tom went for a walk alone. It was a stroll along a cliff path. Small colourful fishing boats lay in the bay bobbing to a growing nocturnal beat of the waves. They sat down on the grassy cliff to watch the twitching boats.

Sally got straight down to reality. 'Have you a best friend?'

'No, I have no special friend. Do you have a best friend?'

'Yes, Becky is my best friend.'

'Oh, I see.' Tom was aware of same sex relationships as an avid soap viewer. 'So will you marry her?'

'No,' she giggled. 'She's my sister.'

It took a few moments for them to make sense of their conversation. Their eyes wandered over the waves while Sally wound the long grass beside her around her fingers. Tom fiddled with his dark blue Fitbit strap on his wrist. He tapped it twice. He had only walked 8K steps so far, that day.

'Do you like my jersey?' Sally asked.

Tom turned his head towards her. 'Yes, I like your jersey.'

They did not say anything else for the best part of twenty minutes but they sat closer to each other inch by inch and eventually their sides met and gave each other some warmth. Then Tom arose.

'We should get back soon,' he said. 'Dad will be worried.'

'Yes, my Mum might be too.'

Both needed to recharge. It was good that they both realised this simultaneously in making their excuses.

On the way back to the hotel Sally took Tom's hand and smiled at him. He momentarily withdrew his hand and gasped. Sally felt awkward. What had she done? But Tom then took hold of her hand and he smiled back at her. They were not happy photo smiles, more of a tense stretching of the lips. They were still holding hands when they returned to find their parents sitting at a table by the pool.

'Did you have a good time, Tom?' asked Eric.

'Yes, I had a good time.'

'And how about you Sally, was it a good walk?' asked Eric.

Sally lifted her sleeve to her mouth and gnawed her jersey gently.

Donkey was now in Elsie's bedroom going through her jewellery. Elsie had obviously not taken the best on holiday but again how much could they take without it being noticed? Donkey settled for a broach with a jade green stone surrounded by small pearls. On its other side was a Birmingham silver hallmark. She put it in her pocket. Meanwhile Bones was going through all of Elsie's pockets and bringing out coins and some notes. In one drawer there was a purse with more than one hundred pounds in ten and five pounds notes. Donkey took £45 hoping the remainder would not arouse suspicion.

It was now after 10 p.m. and they still had another floor to explore.

'Hey Donkey, slow down. Best to sleep overnight here and leave tomorrow morning. You agree?'

'Yeah, up in the attic we can get some kip. I fancy going up to bed, having a second floor instead of being at home on the ground floor.'

'Not yet though. Let's do the spare bedrooms next.'

'Okay darling,' said Bones.

Bending under the windows as a shaft of moonlight pierced one room, Donkey came across a trunk under a bed. She struggled to pull it out. She asked Bones to help. They were pleased to find it unlocked. There was a cloth cover which she removed and saw two boxes. Donkey opened the first. Then the second lid came off the solid cardboard box. Donkey's eyes dropped, comics only, but so many. She took the contents of the last box and looked at the last copy on the bottom of the pile. It had a special cover. "First Edition 30th July 1938" it declared in large bold though slightly faded print. Then it dawned on her and her face lit up. In her hands were The Beano comics in numerical order from the very first edition to edition number 6000.

'Frickin' brilliant, Bones.'

'What d'ya mean, luv?' he asked bewildered at her excitement over comics.

'We've got to take these,' said Donkey flicking through some more magazines then stopping to gaze at the cartoons of Lord Snooty and Denis the Menace.

'What, lots of comics? You're crazy, that's what you are. What's great about them?' asked Bones.

'Yes, but maybe it's big money when you have the full set.'

Bones looked at the boxes packed with comics.

'We've got to be selective. They are a bit bulky. That's all I'm sayin'.'

Donkey was not to be put off.

'Then we take this because they'll not touch this trunk for some time, even years. Keep what we've pocketed but this is the icing on the cake, believe me.'

Her eyes were gleaming bright as she imagined the ching-ching of the cash earned from these boxes of comics in her mind.

'Don't touch them. Keep them in good condition. No spaniel ears.'

'Okay, if you think they'll sell well.'

Donkey nodded enthusiastically. 'They will. Trust me. Now, I'm ready for bed.'

The attic stairs creaked. The door was closed. Donkey opened it slowly then turned to Bones.

'Christ, we're not going to sleep just yet. Look, a bloody snooker table.'

# 5

# Malta Romance

The skies were clear and if an ear was cocked towards the sea, the waves could be heard collapsing on the golden sand near the rocky shoreline. Sally and her mother had arrived at the breakfast table by the poolside. There was already warmth in the air. Not from the hotel kitchen but the fresh sea air was wafting its way through the open breakfast area. Elsie set off to the self-help breakfast table where under fly nets could be found the hams of Europe, the tropical fruits of nearby Africa and the Mediterranean and of course the ubiquitous Cornflakes amid different plain and flavoured yoghurts. Sally returned to her table without anything. She was off her breakfast food and her mother noticed.

'Have some orange juice, Sally,' she said as she balanced the plate of hams and kept an eye on the mesmerising movement of her mug of tea to the table.

'No, don't want any orange juice.'

'But you must have something. A slice of melon, perhaps?' she suggested sympathetically realising the cause of her heart flutters.

Sally went to the table and brought back a slice of watermelon. She had pleased her mother.

But Elsie recognised the ailment of her heart.

'How long have you been feeling under the weather, darling?'

Sally's eyes wandered round the tables. Her heart missed a beat. Tom was approaching with his parents. It was too late to respond.

'Can we join you for breakfast?' asked Eric.

'Yes, do,' said Elsie as Sally stood up and gazed at Tom.

Eric pulled out a seat for his wife next to Elsie and then the seat for his son next to Sally. She remained standing. She continued to stare at Tom. Nothing was said. It was appropriate not to. In time Sally sat down.

There were not one but three skyline windows that night providing sufficient light for them to distinguish the colours of the snooker balls. After the first game Bones took the chalk and approached the board and recorded the score.

'For God's sake. Put the chalk down, ya bugger. Trying to name and shame us?'

'I wasn't. I was only going to write the scores,' said a defensive Bones.

'You don't understand do you? Sally eventually comes up here and sees the board has had an entry. She may be daft but she'd know someone had been up here.'

Bones nodded reluctantly. He wiped the board almost clean with his sleeve. 'Okay one more game and its bedtime. And no smokes either for that matter.'

The next game took more than an hour to complete. That brought the score to one game each. They felt a decider was required. They had that competitive streak. But they were hungry too.

They went down to the kitchen and looked into every tin. Some were empty. They came across Jaffa cakes in one tin and they took two each. Sure, they wanted more but again they agreed that four would not be noticed missing as the pack had already been opened. They washed their biscuits down with a glass of lemon barley water making sure they washed and dried their glasses thoroughly before putting them away where they had taken them from. Then they took four cushions from the lounge and headed back to contest the final game before retiring.

It was almost 1 a.m. when the decider was over. Donkey accepted defeat.

As they prepared for sleep, Bones noticed a rocking chair in the corner. He looked at Donkey with lingering eyes, those same eyes which told Donkey he had further plans on his mind.

'You sleepy, luv?' he said glancing between her and the rocking chair like a metronome. Donkey got his message clearly and it was one which was heightened by the excitement of where they were and what they had achieved that night. It had them aroused. Bones approached and gently lifted her jersey over her head. As her hair fell backwards into place, he felt his trouser zip being pulled down. His trousers flopped to the floor. He turned her around and drew her close to him. His hands came over her shoulders and clung to her breasts. He pressed hard adding a circular movement and Donkey's eyes closed. He stepped out of his trousers and kicked off his trainers. His socks remained on. To remove them would interrupt. He pulled at her bra strap. 'Hey easy, luv.' The release came soon after and he let her bra fall to the ground. He continued to play with her nipples and felt them harden to both his pleasure and hers. Donkey let out a child-like cry. She turned around to grab his manhood and brought it towards her.

'Wait. I've an idea.' Bones tiptoed quickly to the corner of the attic and gathered a tartan rug and draped it over the rocking chair.

'Come here, luv,' he said curling his index finger towards her.

Bones sat stately on the chair his penis proudly aroused and awaiting attention. She lowered herself gently to allow the union to take place. She then leant back permitting Bones' right hand to hold firmly her right breast while the fingers of Bones' other hand teased her softness between her legs. But Donkey was in control. She gripped Bones' thighs and her nails dug into his flesh as she used his legs to propel her forward and backwards to the swaying of the rocking chair. It brought them to new heights of pleasure. The strangeness of the room, the illegal but quick entry to the house, the treasure finds and the excitement of the snooker all conspired to make this a most memorable night. A night which was far from over.

Then they crawled under the snooker table with Sally's duvet over them. It was a hard floor but the discomfort did not delay sleep. Their sexual activity brought instant sleep and both soon succumbed to the powers of

Hypnos, the Greek God of sleep, satisfied with feelings of mutual love.

It may have been around 2 a.m. when a scream came from Donkey's anguished mouth. She had hit her head on the table above her as she prepared to visit the loo.

'God that's sore.'

Bones was disturbed and slowly came to life. He sat up and could see blood starting to run down the side of Donkey's face.

'Don't get any blood onto her duvet. For fuck's sake, you've spilt some on that cushion. Cover your head with your hand and I'll get some loo paper.'

Donkey crawled from under the snooker table. She stood up and made her way to the loo. Her blood started to drop on the floor but it was the patterned linoleum flooring she was on and that could be easily cleaned. Bones found the medicine cabinet in the bathroom and took some bandages, two plasters and cotton wool. He parted Donkey's hair and the source of her injury appeared. He wiped the growing bump with wet cotton wool and dried it with some more. Then he placed a bandage over the wound.

'Get that cushion soaked,' was all thoughtless Donkey could say.

Eric and Beth ran a chemist's shop in Bolton, not a long distance from Wigan. Eric was pleased to see Sally take an interest in his son. So too was his wife. There were signs that family friendship might survive this Mediterranean holiday. After all they were almost

Lancashire neighbours, with a common experience of autism and now Malta.

Tom and Sally left the table and parted at the entrance to the hotel where Sally mounted the stairs.

'She'll be going to brush her teeth,' said Elsie. 'Never leaves any dining table to go anywhere else.'

Beth gave a knowing smile. 'It's good for her to have a routine. Best to leave them in their own silent world. We learned from our mistakes, you know, the denial that your child is really ill. It took us some time to adjust, didn't it Eric?'

'Yes, fifty years ago, they thought it might be cured some day but no, they got that wrong. I suppose we did our best as everyone did but there wasn't a real understanding of the condition. Little support either at that time.'

Elsie nodded her agreement and replaced her cup on its saucer and pushed it further onto the table.

'It was very much the same for us. My husband, Ian, who died four years ago, felt it was a stigma at first. He got frustrated that Sally wasn't trying to improve but fortunately we began to see autism in a better light.'

'Yes, they have their own personalities,' said Eric stretching his arms over his head.

'Not just personalities. Sally plays several different harmonicas really very well indeed.'

'Really? Has she got any with her on holiday,' asked Eric excitedly.

'Yes I think she's brought just one. Goodness knows which one it is.'

Eric smiled. He unbuttoned another shirt button.

'It's getting warmer by the minute,' Elsie found herself saying on seeing more of his hairy chest.

Beth moved her chair further in and tipped it forward. 'Elsie, you don't mind Tom showing an interest in Sally?'

'You mean Sally showing an interest in Tom? She's quite off her food at present and that's not like her.'

'I'm pleased for them. They are relaxed around each other and that will provide comfort for them to explore,' said Eric.

Elsie opened her mouth as she thought through her question. 'Has Tom had many girlfriends?'

'Girlfriends? Thousands. Every holiday, every trip to the supermarket or even the recycling centre he comes back and tells me about them. I ask who they are and he tells me they are all his girlfriends.'

'Oh, so I can relax then,' she said winking at Eric.
'No Elsie,' he dropped his voice. 'It's sad but as a couple they could not survive. They live in their own worlds and they'll never co-ordinate to manage the task in hand,' said Beth.

Elsie agreed through more of her silent nods. 'Has Tom ever worked?'

'He had a job for a few weeks but he stopped going. It was his choice. They could not keep him on their books. He was not reliable enough for them. Mind you I don't think they went out of their way to support him or show him the ropes in a slow gradual manner.'

Elsie's face showed concern. 'May I ask where he worked?'

'Yes, he packed tea at Martin's Supermarket. Well, tea bags and loose tea, Ovaltine, hot chocolate drinks and coffees. You can imagine all the types of coffee there are these days, let alone infusions of all sorts.'

'Yes, that's too much to handle. Probably not the best department with that number of drink items. Perhaps he could have coped better gathering the trolleys.'

'You are right. It is one thing for a company to be proud to employ the disabled but they have a responsibility to make sure the jobs given match their ability. Too often they manage to fit round pegs into square holes,' said Eric shaking his head in despair.

'Sally worked in a store too. Same reason she gave up. Lost interest. Happier at home. So I didn't push it.'

Smiles were seen all around the breakfast table as the realisation and comfort was shared by the common paths their children had taken.

'Sally sees her role in life is to be with me,' Elsie said with a distant look.

'That can't be a bad thing,' suggested Beth.

'It's fine just now but when I die, I really don't know what Sally will do,' she said misty-eyed.

The atmosphere changed. Elsie thought Eric might enlighten her with his thoughts on this grim matter but suddenly there was a shout. Sally had jumped into the pool near Tom and they were splashing around like five year olds.

'They are kids enjoying the moment. It's what they live for,' said Eric placing his sunglasses on the bridge of his nose.

'Yes, when we both die, we hope our son will take on Tom. His wife is fond of him and we see that as the best option.'

'I've two children and I suppose they will come to some agreement. A shared arrangement perhaps. But I feel I should also be part of the decision-making. Death is such an inhibitor,' said Elsie scratching the back of her head. Eric nodded slowly and thoughtfully. It was an understanding they had already reached. It felt good to have had it validated.

Dawn was breaking. Donkey looked at her watch. 'Let's not try and have breakfast here. 8.30 a.m. is the best time to leave. Join the flow of workers to work. And boy do we have some work to do this morning.'

'Yeah? What you got planned?' asked Bones rubbing his hands together.

'Let's get to the auctioneers with the booty before Sally and her mum get back. But first let's make sure we have cleared our tracks.'

They started in the attic leaving the red balls in their triangle at the top of the board just as they had found them. The cue and its rest were returned to the cue stand and the cue ball positioned with the accuracy of a gloved professional, on the spot at the far end. They thought they had made a good spring clean of the attic and were pleased that the blood stain on the cushion was minimal to the eye and unlikely to draw attention. It would dry in the sunshine of the lounge from where it had been taken and returned. They closed the attic door, just as they had found it. They entered each bedroom once more to ensure drawers were closed and contents left in the way they had found them. But with light increasing, they could not risk a sighting from the nearest house.

They walked bent like the backs of hod carriers.

They gathered all their booty and set the house alarm back on. They were mighty relieved when the security bell stopped and silence reigned around the back door. The backdoor key was returned to where it had been located. They had each stolen four Tesco bags from the pantry for their plunder. There must have been over a hundred bags there. Donkey loitered a while in the driveway shrubbery to give Bones a head start. They considered it to be too suspicious if they walked together with such baggage. They agreed to meet at their home in one hour.

# 6

# A Surprise for Sally

It was early evening. The pool still had a few swimmers doing lengths. Both families had eaten and were sitting in a semicircle of the reception area, relaxed, and at perfect ease with Eric gulping his Heineken beer, while Elsie and Beth each sipped their Hendrik's gin. Sally sipped a fizzy orange through a spiral straw while Tom had a half pint shandy of Adman's lager and lemonade.

'Sally?'

Sally looked up at Eric with an abrupt staring pose.

'I hear you have brought your harmonica with you.'

Sally smiled happily and nodded a few times in agreement.

'Which one is it?'

'My favourite,' she replied gripping the sides of her chair.

Eric smiled and continued to pry.

'I see. Is it in F or G?'

'No, it's the chromatic one.'

'Ah yes. Difficult to play all those semitones I bet.'

'No, it's easy,' said Sally looking coldly at Eric then watching her juice spiral its way to her mouth through her fancy straw. How dare he say it was difficult when it wasn't?' she thought.

'What if I played the piano over there, would you play with me on your harmonica?'

'Yes, on my harmonica.'

'Then can you bring it down and we can make some music?'

No sooner had she been asked than Sally was on her way to her room to get her instrument.

'What sort of music does she like to play, Elsie?' Eric asked with a sudden realisation it might be in the order of Jack and Jill went up the hill. Maybe even Frère Jacques.

'That's a good question. She plays so many things I don't know all the tunes she produces.'

'Where has Sally gone?' asked Tom whose eyes were scanning round the area like a spinning top.

'Gone to get her mouth organ, dear,' said Beth.

Elsie smiled then chuckled. 'Don't let Sally hear you calling a harmonica a mouth organ. They are the same thing I suppose but she told me off about that once. I'll never forget.'

Beth smacked the back of her left hand. 'I must remember.'

Sally arrived having brought the harmonica down. It was in its case. She handed it to Eric who opened it to see a gleaming bright instrument bearing the name of Unica Young. He lifted the instrument out and looked closely at it. Sure enough the slide key was in position on the end of the harmonica. It was indeed a chromatic instrument.

'I see it's made in Japan. It feels good to touch but I can't play it. I hear you play well.'

It was a compliment but Sally didn't do compliments well. Instead she pointed the instrument at the piano.

'Okay, let's go and make music,' said a contented Eric.

Eric sat down at the Bechstein piano and ran his fingers up and down the keyboard. This was no honky-tonk piano. It had depth and feeling. Not a note was flat or sharp. Eric was surprisingly pleased with its condition and tone. He thought for a moment, wondering what Sally might be able to play. He decided to play an introduction and then perhaps a few well known bars. If Sally had not caught on, then he'd ask her what she wanted to play.

Eric began to play Adele's Chasing Pavements. Immediately Sally began to play along with him. Tom began to clap, not entirely in time and Elsie smiled. She had often heard Sally play but never accompanied. It sounded good. The song took almost four minutes to play during which a growing group of holidaymakers had started to gather round to hear the impromptu live performance.

'Okay Sally, that was good. Your turn, do you want to play something?'

Eric's fingers hovered over the piano in readiness. He waited to see what tune might emerge. He noticed Sally shield the harmonica by the end of the instrument and he soon heard why. It was the sliding action underway which lent itself to the sharps and flats that Sally required to play Gershwin's Rhapsody in Blue.

People were mesmerised with Sally's performance and Eric gave up playing as he had never attempted this classic masterpiece. The audience grew and in silence they listened to Sally seeing her contort herself to reach lower notes and arch her eyebrows to hit the high ones. Sally was in her element. The audience was enthralled.

When she reached the last note there was an instant of pure silence then the clapping and cheering filled the vestibule.

'More please. Encore,' was heard a dozen times but Sally did not smile or acknowledge their delight. She returned to the table where her mother was still applauding. The audience smiled feeling she was shy.

'They want you to play another tune, Sally,' her mother said with a nod of encouragement. And to please her mother was one of Sally's delights. She returned to the exact spot where she had stood to play Gershwin. Meanwhile holiday makers found chairs to sit down quietly and the large flower pot lips became seats too as the evening entertainment seemed to be developing. Children sat cross legged on the floor.

Once more her lips met the instrument and a silence descended over the area. She gave no announcement. The audience wondered what she would play.

Sally worked her way through Vaughan Williams's The Lark Ascending. It was a piece which heard the harmonica fully stretched to find each trill and sustained note. Everyone could imagine the hovering lark. It was once more a note perfect performance and again she returned to her mother's table without acknowledging the audience's applauding gratitude. Instead Sally went to the toilet after pocketing her instrument.

That night a lady approached Elsie. She smiled as she appeared.

'Excuse me I gather you are Sally's mother?'

'Yes,' she said taken aback while looking at the tall tanned figure of a woman in her mid-thirties dressed in a tracksuit and mauve Tee shirt bearing the logo: I'm not arguing; I'm just explaining why I am right.

The lady pulled out a chair and sat down beside Elsie. 'I hope you don't mind me barging in. My name is Carolee, Carolee Meredith. I am a music agent. Yes, on holiday of course but work is always on my mind. Your daughter is a gifted musician you know. Not many play the harmonica and as well as that. I'd like to take her on to my books. Would she agree?'

'Well...er...an agent....what does that mean?' flustered Elsie who was somewhat taken out of her field of comfort.

'I arrange tours for entertainers, musicians and some six authors. I make the booking arrangements and provide their accommodation. I feel sure Sally will be a great attraction,' she said opening up her iPad sitting on her lap.

'But you don't understand. Sally has autism. She's fine tonight because she knows I am here. But take her to a new place to play to strangers then return her to her hotel room and she is likely to freak out. Like a fish out of water. I do know what I am talking about, you know.'

'Your name is?' she asked, lightly touching her arm.

'I am Elsie Dunning.'

'Mrs Dunning, I assure you I know what Autism is. My nephew has it too. He has concentrated on constructive art. He has built the Angel of the North in fine detail with matchsticks; he works with my late father's Meccano set building moving cars too. He is always creating constructional art. That's his ability. That's when he is in that autism zone. Your daughter, Sally, has concentrated on music...... and that sells.'

It took a moment for Elsie to swallow what she had heard.

'It is good to know that you understand her condition. So I must thank you for your kind offer but I just can't see it working, I'm sorry.'

There was an awkward moment of silence. Elsie thought the dialogue had ended. This young woman would surely leave.

'Mrs Dunning, then let me make a different offer. I'll arrange a hotel for you and Sally and you will be off stage when she is performing. Let's keep it simple. Let's try it at one venue, one local one for you. And assess afterwards how it has been for us all. Now that can't be a worthless offer.'

Elsie felt shepherded into a sheep's pen. 'I suppose then I have nothing to lose.'

'Well, this is my card. Are you on-line?'

'Yes, we are.' Elsie gave her the email required and they parted with a handshake.

'I have every confidence in Sally, Mrs Dunning.'

'Thank you. Thank you very much indeed.'


Bones and Donkey spread out their ill-gotten gains on the carpet. It was one of the larger hauls their housebreaking career had produced. And it could continue if Sally, their golden egg, did not shatter. They hoped not to break the egg and like a productive hen, the golden eggs would keep laying.

'The comics. We should repack them. Get them in the right order.' Donkey threw a plastic bag to Bones. 'One each. Got to find a plausible story for them too,' said Bones, and they did.

Donkey entered auctioneers Harper & Pierpont Ltd. at the Robin Park light industry area of town the following day. She placed on the office desk both boxes of Beano magazines. Mr. Harper opened one box.

'This looks a very interesting collection. How long have you had this, madam?'

'They belonged to my uncle. He died last year and his widow gave them to me,' she lied with the confidence of a professional trickster, which she was. Her confidence grew. 'Well you see, I've no interest in keeping children's magazines and wondered if they were worth anything?'

Mr. Harper put on white gloves and ran his fingers down the spines of the collection. He took out copies randomly to check their condition.

'Your uncle took great care of them, madam.'

'Yes, he did. He was like that, a very careful man.'

'Was he local, I might have known him?' he asked without raising his head.

'Er...no, not local. He was from Cardiff,' Donkey replied feeling her pulse beat stronger.

'Ah a Welshman.'

'No, his wife was Welsh, he came from here. But he left to go to Wales just after he left school,' she lied, as her lies took off on a journey of their own.

Mr. Harper looked up and over his horn rimmed glasses 'And you are?'

'I'm Donna Riley.'

'Ms. Donna Riley, I seem to have heard that name......,' he said, wondering where he might have come across it in the recent past. In the local paper perhaps, he wondered. But it would be too nosey to ask.

'Er ....Riley is quite a common name. There are quite a few of us in the telephone book,' Donkey said feeling for her cigarette packet in her pocket and tapping it in time with her breathing. She'd have to wait till she was outside.

Mr. Harper returned the comics to the box. 'Well Ms. Riley, do you have an address or email you can give me?'

'Why?' asked a suddenly nervous Donkey.

'Because, Ms Riley, you have an interesting collection here and I intend to contact a special comic auction in London. That is if you agree of course. I'll let you know if they are interested and if they go to auction, as I am confident they will, so you can attend if you wish. How else may I contact you?'

'Of course, I was not thinking. My email address is braytimegal@hotmail.com so how much do you think it will make?'

'The market is difficult to second guess. That's why I am waiting for a comic auction as opposed to a local sale. This may take some time. And of course, the auctioneer receives his percentage too.'

'Yes, but after the deductions, what is it likely to be?' Donkey asked to have a greater idea of its worth.

'On a poor day it might be around £800 but if there is interest on-line, as there are real collectors of magazines, you know, and your uncle kept them from the very start in an almost perfect condition, then we could be talking upwards of even £10K and even more if there are international on-line bids.'

'Ten thousand?'

'Yes, you heard me correctly. That's if the market is interested. Yes, that's what I said the comics could definitely make. Are you surprised?'

Donkey swallowed her shock. 'Yes, I don't think my aunt knew their worth. I should make sure she gets some of the proceeds,' she said like a wonderful, loving niece.

Mr. Harper smiled as he proffered his hand forward. 'Yes, that would be very thoughtful, Ms. Riley, very thoughtful indeed.'

'I'm pleased to have done business with you,' said Donkey in the most professional voice she could muster as she withdrew her hand.

No sooner had the auctioneer's door closed than the first deep draw of nicotine hit the back of Donkey's throat. She had got rid of the comics and for possibly an amount that could see them sunning themselves on a Floridian beach before too long.


Sally returned from the loo to join her mother and their new friends.

'I hear you will be playing to a larger audience, Sally,' said Eric approvingly.

Sally looked at her mother with the anxiety of a cow at its slaughter.

'Yes dear, a lady came to arrange a local night for you to play the harmonica in front of some people just like this evening. Wouldn't you like that? I would, I am sure.'

A green light had been given for her reply. 'Yes I'd like that, mum,' she said without showing any surprise or pleased emotion.

Eric smiled at Sally. Sally ignored him as she thought through the prospects of another public performance suggested by her mother.

'I'd come along with you of course, dear.'

Sally started to roll her thumbs round each other in clasped hands.

'It is to be a local performance, Sally,' said Beth.

Sally stared at Beth with piercing eyes. 'In Wigan?'

'Well, I was wondering if you would like to play in Bolton.'

Sally's eyes turned from Beth to Tom.

'Play in Bolton,' she asked raising her voice in delight?

Tom smiled at her and Sally managed to smile back. 'Yes, Bolton is good.'

Elsie was relieved. It seemed like a new dawn for Sally. If it worked well then.....but that was jumping ahead too many fences.


'Eight hundred minimum, that would do us nicely,' said Bones.

'Might take some time though.'

'We can wait. Yeah, so eBay the rest?' was Bones' instant suggestion.

'Suppose so, but the jewellery. Perhaps we can sell

to guys we know and trust. Good quality prezzies for mums and girlfriends.'

Bones rubbed his hand together. 'Izzy whizzy let's get busy. Let's start with eBay.'

The pair was not short of money. Sally's investments were the ready cash for drugs, food and drink and that kept them happy and under the radar of the local police. That's where they wanted and needed to be.

# 7

# Harmonica

Before they flew home, Carolee Meredith met Sally and learned of her motivation to go to Bolton and see Tom again. This made a contract to play at the Octagon in Bolton with their Symphony Orchestra feasible, she told her. Sally had simply to email Carolee with a selection of her intended music to last no more than 20 minutes. She told her that her mother would do that. She would arrange a pre- and post-interval performance. Sally learned that she would be with a full orchestra for the latter performance. Elsie who sat in on the discussion was excited and reserved at the same time. Sally regarded it as a real challenge but did not say so. Carolee felt the risks were worth taking.

Their return home was uneventful but sad for Sally to know Tom was not on her flight. He would be flying home later in the day.

Four days after their return, there was a phone call which Elsie took.

'Can I speak to Sally, please?'

'And who's calling?'

'Er...it's Sally's friend.'

'Ah..... Donkey?'

'Yes. Oh.... and thank you very much for the card Mrs Dunning. It was much appreciated.'

'Not at all. You have been very kind to Sally. One moment please.'

'Sally, phone for you. It's your friend Donkey,' she shouted.

'She's on her way,' she told her and held the phone covered by her hand. A few moments later Sally arrived and took the phone from her mother.

'Sally, did you have a good holiday?' asked Donkey.

'Yes it was a good holiday.'

'Lots of fun?' she enquired making the conversation flow like melted butter.

'Yes. I went swimming.'

'Did you like that?'

Elsie overheard the start of the conversation and walked away pleased.

'Yes, I liked swimming. I have a boyfriend now.'

Elsie smiled as she just got the jist of what her daughter had said. She knew Sally was pleased with life.

'I will see him soon.'

'Is he coming to see you?' asked Donkey.

'No, he lives in Bolton. I'm going there to play my harmonica.'

'Listen, we should meet up. What are you doing tomorrow afternoon?'

'Tomorrow afternoon. Er....not sure...oh yes, I'm doing nothing.'

'Well, can you get to the bank? Your money is making terrific amounts. Another £500 and your profits will be growing like a baby elephant. Can you manage that?'

A baby elephant, thought Sally. The strange saying perplexed her for a moment. 'Yes, I can get that for you.'

'Okay tomorrow 2.30 p.m. we meet at Krum's cafe on Rodney Street. Know where I mean?'

'Yes, Krum's cafe.'

'Okay Sally, luv. Don't forget the money. See you at the cafe. Bye,' she switched off her mobile. Donkey thumped her thigh in delight.

'Okay, bye.'

Sally put the phone down as her mother moved from the kitchen doorway into the centre of the room.

'I'm going to meet Donkey at Krum's tomorrow.'

'Donkey? It really is a funny name for a girl,' said her mother shaking her head and tying her apron on.

Sally smiled. 'No, it's her nickname. I told you. Donna is her real name. Donna, Donkey, you see?'

'Ah that explains it. A pet name made from her real name.'

Sally then went up to her bedroom and began to play her harmonica. Donkey lingered in Elsie's mind. Nickname or not, what was wrong with her name Donna, she wondered.

Krum's cafe was in the heart of town. What Donkey liked about it was that it had a secluded area at the back and so they would not be overheard.

'Good to see you again, Sally, luv,' said a smiling Donkey.

'Yeah. Had a good time in Malta then?' asked Bones while hitching up his jeans.

'Yes, a really good time.'

67

'You've got a tan, Sally.'

'Yes, Donkey, it was very hot,' she said starting to shake.

The waitress approached. 'Okay you guys, what are you having?'

'I'll have you, ya stunner,' said Bones blowing a kiss.

'Get away. You're all talk. Now what are you having madam,' she said to Donkey.

'A latte, two sugars, an' a slice of fly's cemetery.'

'We don't make fly's cemetery,' she said with an air of superiority. 'It's a lovingly made currant square around here.'

'Okay, that's my order,' said Donkey duly reprimanded by the cold glance.

'And you, madam?'

'Tea please.'

'That it?'

'Yes, thank you,' said Sally feeling uncomfortable with Bones' chat up line.

'Now, smart Alec, what are you having?'

Bones coiled from her rejection. He tried to make it up to her.

'What do you suggest from your marvellous counter?'

'For you, sir, there's the baked Alaska. You're the one with the charm and wit; expensive tastes, I know your kind. A slice of baked Alaska?'

'Okay and a latte too.'

'The cake will cost you £6 a slice. Not easy to make ...... expensive ingredients...takes time.'

'That's fine. I'm not paying anyway. You'll pay, Sally, won't you?'

'Yes, I'll pay,' she said reaching for her wallet in her jacket pocket.

The waitress left with the orders with a twirl of her skirt which caught Bones' lecherous eyes.

'Pretty girl that,' he said.

'Steady Bones, I'm your gal have you forgotten? And I'm sure Sally will get embarrassed with your antics. Anyway, I know you are all bluff or I'd not let you say such things.'

'I've got a boyfriend,' said Sally quite out of the blue.

'A boyfriend, yeah?' a surprised look covered both of their faces.

'Yes, his name is Tom.'

'You've kissed him then I suppose?' teased Bones, grinning as he did so.

'No, not kissed him.'

Donkey looked at Bones. They sniggered. Perhaps her boyfriend was a figment of her imagination. Nevertheless teasing Sally was so easy to do. But it had to be limited.

'So, where did you meet Tom?' asked Bones.

'On holiday.'

'I know that, you mean on Malta?'

'Yes, in the hotel we stayed at.'

'But....if you met him on Malta, was he Maltese?'

Sally laughed. 'No, not Maltese, he's from Bolton.'

'Bolton? That's a stone's throw from here in Wigan,' said a surprised Bones.

'So you will be going over to Bolton to see him then?' asked Donkey making Sally reveal her plans.

'Yes, I'll be playing in Bolton,' Sally replied with a blank expression on her face.

'Playing?' asked Bones.

'Yes, playing my harmonica.'

Donkey remembered seeing the mouth organs laid out in a line in her bedroom. She seemed to have a few. But she was very surprised that Sally would go to Bolton to busk.

The tray arrived with the manager carrying it. He laid the drinks down. 'Now, who's the big head getting the baked Alaska?' he asked.

Bones raised his hand a few inches above the table.

'Then listen mate, keep your eyes and hands off my lass if you know what's good for you. Any more of your nonsense and I'll report you to the police. Understand? Aye, harassment in case you were wondering, okay?'

Bones nodded with his mouth open.

'Enjoy the cake, sir,' the manager said sarcastically as he left.

The atmosphere was cold and tense for a few moments. They ate and drank in silence. But they had met for a reason.

'So, Sally, did you get the money?' asked Donkey in a whisper.

'Yes, here it is.'

'That's good of you,' said Donkey. 'We're well on the way to paying your fare to Bolton three times a week,' she said winking at Bones.

'Oh, I'd say five times a week Donkey. And enough for a night out with Tom, too. Hey, how does that sound Sally?'

'That's not much, bus fares are not expensive.'

'That's right Sally. I didn't mean bus fares. I meant

taxis and the taxi waits for you to bring you home again. That costs money,' said Donkey.

'But I don't need a taxi. I'm going to Bolton with my mother.'

Donkey lifted her latte and sipped. She almost felt sorry for Sally. It seemed time to call off the next £500 demand for the time being.

There was no need to meet again in the near future. They needed to cool off. They had enough money to keep them in drugs for some time now and a slight niggle that Sally's mother might have some doubts about her daughter's relationship with them crossed their minds. In fact, the golden goose should hibernate a while. Bones agreed with his co-conspirator.

The following Friday night, Bones sat on the floor draining his second beer and flipping through the local paper. He did not read any of it. He was not good at reading. Good enough to read the names of the recently deceased and also the court pages. Little else interested him. Car sales, sports pages, letter's page; all had no interest for him. Just pictures filled his mind as he began to feel alcohol muddled.

On page 12 was a picture which startled him. It was a picture of Sally playing her harmonica. The text was quite expansive. He called through to Donkey.

'Hey, you seen the Wigan Post this evening?'

'No, why?' she asked with caution from their bedroom.

'There's a picture of Sally playing her mouth organ.'

'Yeah? What else does it say?' Donkey was intrigued.

She ran through to grab the paper and sat down on the dining room floor, cross legged.

'So, what's it about?' asked a perplexed Bones

'It's a long piece. I've not read it yet. Bring me a beer too, will ye, luv?'

Bones duly obliged anxious to hear the words which went with the picture.

Donkey pulled back the can's ring and watched the froth rise.

'Okay, let's see what Sally's been doing,' she said taking a swig of the can. The next few minutes passed by in silence as Donkey read the article. She took another mouthful.

'Christ. She's not a busker at all. She's performing with the Bolton Symphony Orchestra. Blimey, strike me down with a barge pole.'

'Would if I could, Donkey. You mean playing her harmonica?'

'Yes. They say it's wonderful despite the fact she suffers from autism but she's turned her difficulties into music. They say she's appearing at the Octagon in Bolton.'

'What, you mean our golden egg, Sally?'

'Yeah, playing the Elizabethan Serenade in the first half as a solo and in the second half, with the string orchestra, she plays the bloody Beethoven clarinet Concerto - for the first time on harmonica. A fuckin' world premier no less.'

'Wow, god almighty. What a surprise. Bet her boyfriend is in the orchestra,' Bones said with a flighty mind.

That night a key turned in the front door.

'Hey, anyone at home? Sally? Mum?'

'Oh darling, it's good to see you, Becky,' Elsie said running to the door and drying her hands with a dishtowel at the same time.

They gave each other a warm hug.

'Where's Sally?' asked Becky straining an ear to the floor above.

'Upstairs as usual, she's been playing her harmonica most of the day.'

'Yes, I read about her in the Manchester Gazette.'

'Yes, now I can say she's really looking forward to going to Bolton to play.'

'Are you sure Mum?' asked Becky holding her mother's arm. 'I mean she's never done anything like this before.'

Elsie's eyes began to water. She looked away so that her daughter would not see the tears pricking the corner of her eyes. Then a tightening of her throat made her lips quiver. 'To think....we've missed all those years when she could have made her name as a well-known harmonica player.'

Becky led her mother through to the lounge with her arm in support. 'Don't worry. Life is like that. Carpe Diem. Seize the day, let her enjoy herself.'

'Oh yes, she will.' Elsie regained her composure.

'I should tell you too, that she has a Bolton boyfriend.'

'What Sally has? Bolton?' Becky opened her mouth in astonishment. 'A real boyfriend? Not easy for her to get there and back. I mean, does this man realise what Sally can be like?'

'Well, he's autistic too. We met Tom and his parents on holiday.'

Becky smiled as she placed a hand on her mother's shoulder. 'A holiday fling I suppose. Can't see it going anywhere.'

'No, probably not.'

Becky spent the weekend in her parental home. One reason was to discuss with her mother what present she could get for Sally's birthday the following week. On the Saturday night she retired to her former bedroom which she felt would always be hers. She looked about the room and investigated what she had left in the drawers before she went to live in Manchester. She made a worrying discovery but chose not to rouse her mother there and then as she heard Elise and Sally were already snoring, loudly.

Becky did not get to sleep till 2 a.m. Her mind could not contemplate its disappearance. Had she taken it to her city home, she wondered. She must have. How else could it be missing from the room? With that thought in mind she slept soundly.

At breakfast Becky still had the necklace on her mind. She asked Sally about it.

'Have you seen it? I mean seen it anywhere in the house?'

'No, I haven't seen it.'

Becky scratched her head. 'Well, Mum, it's a mystery, that's all I can say.'

'Don't worry dear, it will turn up. I am sure it will.'

'Yes, it will turn up, Becky, it will turn up,' said Sally with a warm look of love towards her sister.

Becky smiled at her. She approached her and gave her a warm hug and patted her back.

'Of course it will, Sally, of course it will turn up.'

# 8

# Sisterly love

Inspector Mark Rawlings sat nursing a coffee at 11.10 a.m. in the police canteen when Sergeant Jim Boyd came in.

'Over here Jim, have a seat,' he said raising his arm.

'I've been looking forward to this coffee. It has been a hard morning.'

'Hard?' questioned the Inspector leaning back as Jim pulled out his chair.

'Paperwork. Can't say I like it. Targets, reports, you know, that sort of thing. It's not what I became a bobby to do.'

'Yeah, know what you mean,' the inspector said stirring his drink and tapping it with his teaspoon on the lip before returning it to the saucer. 'I don't like it either. It's too quiet. That's when the paperwork increases.'

'Too quiet, sir? Yes, I've had that feeling. ....Do you think..... Bones and Donkey have hibernated or are they just under the radar?'

'Maybe, maybe they are growing out of delinquency. You know, beyond the peak age of criminal responsibility?'

'And into........?' asked Jim following his thought.

'If I only knew, if I only knew, Jim.'

'Perhaps I could drive by there and recce the area?' Jim said with a sudden impulse.

Mark sniggered. 'You mean get away from the deskwork?'

Jim threw his hands in the air. 'I'm obvious, aren't I?'

'Yes, but you do that. Let me know if you find anything of interest.'

Becky's long weekend at home was coming to an end. She would return to the family home the following week when Sally would celebrate her fifty-fourth birthday. But before leaving Wigan on the Monday morning, she called at the local TSB bank where Sally had a dormant account.

'Good morning,' Becky said to Gwen, the young female desk teller who flicked a hair from her white blouse. 'I'd like to transfer £100 from my account to my sister's account.'

'Certainly, do you have the account numbers handy?' asked the teller with a provocatively low cut top bearing her name under the bank's logo.

Becky brought out her card and inserted it into the card holder.

'And your sister's account, I mean accounts..... Which one is it you wish to credit?'

Becky thought for a moment. Could she possibly have two accounts?

'I thought she had just one,' she said grasping the counter with a strong grip.

'She has one, that's the active account and the other which seems to be more spasmodic.'

'I wonder... you know my sister Sally is autistic? She's not very good about money. I sort of unofficially keep an eye out for her in that department. I am a little concerned about her active account. Can I see it please?'

The bank clerk thought for a moment with her hand on top of the computer showing Sally's transactions. She turned the screen further round and away from Becky's eyes.

'Just one moment please, madam,' said Gwen.

Becky nodded and remained standing at the desk. She saw the young lady trot like a filly to the manager's office. She chided herself for not having made her role more official in the eyes of the bank.

A few minutes later the door opened and the manager looked towards her.

'Dr. Becky Dunning, it's good to see you again. How's Manchester?'

'Ah.... you remember that's where I am.' Becky glanced at his name tab near his bank logo. Indeed she remembered the spotty faced sixth former whose name was Nigel Lees.

'Yes, it has been quite a while since we've seen each other but my sister is at your hospital. She's a nurse.'

'Really?'

'Yes, Susan Clark, paediatric nursing.'

'Of course, yes, I know Susan and I can see the family similarities now, but the married name threw me completely.'

'It does, doesn't it? Come, come into to my office for a moment please.'

Becky was pleased to be remembered by an old school friend and hoped the pleasantries would lead to an understanding of Sally's finances.

'Now tell me, have you the power of attorney in Sally's affairs?'

Becky's eyebrows arched and she breathed in through her teeth. 'I should have, shouldn't I? However we've been caring for Sally all of our adult lives. When our father died, a lump sum was placed in Sally's name in an account here. We presumed she knew it was her nest egg for after Mum dies. The care she would need would be expensive. That's why I am surprised she is using it.'

'Well I suppose this comes under discretionary powers. I don't like using them but I think common sense prevails and is stacked in Sally's favour..... her best interests, you realise.'

Nigel Lees switched on his computer and logged in. It took seconds to enter unlike Becky's home computer. Sally's account was opened.

'Her first account is her main, functional account. Her standing orders, direct debits and occasional expenditure usually come from this. Fairly low amounts and mainly monthly expected transactions as you can see. She keeps in the black. Her shares income and her benefits are both linked into this account. There, look at the list,' he said turning the screen towards Becky.

She scanned her eyes down her transactions. 'Nothing untoward there. She keeps it well in credit. That's reassuring.'

Both felt all was in order. Then they laughed with embarrassment at the poor bank returns. Nigel switched accounts and drew his chair nearer towards the screen.

'Her second account is the one in which she has inherited some money from your father's estate, you say,' he said.

'Yes, that's right. Most of it is in our family accountant's hands but we thought some money should remain in the bank gaining interest, albeit at £5 a month at the present rate. Spreading the risks, sort of thing,' she found herself saying with little conviction.

Mr. Lees tore off a slip of paper from a pad. He made a column of dates and alongside each wrote £500.

'Sally has been bleeding this account at £500 almost every ten days, on five occasions to be precise. It's always the same amount. That's a total of £2,500 so far. She withdraws cash each time, the same amount as I said, always £500.'

Becky's eyes grew larger and her breath was held for a moment.

'Can I put a stop to this?' she asked determinedly.

'No, but you can speak to Sally to see what she's spending it on and, if she agrees, then you can either come in with her and we can arrange a double signature for withdrawals in the future. Or, if you are satisfied with her response, then we carry on as normal.'

'Thank you, Nigel. I'm beginning to see what I can do. But I came to deposit £100 in her account. I'd better do that now.'

'Of course, you may, but why not give her £100 in cash? Get her out of the habit of coming in to bleed her savings from the bank.'

'Makes sense to me. So I'll get that from the hole in the wall outside?'

Nigel nodded. He stood up and he offered her his hand. 'We'll keep an eye out for Sally.'

They shook hands. 'That will be appreciated. Thanks for all your help.'

'My pleasure. I trust I shall not be requiring your services in the near future, Dr Dunning.'

'But if you do.....' Becky smiled; satisfied with the business she had attended to in his bank.

On the way back to the car she stopped. She took out her mobile phone from her handbag and leant on the back of her car door and called her mother.

'Mum, I've just come from the bank. Sally has been taking large sums out of her account. Did you know?'


Sergeant Jim Boyd was in his police car going around Wigan's most troublesome estate. Graffiti was scrawled on almost every end-facing building and everywhere bundles of used chip paper and cans of juice lay on the grass verges. Dog owners let their pets walk themselves and hence there was dog mess almost everywhere. In the gutters lay some used needles. Local Mums had drawn attention to the state of the area but despite front page coverage in the local press, it made no difference. Outside Bones and Donkey's home was no exception.

Sergeant Boyd parked. He lowered his window and breathed in the air. Then looking through his rear window he saw Donkey approach with her hands in her trouser pockets. He got out of his car.

'Hi Donkey, so how's life?' he asked nonchalantly as much as his uniform would permit.

Donkey lowered her eyes into the car to check if he

was a lone officer. Two meant trouble. One a recce and that was fine.

'Life's okay, can't grumble.'

Sergeant Boyd nodded while thinking his next approach.

'Still on benefit?'

'Yeah, not much suitable work for me, you know poor back and bouts of depression. Doctor laid me off for a while. But I keep looking. Too many offers of so-called 'light work', can't take them on. Wish I could, but... well...you know?'

The sergeant had heard enough. 'So, where's Bones these days?' the officer asked changing the subject.

'Oh, er....at home. We have settled down these days. Crime don't pay. Guess it took a long time for the penny to drop for us.'

'Is that a fact?' the officer said looking up into Donkey's shifty eyes.

'I got other friends too, ya know.'

'Seems like your new friends are having a good influence on you,' the officer said taking off his police chequered hat and placing it on the roof of his car.

Donkey hesitated. She wondered what that was all about. 'What d'ya mean?'

'No reports of housebreaking, robbery, at least none in these parts involving you, Bones or your friends,' he said hitching up his trousers and in so doing revealing his spray gas canister.

'Well, that's maturity for you, isn't it? But at the same time, I don't want to put you out of a job,' she said, scratching her head and laughing at him.

Boyd stroked his day old facial growth.

'So you mean you'd now grass on anyone out of line?'

'That's going too far Sergeant. Just you be satisfied, Donkey and Bones want to settle down at last. Life is just fine.'

Sergeant Boyd grunted as he turned to open his car door. He lifted his hat from the roof and threw it onto the passenger seat. He flopped down into his seat and started the engine. 'Good, glad to hear it.' But it was unlikely Donkey heard the end of the sentence, as the side window was wound up and a call was coming in over the car radio.

Later that day Donkey took out her mobile and prepared to put her best accent to the test should Sally's mother answer. It rang six times.

'Hello Mrs Dunning. Sally's friend, here. Can I have a word with her?'

'Oh yes, certainly. Er..are you the accountant friend?

'Um...no, not the accountant one. He's on leave at present. I think in the south of Italy on holiday with his wife and children. Got a post card from them yesterday,' she lied with ease.

'How pleasant. I'll just get Sally.'

'Thank you very much Mrs Dunning.' Lies and charm, the very tools of her trade and Donkey was a master of them both.

Sally heard her mother call her loudly as she played Erich Wolfgang Korngold's violin concerto on her harmonica.

Remembering the reprimand from Bones for not

answering promptly she stopped playing and ran to the phone.

'Hi Sally. It was good to speak with your mother just now. She's a very pleasant lady. Now I've got some good news for you. Bones has just informed me that the money so far is doing very well, taking advantage of the Chinese market. It's a good time to invest there at present so if you bring another £500 we will ensure you have a solid bank account very soon. Good deal, isn't it?'

'Yes, that's good.'

'Okay, meet in two days time, that's Wednesday 7 p.m. Top of the Plantations walk. Got it?'

'Yes, I know where it is.'

'Great, so see you then with the money. Bye for now.'

Sally was elated that her money was doing so well and with the Chinese economy making it work faster, she was sure to have a good bank account before too long.

Becky took a break from Ward 7 and took a moment to phone her sister from the Manchester Royal Infirmary's staff rest room.

'Mum?'

'Oh Becky, the phone hasn't stopped ringing today it seems. Yes dear?'

'Well, it's really Sally I want to speak to. Is she in?'

'My, she's popular this afternoon. Sally, it's your sister on the phone,' she shouted at the top of her voice.

Sally came running down the stairs and lifted the phone slightly out of breath.

'Sally, I was at the bank this morning, in Wigan, your bank.'

'Yes, my bank, TSB it is,' said Sally fiddling with the telephone cord as she listened following the conversation closely.

'I spoke with the manager.'

'Yes, the manager. I don't know his name,' she said feeling the message was about the nameless manager.

'It's Mr. Lees.'

'Oh, Mr. Lees?' she confirmed. She made an effort to remember this important man's name.

'Yes, he told me that £500 has been taken out of your account a few times and it's always the same amount and in cash.'

'Yes, always the same,' she confirmed.

'What are you spending it on, Sally?' she asked trying hard not to imply an accusative question had been delivered.

'I'm not spending it. I'm investing it. In the Chinese market, my accountant tells me. They have opened up their stock exchange, did you know?'

'Your accountant?' Becky repeated as she recognised Sally was coherent and was answering her questions without any doubts or delay.

'Yes, so I give the money to him.'

'Well, Sally, I am not wanting to burst your bubble but until you see the rewards on your investments, I suggest you, ....no, in fact Sally, I am telling you, do not give the accountant any more money. Is that clear?'

Sally felt cold. She always respected her sister. She now found herself caught between her two advisers.

'I can get my accountant to speak to you. Would that be a good idea?'

'Yes, Sally, that would be a good idea. Ask him to phone me. Yes that's a very good idea. It will put my mind at rest. But in the meantime, no more money out of your accountant, understand?'

'Yes, Becky. No more money.'

# 9

# A&E

Donkey and Bones stood under the horse chestnut tree at the entrance to the Plantations, lighting up their cigarettes. They had arrived early, a few minutes before 7 p.m. They were relaxed confidently awaiting their latest gift of £500.

'Did you not say we should cool off the requests for a while Donkey?' Bones asked, then drew a lung full of nicotine in a mournful drag of his cigarette.

'Yea, but I'm sure we can get away with it a few more times. Her Mum isn't suspicious luv, believe me.'

Sally entered the gates and started to walk down the driveway of the park. Her legs were heavy as she thought through the disappointment she would have to share.

'Hi, over here luv,' said Donkey.

Sally looked up and smiled at the pair.

'You okay, my friend?' asked Bones.

'Yes, thank you.'

'We've got something for you,' said Donkey leaving her cigarette in her mouth while searching in her pocket. She brought out two twenty pound notes and a tenner.

'Here's £50.' She handed the rolled notes to Sally.

'That's just a thank you from the city trader, Mike. He's making you the money in Hong Kong,' she said with a genuine smile to a surprised and pleased Sally.

'Thank you, Donkey.' She put the money in her left hand pocket of her trousers.

Donkey looked up at Bones who smiled. Their golden goose seemed genuinely thankful for her sudden good fortune. It should ease a few more requests.

'Now, Sally, luv. You got the cash?'

Sally looked around but nobody was in sight. She made no effort to check her pockets.

'I've not got the money.'

Bones' face looked threatening. Donkey raised her hand as if to say she would deal with the tense situation.

'That's okay Sally, we all get forgetful. You can get it tomorrow morning and we meet again tomorrow afternoon, same time. Okay, my friend?'

Sally moved from one foot to the other and started to sway to and fro.

'I said okay, Sally?'

'No, not okay. I can't give you any money.'

'What do you mean?' said Donkey with an anxious look on her face.

'I was told not to give you any more money.'

A cold current of fear went through Sally as she sensed the changing atmosphere. She felt the hairs rise up on her neck.

A similar feeling came over Bones and Donkey as they feared the end of the arrangement. Bones pulled out a small blue glass bottle from his pocket. Donkey's face was serious.

'Who told you, Sally? Who said no more money?' she said in a slowly spoken voice.

'My sister told me,' Sally replied with confidence for that was what Becky always gave her.

'Do you always do what your big sister tells you?' asked Bones as he stepped nearer Sally.

'Yes, she's my sister. You can phone her if you like. She would be happy to talk to you. She wants you to phone her.'

'Well I can when I get home but not now, Sally.' Bones said with more pressing matters on his mind as the golden goose was becoming egg-bound.

'And we are your friends,' reminded Donkey.

Sally saw they were saying the right words but she felt ill at ease.

'That's not a kind way to treat your friends, is it Sally? But I know..... we all make mistakes. So will you get the money tomorrow?' she asked in a more conciliatory tone.

Sally was very direct.

'No, Donkey, I won't get the money.'

Donkey stubbed out her cigarette with her right trainer shoe and ground it into the damp foliage underfoot.

'We usually celebrate our profits to date with a small drink,' said Bones as she took off the bottle top and handed it to Sally.

Sally sniffed and did not know what the liquid was. She hesitated. It would be some alcohol and it was a small bottle. Perhaps she should enjoy the success of her financial contributions to date.

'Go on Sally, celebrate,' urged Bones. Donkey looked around.

Sally raised the bottle to her lips and took a sip. Again she hesitated. It was not a familiar drink.

'Enjoy it. Sally, take it all in one go,' said Bones. Sally finished the bottle in one huge gulp. A few seconds later Sally's legs buckled and she sank to the ground like an anchor to the sea bed.

'We're not gonna get any more from her, Donkey.'

Donkey nodded. She pulled out the £50 from Sally's trouser pocket. Their luck had ground to an end and they were bitter. It was time to conclude their relationship and in a way only they knew how. The process began. As Sally's child-like pose lay on the ground the first solar plexus kick landed. It was followed by kicks to the head which made her nose bleed and more to her stomach and chest. Each seemed to take turns in administering the torture. The assault was fuelled by the realisation Sally was no use to them anymore, after such a promising start. It was unnecessary and spiteful but part of their modus operandi.

A dog walker approached. The attack stopped.

'Hey, what are you doing to her,' the dog walker shouted with concern and with adrenaline rushing through his veins.

'Mind yer own fuckin' business,' said Bones.

'Mind your language or I'll set my dog on you.'

Donkey looked at Bones, then at the canine threat. The dog was a mongrel to Bones and Donkey with a long black tail. Its teeth were showing and a growl came from its throat. The dog sensed the situation accurately.

It could defend its master and on command attack confronters. There was no time to ask about its mixed pedigree.

'C'mon, let's go,' said Donkey with an eye on the restrained dog. They raised their collars as if to hide their faces as they ran up the path and out of the Plantations gate to the main road.

The dog walker approached the victim. He wound the lead round his hand as his dog was very keen to sniff the body.

'Are you all right, my dear?' he asked towering over Sally's foetal position.

There was no reply. The man prodded Sally but it did not rouse her.

He stood back pulled out his mobile and phoned 999.

'Which service?'

'Ambulance and police. Woman beaten up by two youths who have just left the Plantations. One male one female.'

'A police car will be with you shortly. Can you place the woman in the recovery position?'

'You mean turn her on her side? She's already in that position.'

'Good, then make sure she's still breathing and if she comes to speak to her. Reassure her, got that?'

'Yes, okay. I hope the ambulance will be here soon.'

'It will.'

He tied his dog to a nearby tree and it resumed a seated position looking at the body just out of reach.

In the distance the man heard a siren but had no

idea if it was a police car or the ambulance. Soon after, a bright luminous vehicle stopped nearby and two paramedics approached Sally wearing thin light-blue rubber gloves.

'Madam, can you hear me? I'm Ricky, a medic. Can you hear me?' What's your name luv?'

Ricky shone a light in her eyes. There was only a flicker of an eye in response. 'She's out for the count.' He took a pulse reading. 'Pulse normal. She needs some cautionary x-rays. Let's get her aboard.'

'It's probably a drug case. Her lips are blue,' his colleague informed Ricky.

Sally uttered a painful groan as she was carefully lifted onto a ridged plastic board. She lay there for a moment. The police car arrived. A sergeant got out together with a female constable. They recognised the ambulance crew.

'What have we got, Ricky?' the sergeant asked.

'Looks like an overdose and assault. Her face took a beating,' he said. 'Unusual, she seems an older woman.'

The female officer approached the dog walker taking out her notebook.

'I'm Constable Karen Dunbar. Did you see what happened?'

'Yes, well probably not all of it.'

'Your name please?'

'Ronald Pattison.'

'Double "t"?'

'Yes. I had just entered the Plantations and the two thugs had been kicking the woman when she was down. She put up no fight.'

'Did you see the attackers clearly?'

'Yes, but I didn't know them. Never seen them before.'

'Would you know them if you saw them again?'

'Yes, I might. If they were together.'

'How old were they? What were they wearing?'

'Mid-twenties, maybe early thirties, I'd say. Both in dirty old trainers. The taller one, the man, had a grey top and the woman a blue one. They were both in tracksuit bottoms. One pair was a sort of maroon with a white stripe down the sides, that's what he wore. The woman's tracksuit was plain light grey.'

'And did you see the actual assault?'

'Oh yes, both of them were kicking her.'

'On the body?'

'Yes, and kicks to her head too. That's when I shouted out at them and they stopped.'

'Right sir, I just need some personal details. Your date of birth and address please.'


Sally only saw a light flooded ceiling as she lay in bed 4 in the A&E triage area of the Royal Albert Edward Infirmary, on Wigan lane. Slowly the effect of the drug eased and when a nurse approached she made some tentative enquiries.

'Can you tell me your name, luv?'

Sally wondered who this woman was. She had not seen her before. Why was she asking for her name?'

'Where am I?'

'You are in hospital. You had an overdose of drugs. Remember?'

'No, I don't take drugs,' said Sally trying to sit up and

protest the suggestion. But why, she wondered, was she there? Why was she in pain?

The nurse looked at her wrists. There was a grazed mark which showed a slight swelling over a web of red scratches.

'Looks like you've tried to inject, love?' she said raising her wrist.

'No, I don't,' said Sally raising her voice with a dazed and confused look in her eyes. Tears seemed to be forming behind her glazed eyes.

'The evidence is that you do drugs my luv. I've seen many cases like yours over the years,' she said twisting her arm so that the scratches were brought to Sally's sight.

Sally looked down at the wrist the nurse was inspecting.

'I was cleaning Mum's gutters. I was up the ladder clearing the soggy leaves. The gutter scratched me.'

The nurse made a note of her comment and twisted her head as if to ask herself if she was telling the truth.

'Tell me your name and address,' she asked.

'I'm Sally Dunning. I live with my mum in Wigan in Leyland Mill Lane.'

'And where do you work?'

'I don't work. I look after my mum.'

A full-time carer, thought the nurse. The interview stopped abruptly as two policemen arrived. They took off their hats and drew alongside Sally's bed.

'You are the patient found in the Plantations an hour ago or so?'

'Yes. I was in the Plantations.'

'Okay I'm Constable McGuire and Constable Sinclair is my colleague. We'd like to ask a few questions.'

Sally tried to sit up but the pain in her midriff caused her to sink back flat on her back.

'So you were in the Plantations, yeah?' asked Sinclair.

'Yes, I was.'

'And you were beaten up?'

'Yes, that's why I am here, isn't it?'

'I guess so. So who hit you?'

Sally thought for a moment. Nothing was coming to mind. She was clearly stressed.

'I don't know.'

'You mean you don't know or you won't tell me who beat you up?'

'I don't know who beat me up,' she said drawing her knees up and clenching them over the bed sheets.

Dr Basil Ainsworth approached, his stethoscope swinging with each step. 'Officers, if you have finished with my patient, I will require a CT scan quite soon.'

'Doctor, I think we are almost finished. Sally, one last go eh? Who hit and kicked you?'

'I don't know, I really don't. I can't understand it. I walked into the park. I remember that. It must have happened very quickly. Why me? Why was I hit? I've done nothing wrong,' was all Sally could say and it was all Sally knew about the assault.

Elsie bit her lip and walked up and down the hall like a caged panther. Sally had not come home and it was past 11 p.m. Perhaps she had got lost again. Maybe she was out with her friends. She called her mobile but it wasn't turned on. Perhaps she was with new friends. They would surely look after her. Wigan was a friendly town after all. It was this thought which prompted her off to bed and sleep overcame her anxiety.

She woke before the usual time of 6.55 a.m. and turned on Radio 4. She lay in bed dreaming, awaiting the 7 a.m. news bulletin. But before the BBC gongs of the hour struck, she called through to Sally as the previous night's anxiety returned. There was no reply. She got out of her bed and went to her room. She opened the door only enough for a shaft of light to enter, but enough to see that her bed had not been slept in. Never had this situation arisen before. She shivered. Had she been run over? Had she had a heart attack? Morbid fears grew in her mind. What should she do? No point informing her sister or brother at this stage; they were too far away. The thoughts kept flooding her mind. She put on her dressing gown and dialled the police.

'Can you help me, I've lost my daughter?'

'Your daughter? How old is she? When did you last see her?'

'Sally is fifty-three; fifty-four later this week and she's autistic. Sally Dunning.'

'I see. Can you describe her?'

'She's about five feet eight, with bubbly brown hair. She has tics which make her shiver from time to time. Oh and she was wearing a light blue pullover last night when she went out.'

'Good. And when you say that you have lost her do you mean she did not come home last night?'

'Yes, I suppose so. She was not in when I went to

bed,' she said twisting the telephone cord around her fingers.

'Does she have friends? She might have had a sleep-over? Does she go to any place often, a dance hall for example?'

'Not really, no nothing like that. She sometimes goes for a walk but that could be anywhere.'

'Was she at a pub last night?'

'Oh no, I can't see her going into a pub.'

'She might ring you soon or arrive back. She is a grown woman after all.'

'Yes she's an adult but she is autistic. I'm not sure where she'll be. But you mentioned a friend. Yes, she's got an accountant friend. Perhaps that's where she's been.'

'I'll put out an alert. We'll get back to you if we trace her.'

The call eased Elsie's mind. A first overnight for Sally, she smiled. Well, better late than never. She dressed and had breakfast. As she was drying the dishes, a patient van drove up to the front door. She threw the dishtowel over the drying rack and made for the door, rubbing her wet hands on her apron. A man in a charcoal sports jacket opened the vehicle's rear door. A car accident was all Elsie could think of, poor Sally.

'Back home for the wounded soldier. Be prepared for a daughter with a smashed up face. But she'll recover,' the volunteer driver said.

Elsie saw Sally step down the couple of steps unaided. She smiled at her mother. She came forward to inspect her and support her.

'What in the name of....'

'She'll be okay in a couple of days,' said the man returning to his patient van and the engine started up. It glided down the drive and was soon out of sight.

'Now in you come and tell me all about it, Sally. I was really worried when you did not come home last night.'

'I was in the hospital last night,' said Sally holding her mother's hand.

'But your face dear, what happened?' she asked looking at her swollen face and bruised haematoma above her right eyebrow. Evidence of some sort of attack surely, she thought.

'I don't know Mum, I don't know,' she said and her face told no lies.

Shortly after, they heard a car draw up to the front door. Elsie went to investigate. She saw its diced colours.

'It's the police Sally. What do they want?'

Sally did not reply. She merely stood still in the hall like a grandmother clock and waited for the front door to open.

When it did, Constable Andrew Barnett stood before them along with his colleague Constable Pam Eddy.

'Ms. Dunning? Ms. Sally Dunning?'

'Yes,' said Sally looking through the officer.

'Can we ask you a few questions?'

'Can I help, officer, you know Sally is autistic.'

'I'd prefer not, at least not at this stage of our enquiry. Maybe later. We've got to know what happened to your daughter,' said Constable Barnett.

'And so do I, I assure you.'

'We all do. This is however an enquiry, as my

colleague said, we would like to talk to Sally alone first,' said a sympathetic Pam. Elsie nodded.

'Are you going to charge Sally?' she asked with her hand almost over her mouth.

'No, she's been a victim of a crime. I assure you Sally will not be charged.'

Elsie's hand dropped and she ushered the officers into the lounge.

'Would you like a coffee?' she asked them.

'No thank you. We hope we will not be too long and we are very busy today,' said Pam wondering how this autistic witness might respond. They sat down with Sally as Elsie left, closing the door behind her.

'So Sally, tell me about what happened yesterday. The whole day so I get an understanding,' said Constable Barnett.

Sally took a moment to gather her thoughts.

'I got out of bed and had Shreddies and toast. Then I went to brush my teeth. After that I got dressed. In the morning I hoovered the hall carpet and dusted around the shelves......'

'Okay Sally, take it from when you left the house.

Sally stopped. Had she upset the officers? They asked her to tell them what happened and now they did not really want to know, she thought.

'In the afternoon I had lunch. I finished an apple and then I went to clean my teeth.'

Constable Barnett looked at his colleague and she showed the blank page in her notebook. Her eyebrows lifted an inch or so. Then she pouted her lips. No point upsetting this autistic witness. Her ability to remember detail might just solve the case, thought Constable Eddy.

'Then I went out to meet my friends....'

'Who are your friends Sally?' asked Pam, glad that they were making progress with the interview.

'My friend is an accountant.'

'An accountant? Hmmm. Do you know his name and his firm?'

'Er....that's Bones. It's not his real name. It's a nickname. He does not have an office. He works from home.'

'Bones, you say. And you mentioned friends. Was there another friend with him?' asked Pam who now was writing with confidence.

'Yes, she has a nickname too.'

'Really? What was her nickname then?'

'His friend, his partner, is called Donkey.'

'Bones and Donkey, I'm not surprised.'

Sally smiled. 'You know my friends?'

'Oh, yes, Sally. We know your friends Donkey and Bones, don't we constable Eddy?'

'We sure do. But how are they your friends, Sally?' she asked.

'I got lost in the Plantations and Donkey brought me home.'

'That was good of her, wasn't it?'

'Yes, and they bought me a ticket to go to the cinema.'

'Can you remember what film you saw?

'Yes, it was very funny.'

Constable Eddy smiled supportively. 'Do you remember the title of the film?'

Sally thought hard. 'It was...about a man....'

'A Western?' asked Constable Barnett.

Sally frowned at him. 'The film was called, A Man... Called Ove.'

Constable Barnett sucked his pen. Then he tapped it against his notebook. 'Sally, has either of them given you any drugs?'

'No, no drugs. I don't take drugs.'

'The fact is Sally you had been given a drug and that's what made you fall to the ground.'

'But I don't take drugs.'

'No, I agree, but you had been given a drug before you were beaten up,' said Barnett engrossed in Sally's child-like delivery.

'So, who gave you the drug?' asked Constable Eddy.

'I don't know. I can't remember.'

'Okay, Sally, don't worry you've been a good witness. You have given us something to be getting on with.'

After the police left, Elsie made a cup of tea for Sally. She took it to her bedroom where she found her polishing her harmonicas. She wanted to ask so many questions but felt Sally was not ready to tell her. She knew she would tell her in her own time in her own way.

She returned to collect her cup half an hour later but the cup was still full. Sally was sound asleep in a world of her own.

# 10

# Identity Parades

Ronald Pattison hesitantly entered the Wigan police station. He had never done so before. He had phoned on a couple of occasions about things he had now forgotten about, in the distant past. He climbed the steps to the front door feeling unsure. It was a new experience.

'Mr. Pattison, come this way,' said a man whose shoulder tab indicated Special Constable. Ronald thought he was either a special volunteer policeman or in the special branch. This menial job suggested the former.

'Have a seat in this room while we get the identity parade ready,' he said ushering Ronald into the sparsely furnished room.

Some twenty minutes later after Ronald had sat looking at a blank wall save for the "Have You Seen This Man?" Poster, he was asked to follow the Special constable and was taken along a solid concrete corridor. It led to three or four steps and after climbing them he noticed a glass window on the left and a seat half way down the aisle.

'It's a one-way glass mirror, sir. You can see the men but they can't see you. Now, do take a seat. When they are standing to face you, you will see they are all holding a number before them on a card. Write down the number of the alleged male attacker you think you remember seeing. Or perhaps you'll remember him as he fled from the Plantations. Okay, any questions?'

Ronald shook his head. 'No, I understand,' he said still feeling tense but secure with the arrangements. A side door was opened and in walked a line of out-of-step men. They turned right in no certain fashion, each holding a number from 1 to 8. Ronald realised another lineup would be required for the female attacker. Nevertheless he was confident he would be able to identify the male offender. He passed his eyes from left to right and then right to left and back again. It was not such an easy task after all, he thought. Their statuary stance made it tricky to come to a quick conclusion since both assailants were bent and running away on that dreadful day. Indeed, Ronald could not remember their faces with great accuracy. The officer asked if he had come to a conclusion.

'Yes and no. Numbers 2 and 8 have caught my eye.'

'You sure about Number 2?'

Ronald hesitated. He gave the man another look.

'Yes, particularly him, No 2. Yes, he's fixed in my mind, but.... perhaps.... number 8 is a very close second.'

The officer pouted his lips. He realised his plain clothed detective inspector, who had been asked to stand in as he came off duty, had just been identified as No 2, one of Sally's attackers. It was hard for the Special to hide a broad smile. However No 8 pleased the policeman. It was a definite result. It was Bones.

Half an hour later eight females arrived and stood in

line. Once again Ronald took to the one-way mirror and ran his eyes along the line.

'Number 4 yes, definitely. That's the woman,' Ronald said pointing and nodding his head at the same time. He was sure. Donkey had been identified.

A shout came from the attic.

'What's the matter, Sally?' asked her mother putting down the Daily Mail newspaper.

Sally came running down two flights of stairs and arrived in front of her mother.

'What did you do with my comics?' she said with a furrowed brow.

'Your comics? What do you mean, Sally?'

Sally's arms shook by her side and her open mouth was fixed for a moment. 'My comics. They are not there.'

'Your comics are not in the boxes?' she asked with a puzzled face.

'No, not in the boxes.'

'You are sure? Let me see for myself.'

Elsie walked up the stairs breathing harder at each flight. A missing necklace and now Sally's comics, she wondered what next she might discover. She entered the bedroom. She got down on her knees to look for the comics. 'You are right, the comics are not there and I've certainly not moved them.' She looked at Sally who returned the look of astonishment. 'Goodness me, they are definitely not here. I don't understand it. Sally are you sure you did not move them?'

'No Mum, I did not move them. Honest, I did not move them.'

Elsie got off her knees, stood up and sighed. 'I don't like this. Let's see what else is missing. Let's start from the attic.'

She entered the top floor and saw the snooker table with all its balls in place but on the blackboard a score was almost rubbed out. Sally never used the blackboard. She stared at the writing through her reading glasses perched on her nose.

'Sally have you been playing snooker with anyone recently?' she asked turning round with an accusing face.

Sally did not like to see her Mum upset but her answer was clear. 'No, I don't play with anyone, not since Dad died.'

'I thought so. But the...see...' She pointed to the scoreboard at the smudge. She looked around the attic. Everything else seemed in order.

Elsie's thoughts turned to the other worldly possessions. She returned to the bedroom and opened her jewellery box, the one which she never took out of the house, let alone took on holiday. She opened the box. Instead of two rings, her engagement ring and her wedding ring, only the wedding ring was present.

'Sally, my engagement ring is missing too. Now I'm definitely sure we've been burgled.'

'Robbed? We should tell the police,' said Sally nodding and shaking at the same time.

Elsie was in agreement. 'Yes, I just can't explain these things going missing in any other way.'

Elsie returned to the lounge and sat down. She dialled the police and a civilian took the details of her missing items.

'Missing, no they are not missing,' she said shaking her head. 'They've been stolen.'

At 9.30 a.m. the next morning, almost on the dot, a car arrived at their front door. Constables Barnett and Eddy got out and knocked on the front door lion-head knocker.

'Good morning. You rang about a burglary,' said Constable Barnett.

'Yes, I have no other explanation.'

Constable Eddy's notebook was already in her hand poised to take any information coming her way.

'Can you say when this happened?' she asked setting the parameters.

'I suppose it must have been when we were on holiday in the Mediterranean. After all there's always been someone in the house since then. And we've been back ten days already.'

Constable Eddy was scribbling at pace. 'Let me clarify, you said you lost a necklace, a box of comics and an engagement ring.'

'Yes, that's all I've found missing, so far. Oh and my daughter's necklace, too. It's not around either. I nearly forgot that.'

'If you do find anything else missing, do let us know won't you?' asked Constable Eddy.

'Apart from the box of comics, it looks like they went for things of value,' said Constable Barnett.

Elsie moved to the edge of her seat. 'No officer, the comics are very valuable.'

Elsie could see the officers doubting her assertion that the old comics were nothing other than emergency loo paper.

'You see they are all the Beano magazines, from the first issue up to the 6,000th edition. They must be worth something.'

Constable Barnett nodded and seemed to have a lemon sweet in his cheeks.

'Oh, and in the attic, there's a snooker table.'

'Don't tell me they took that too. They'd need a lorry to move that,' said Constable Barnett.

'No, not the table but the score blackboard, it has some rubbed out scores.'

'Writing perhaps?' asked Pam Eddy.

'Maybe it was, but Sally does not use the board. She's not good at writing or figures. I suspect the thieves played a game or two. It must be their rubbed out scores.'

Constable Eddy's eyes looked round the large lounge. Nothing seemed to have been disturbed but the evidence must still be checked.

'We will send in the scenes of crime officers. No one should go to the attic until they have been there. In fact I suggest you go out after they arrive. They will do a thorough search for evidence. You understand?'

Elsie looked at Sally. Her gaze seemed to be on the neck of Constable Barnett.

'It just does not make sense why this happened. Are you sure it's a robbery?' asked Elsie opening her cupped hands.

'Didn't you say you had been away? Sally said you were in Malta. Is that not so?' queried Constable Barnett.

'Yes, we were away for a fortnight but the alarm was on when we left. Well, I think it was on. Anyway, it must have been because it was on when we returned, and I turned it off. I haven't seen any damage to doors or windows. Perhaps I left a ground floor window open. Oh, I just don't know, I really don't understand what has happened.'

'I appreciate your doubts. But there's more than enough evidence to investigate and hopefully we will bring the culprits to trial,' said Constable Eddy returning her diary to her breast pocket.

Sally opened the door and walked outside. She stood staring at the lawn and the police car. She too did not know what was happening.

'My daughter tells me large sums of money have been taken from Sally's account. Well, she withdrew it herself but it's not clear what she used the money for other than give it to her new friend, the accountant.'

'The accountant?' repeated Constable Barnett with a sniff to catch a runny nose. She produced a white handkerchief. She blew her nose as she began to speak. 'I...I think Sally should come to the station with us.'

Elsie gasped. 'Oh dear you don't think this is all Sally's fault, do you?'

'No, no but she may be able to give us a better picture of when all this started and we'll see if she can recognise some of our local offenders,' said Constable Eddy putting her diced hat on her head and securing it in position with both hands.

At 2 p.m. that afternoon, Sally found herself in the same area Mr. Pattison had occupied before her. Sally was led along the passageway by one of the investigating officers in the case. They sat in the centre together awaiting the trail of potential suspects. Sally's remit was clear. Identify anyone she knew and especially the accountant, if he was there. She was told twice that the glass wall was one-way and she could not be seen. Instead of pacifying Sally, it was an unusual glass and therefore a challenge for her to experience.

The six men and six women arrived and turned right to face the unseen Sally.

'Well, do you recognise anyone, Sally?' asked the police officer whose pen and paper were to hand.

Sally took her time. She stared at each figure for some time. She wanted to tell the truth as best she remembered. She hoped by doing this that the police would be pleased. That was her focus. But she knew she would fail. She did not know everyone. 'Yes, No 3 is the baker from the bakery across the road,' she said confidently.

'Good. Anyone else?' he asked, smiling out of her sight.

'Number seven I've seen in the post office but I don't know her name. Oh I know the next one, that's my friend Donkey.'

'Which number please?'

'Donkey is number 8 and that's ...yes, that's Bones, Number 1. He's my accountant.'

The officer drew a breath. Things were taking shape in his detective mind. 'Your accountant?' he clarified. If ever there was a less suitable banker it was Bones, he thought. 'Do you give him any money?' he asked in view of Sally's description of number 1.

Sally looked at the officer. How could he know she had brought him money, was her thought. 'Yes, but only when he asks for it.'

'I see, and how often does he ask?'

Sally looked at the ceiling. 'About every two or maybe three weeks.'

'And is it a ten pound note you give him each time?'

Sally looked cross. How could £10 make a good profit? 'No, five hundred pounds each time,' she replied. 'The money is doing well in China.'

'Hmmm China, you say?'

'Yes, that's what Bones told me.'

The officer now had the full picture. What he needed now was a statement from Sally. He invited her into an office near the front desk.

'Now, can you write down what you told me about your banker, Bones?' he asked handing over a pen and an official notepad.

Sally looked at the pen and paper. She looked up. 'No, I can't.'

'You can't or you don't want to?' he asked in a gruff voice.

'I won't cos I can't write well.'

The officer realised just how damaged her mind must be and started to write each sentence by sentence recalling what he had heard Sally say earlier. After each sentence he looked up at Sally and asked if it was true. On each occasion, Sally gave a clear YES.

'Now I need you to sign down here to show you agree with what I have written. The pen was given to Sally who took it and she carefully wrote her name slowly and without any flamboyance.

'That's fine. Okay, Ms. Dunning, you are free to go now.'

'Is that all I have to do? Can I see my friends now?'

'You can see your friends anytime but Donkey and

Bones are no longer your friends. They are about to be locked up,' the officer said as he found Sally holding onto the table staring at the wall, trying to comprehend what she had just heard.

On Saturday it was Sally's birthday. Her brother Alec and Becky had arrived late the previous night. They slept in till 9 a.m. but Sally was up with the lark. She was keen to make the most of her special day. She was quick to open the cards which lay on the kitchen table. She was a child at heart and had always been so. She placed the cards on the Welsh dresser in her own special order of sister on top shelf and mother and brother on the second row. No one questioned her reasoning. Then she had some breakfast eating two boiled eggs and four brown toasted soldiers.

By 9.15 a.m. the family had gathered in the kitchen. Becky was keen to find out what recent events had been happening but perhaps not so early on her fifty-fourth birthday.

Her mother gave her a new jersey and she kissed her expressing her thanks. She immediately took off her jersey and donned her new birthday one with seagull motifs. Becky handed over one hundred crisp pounds in £20 denomination notes tucked into a fruit and nut chocolate bar cover then gave her a little something else. It was not packed and it squeaked in front of Sally as Becky handed it over.

The family could see Sally was unsure about this present. 'You will find it very useful, I assure you, Sally.' She came and gave Becky a hug and a kiss.

'Thank you for my chocolate bar, the money and this squeaky cat, Becky.'

Alec knocked on the table. 'Happy birthday to you...' and the family joined in singing the traditional verse.

'My present for you is not here yet. I've still to collect it. So we leave in ten minutes. Who's coming with me? Becky put her hand up but Elsie, who was in on the arrangement, said she had too much to do at home. Sally put her hand up, jumping in the air as she did so.

'Of course you're coming Sally, it's your birthday present and we need you there,' said a smiling Alec.

With her teeth brushed and her hair groomed Sally joined her brother and sister in the Land Rover and Alec set off heading away from town. It was a cross country route which ended up on a minor farm road.

'I'm going to ride a horse,' said Sally getting excited.

'No, not today, something quite different,' said Becky.

The car drove to the front door of the farm and the farmer's wife greeted them.

'And you are Sally. Happy birthday young lady.'

'I'm fifty-four today,' she said.

'My, that's the best age to look after a....well...come this way and see.'

They followed her to a barn and entered. Inside there was a straw box with a bitch feeding her young.

'They look so cute,' said Becky. Sally was unsure and grabbed her brother's hand.

'What are they?' asked Sally.

'From good Schnauzer stock, they are miniature Schnauzers. Very friendly and loving. With a good strong bark to warn off strangers.'

'Just what you need Sally,' said Alec.

'Yes, to warn off strangers,' she replied.

The farmer's wife took some selected dogs from their mother. 'Well you see five puppies in total. Two are already accounted for but you can choose any of these three. This one is a male and the other two, female.'

'Well Sally. It's to be your dog. Which one do you like?'

'I like them all.'

'So do I but I can only afford one,' laughed the wealthy and smartly dressed Alec. 'These are pedigree dogs, you realise Sally?'

Sally ignored her brother and went down on her knees. One of the puppies approached and sought loving attention. She picked up the pup. 'This is the one I want,' she said triumphantly.

'Now you know why I gave you a squeaky cat, Sally,' said her sister.

'Yes, so she can play with the cat.'

'Yes, and the squeak will be fun too,' said Alec.

And so Molly joined the Dunning family, took up residence and barked at the postman. This gave the family additional security but the mystery how burglars had entered still remained.

At police Headquarters the evidence was gathering pace. Harper & Pierpont auctioneers informed them that the comics had not been sold. In fact the comic auction in London had not yet been arranged. They were happy to give the comic stock back to the police as evidence. It would however take a few days for a courier to return them. Mr. Mike Harper, the manager, also recalled the woman who had brought the comics to his firm and so was identified as a crucial witness. Mr Harper was brought to the police station by appointment and shown a book of 'mug shots.' He had no difficulty in recognising the comic seller as Donkey.

The police rightly assumed the jewellery had been sold on eBay and that meant a raid on the gang's house. From their home they took away their computer to trawl for emails to eBay. They also discovered a large amount of drugs; indeed a concoction of an alarming amount. Amphetamines, LDS, acid drops, marijuana and a collection of legal highs. They were found in the toaster base, behind the loo, in a pillow and to the delight of the police, more drugs were spread out on Donkey's bed for the entire world to see. Police estimated the street value to be several thousands of pounds. On a card found under the settee seats their client group requiring drugs was listed and named. Both Donkey and Bones were now in police custody in separate cells and as a consequence, charged with the possession and supply of category A and B drugs.

Meanwhile the Crown Prosecution Service received the police report and was informed about further charges likely to follow. A new folder was not required by the Crown. The alleged two local offenders still had room for several blank pages in File number 4. Their names filled three chubby files gathering dust as they lay on the shelf.

Constable Pam Eddy returned to see Sally in her home.

She informed her that she would be regarded as a vulnerable adult for court purposes. This status would give her some protection from the Judge against bullying questioning from the defence agent. However Sally would have to provide evidence against Donkey and Bones which might incarcerate her old 'friends.'

This was a worry for Sally. It was difficult for her to differentiate their good acts from those she was being told about. Elsie was informed there would be a plain police vehicle stopping by the house from time to time just in case bail was granted to the accused. As a vulnerable adult, the police would prioritise her case and respond promptly and appropriately when deemed necessary.

# 11

# Romance

The following weekend, Elsie drove Sally to Bolton where Sally's agent had arranged for her to perform at the Octagon Theatre. When they arrived, Eric and Beth welcomed them while Sally and Tom stood back and stared at each other awkwardly, as if they had never met. They were met by Carolee Meredith who took Sally backstage while Elsie joined Eric, Beth and Tom in a box overlooking the stage.

'Are you feeling okay, Sally?' Carolee asked switching off her iPad as they walked together.

'Yes.'

'Look up there.' She held Sally's arm and guided it to the box. 'There's your mother. She'll enjoy the performance I am sure. You will be with her after the performance. Okay?'

'Yes, after the performance.'

Elsie waved to Sally and then so did Tom's parents. Tom stood up and waved more enthusiastically.

Carolee moved more slowly. She hoped Sally's Malta performance would not be a one-off impromptu performance because the Octagon's rows were filling and behind the curtain the musicians of the Bolton Symphony Orchestra were tuning their instruments.

The formality of the occasion and the paying numbers attending were the concern of Carolee. But not for Sally who sat in the wings oblivious to the audience's murmurs, accepting the orchestra's preparations and awaiting her turn to perform on stage.

She sat motionless as the concert proceeded. Carolee noticed Sally did not clap when each piece of music finished. She presumed nerves had got to her.

'Would you like a glass of water? Good for calming nerves.'

Sally looked straight at her agent. 'Water, no. Anyway I am not thirsty.'

Carolee smiled a reassured grin. It was so different to have Sally on her books. A straight talking client was always welcome to her, used to the idiosyncrasies of some of her more demanding authors.

As the interval approached and many of the audience's thoughts turned to an interval drink in the bar, Sally took to the stage. She was told to go to the centre where there would be a gold spot on the floor. That was where she had to stand – mid stage. She marched on with her head lowered to find the spot. As soon as she found the exact location, she turned a military left turn to face the audience then raised her harmonica to her lips, catching the conductor by surprise as the applause had not quite died down. She began playing the Elizabethan Serenade. The conductor held his baton across his chest. The orchestra was silent till the first twelve bars had been played. Then the strings joined in and Sally continued to play. The audience saw no false start. Instead it seemed a pleasant and planed approach.

It was certainly not intended but the conductor's smile encouraged any frowns on the players' faces to disappear. This five minute piece of music received a firm hand clapping. Rather than await the applause to die down or even remember to bow, Sally made for the wings. Her first performance was over. The audience was talking. It seemed to have gone down well.

During the break, some of the orchestra approached Sally to congratulate and thank her on her performance. It was just another occasion to play for Sally and so her cold stare seemed to reject the praise offered until one member mentioned Sally was autistic and the word flew round the orchestra players like a scherzo volante.

The finale in the second half was Beethoven's Clarinet Concerto. But of course there was no clarinet as the programme stated. The conductor introduced Sally after announcing that Bolton would receive a world premiere performance of Beethoven's Harmonica Concerto. Initially, this news was met by audience titters but applause broke out and swelled the chests of the good and worthy citizens of Bolton at this special occasion for the Lancashire town.

The harmonica had to wait several bars before entering and this gave the conductor a missed heart beat in case Sally set off prematurely like an errant Ascot horse. But her introductory notes were seamless and the years of perfecting the work in her bedroom came to fruition. After the final chord was heard the conductor stepped down from his rostrum and held Sally's hand up high to the appreciative orchestra. Then he lifted it aloft to the audience as Sally faced the applause of the proud Bolton town. She was restrained. She could not leave the stage – and the conductor made sure. As the applause began to die down the audience called for more. "Encore!" they shouted and the conductor asked Sally if she had a favourite tune to play.

'The Romance,' said Sally.

'You mean Shostakovich's Romance from The Gadfly?'

'Yes,' said Sally with a frown. What other Romance had he in mind she thought as her stance briefly turned towards the box where Tom was seated with his parents and Sally's mother. She smiled at them as the conductor informed the orchestra of the selected music. Then she saw the audience before her. They were expecting more music and she would give them that. She could play many different pieces and wondered if the Romance would be appreciated. She moved toward the front of the stage where a young lady sat with her parents. Sally's eyes focussed on her like a narrow beam of light.

'Do you like Shostakovich's Romance from the Gadfly?' she asked.

The girl did not speak. She was dumfounded at being asked. She smiled at her and nodded. It was a good enough signal for Sally to return to her spot on the stage.

The orchestra keyed in the music on their iPads and placed them on their stands. All knew the piece with its melodic tune but of course no one had ever heard it on the harmonica. Expectation on the audience's minds was mirrored in the thoughts of the symphony orchestra of Bolton that evening.

Once more a note perfect performance was heard on

that warm June night at the Octagon. The local paper music journalist looked forward to writing her report over a glass of claret at home that night. She was inspired by what she had heard.

The following morning Inspector Reeves appeared at the Dunning house.

'Good morning Mrs Dunning,' he said, showing his identification. 'I'd like to take one more look in the attic again. Pieces of chalk from the snooker room board are not showing any conclusive fingerprints. I'd just like another look. Will that be convenient?'

'I see you have a camera. You mean look for evidence?' asked Elsie, as she untied her kitchen apron.

'Yes, a thorough look. That's why I have the camera,' he replied with one foot on the door mat.

'Yes, I suppose that might catch the villains,' she said as she absent-mindedly adjusted her hair.

'That's what I am hoping too,' the inspector said with a pleasant smile. 'You know, we think we can get them for a long jail sentence. I'm just hoping I can find some more to lengthen their stay at Her Majesty's pleasure.'

At that moment Molly escaped. She ran out of the house and round and round the police officer's car. She barked incessantly. Sally was in hot pursuit.

'Molly, come to me Molly,' but it had become a game and Molly would not come back to Sally until she was exhausted. The Inspector took his time. But after only a few minutes he had taken a very significant photo of a chalk fingerprint from underneath the snooker table lip. He felt sure he now had the icing on the cake.

Sally returned to the house holding Molly in her arms. 'I don't think she'll run away, Mum. She does like to chase me though,' she said as happy as a young child without a care in the world.

# 12

# Light at the End of the Tunnel

Sally did not often have mail addressed to her. This was a rare exception. Her mother brought the letter through to her as she played her harmonica. She handed it over along with a paper knife. Sally did not stop to open it until she had concluded her music. She was playing Bist du Bei Mir by J. S. Bach. Elsie sat down to enjoy the classical piece.

'Beautiful. That was beautiful Sally. You have not played that for a long time.'

Sally, as usual, did not have a smile even for her mother. She had played the music before many times in her head as well as on her harmonica. It was not a special moment in her mind. Her mother handed the letter to her. Sally opened it and passed it back to her to read.

The letter was from Carolee. Elsie read it silently before informing Sally if its contents. It was, however, good news as Sally could see from her mother's wide open smile.

'Sally it seems you have got a record deal, you know, a CD to record. Isn't that good?'

Sally took a moment to understand the deal.

'What do I have to do?' she said, as she tried to cope with the consequences of the information.

'Carolee says you will record twenty pieces of music. You will be going to London to discuss the contents with a record producer. She'll make arrangements for that. It seems the local review in Bolton got the music world thinking a harmonica played so well with an orchestra was unique. It's a selling point.'

'I'm not selling my harmonica,' she said as her body tensed.

'No dear. You are selling nothing but you might be making some money.'

Inspector Mark Rawlings pinged the Dunning case over to the Crown Prosecution Service, turned his computer to solitaire and made a coffee. His part was done. As he lifted his mug to the ceiling, draining the last black grains of his four star strength coffee, the phone rang. It was the Crown Prosecution Office wishing him to come down to talk about the case he had just submitted.

He enjoyed his official walks. Today the sun shone as he made his way down through the shopping mall to the Crown Offices and entered.

'Good morning,' he said to the desk official, Simon.

'And it is a good morning to you too sir. So what can we do for you today busy Inspector?'

'A request from prosecutor Helen Regan,' he said with a grin. 'She wants to see me.'

'Helen Regan? I'll give her a ring.'

As he did so Inspector Mark Rawlings wandered round the vestibule. Domestic Abuse and Neighbourhood Watch posters caught his eye. He speed read them, hoping they had an effect in the communities of the town.

'She'll be with you in a moment, Inspector,' said Simon returning the phone to its cradle.

The moment took two minutes before the swing doors opened and Helen Regan appeared. She was dressed in a two piece grey suit. Her heels were at least two inches high but she walked with confidence, grace and rhythm. Between two fingers on her right hand were the stains of a smoker.

'Hi Mark. Glad you could make it,' she said throwing the file on the table at reception.

'Heard of Donkey and Bones?' asked Mark while Helen smiled with raised eyebrows as if the names were not unknown to her.

'God, I used to live, breath and dream about these two. They've been quiet for a while but they went far too far with this one,' she said shaking her head from side to side and tut-tutting at the same time.

'So you dreamt about Bones and Donkey did you?' laughed Mark.

'Oh, yes, I did but not the way your dirty mind is telling me,' Helen said digging a playful elbow into his ribs.

'Ouch,' that hurt.

'Police assault then?'

Mark laughed. 'I bet you get enough of those.'

Helen did not need to say any more.

Then she saw the gravity on Mark's face.

'Okay, let's use this room,' she said pointing with her raised arm.

They entered an interview room where they sat down opposite one another.

'Run over the case for me. I haven't the time to take all of this in right now,' she said flipping her fingers through the bulky papers.

'Okay, we've got housebreaking, fraud, assault, selling stolen goods, possession and selling of drugs, oh and a breach of the peace on Bones who went berserk in the police station,' then he took a deep breath.

'Both in custody, I presume?'

'Yes, you bet,' he said adjusting his black tie.

'Since when?' asked Helen

'9 a.m. this morning.'

'Okay first appearance tomorrow. Any bail requests?' she asked looking over her glasses at Mark.

'Not that I know of.' Mark shook his head with pursed lips.

'What's your position on that?'

Mark sat forward and spoke slowly. 'Must be detained; victim at risk and that brings me to the issue.'

'An issue?' queried Helen. 'What's on your mind then?'

'It will be on your mind too when this goes to trial. There is the only one victim but she's autistic and brain damaged. You'll have to tread carefully or we might lose the case.'

'A possibility?'

'A probability on Sally's evidence. Sure as can be. She's a Yes woman. She'll see the accused as friends perhaps and cave in on cross examination.'

Helen looked up at Mark. 'Vulnerable witness, special measures required then. I'd better inform the bench.'

'Will that make any difference?' wondered Mark.

'It will keep the case on track. As long as I'm not up against Ralph Brown, I'll have a fairly easy ride.'

'Yeah, Ralph Brown would defend a mass murderer with all his tricks, get him off and let him roam the streets for his next victim. God, I hope it won't be him.'

'I hope so too for my sake and for this Sally girl too.'

The next day Bones and Donkey were taken from the police cells to the Magistrate's court. The duty solicitor was Peter Kushner. He had spoken to the accused and was ready to proceed.

Miss Helen Regan was pleased to see Peter representing both accused until she remembered he was from the same partnership as Ralph Brown at Brown and Meadows Solicitors. Presumably first appearances were for the rookies in his firm.

Judge Peter Tuchman entered the courtroom. He was a man past retirement years which meant he was thoroughly acquainted with the laws of the land as he was with the couple of accused before him. He turned towards Helen Regan and nodded slightly for her to begin the proceedings.

'My Lord these are the joint cases of Ms. Donna Riley also known as Donkey and Mr. Barry Ritchie also known as Bones. They are jointly accused of housebreaking, fraud, assault, possession of stolen goods and possession and distribution of class A and class B drugs. Mr. Ritchie is also accused of a Breach of the Peace. The Crown opposes any bail conditions for both accused due to the very serious nature of the offences and as the victim in this case is classified as being a vulnerable adult,' she said and sat down, the case against release having been expounded.

Peter Kushner took to his feet. 'My Lord my friend has stated this is a serious case. Well, fraud and housebreaking are, but as the accused have been properly cautioned and charged, the seriousness of the offences have been taken on board and understood by my clients. They will be of good behaviour until the case is called, my Lord.'

Peter sat down and they both awaited his Lordship's decision. The Judge returned his pen to his inside pocket after a few moments. His decision was not long in the making, nor, it must be said, a very demanding one.

'Mr. Kushner, you forgot to mention they have also been charged with assault and drug offences. I have not forgotten. You tell me the accused will be on good behaviour till the proceedings take place. Good and behaviour are two words I suggest your clients do not fully understand. Both the accused will be detained on remand for the following reasons: Firstly because of the seriousness of the offences, secondly these alleged offenders are as familiar with the court as I am and therefore not first time offenders and thirdly and last but not least, the vulnerable adult victim needs protection in the intervening time and, I am sure, subsequently too.'

Helen relaxed with a sigh. Mr. Kushner's pen scribbled away for a while before his file closed.

'The case is adjourned and will proceed to trial at the Crown Court on Monday 23rd August.'

Helen closed her file, left the court house as soon as the Judge had disappeared and before returning to her office, lit up one of her French Gitans. A trail of smoke danced along behind her bringing to noses the French essence as she walked, slowly, back to work.

Elsie and Sally went to London and met Carolee. They were driven to Abbey Road and after coffee, Geoff Cook, the music director, informed them that what Sally had performed at the Bolton concert had been recorded and her harmonica had come over very well. The concerto was quite long and so he hoped, for variety's sake, that some shorter pieces of Sally's music could be recorded.

Sally had already thought of some more music and Sailing By, the tune she never failed to hear each night on Radio 4 before she turned out the light and fell asleep, was accepted.

The orchestra was far from the formal players in Bolton. They seemed to be a ragtag of session musicians but the quality of their harmonies were superb. Elsie had a grandstand seat in the adjoining room where Geoff played with many buttons and slide knobs. She wore headphones while his expertise was in bringing the music to tonal perfection and to the personal modern apps folk had these days.

After lunch Amy McDonald arrived to sing some jazz to accompany Sally. When she sang That Old Devil Called Love and I Want To Know What Love Is, Sally was in her element. But the last track was Spring from Vivaldi's Four Seasons. It was her virtuoso spot. It gave the CD depth and quality having some classical music as well as some popular melodies and Geoff was pleased with the production. It was now left to the Warner Music Group record company to promote the disc and they did, so effectively. It was played regularly on Classic FM and its position on the classical chart began to rise.

Sally took her radio to bed for the next three nights and with Classic FM being played till the small hours, she heard her performances time after time. Eventually it bored her. She lost interest and slept soundly.

As the popularity of the disc increased, Geoff was quick to suggest another set of tunes but Sally was not sure about all the fuss around her and had to be persuaded by Elsie before she chose a further set of performance delights.

The following week Sally had a visitor. She was a long haired pale faced woman in her forties wearing chinos styled trousers and some solid loafers on her feet. She introduced herself as Joyce, a criminal justice social worker.

'Sally it's my job to make the court case as simple and comfortable for you at each stage.'

'Yes, I see.'

'You don't mind if I sit in on the interview? I can reinforce what you are saying to Sally later on. You understand?' asked Elsie holding onto the back of an armchair.

'Yes, I understand. It's not an interview, however. I'm simply preparing Sally for a difficult time in Court. Please join us Mrs Dunning,' said Joyce ushering her to a seat with her right hand.

'Of course, if they accept all the charges, then you will not have to give evidence. But perhaps we must prepare for the trial entering a second week. That's the worst scenario.' Joyce sat back to gauge Sally's response but it came from her mother instead.

'Oh, I don't think that's the worst scenario,' said Elsie ringing her hands. 'If they are found not guilty then that will only be the start of Sally's troubles, surely?'

Joyce scratched her head with her pen. 'I think a finding of guilt is more on my mind. But in the unlikely event that there is no case to answer, that would mean additional support which we would provide. Personally, I am not expecting a guilty plea. I feel it will go to trial.'

Joyce spent the next three quarters of an hour making suggestions, some of which left Sally perplexed.

'If you have a book, a comic or something to distract you in the waiting room that would be helpful,' she suggested.

'I've got my harmonica,' said Sally.

'Hmmm...well... bring it along anyway but you might not be allowed to play it.'

'So why bring it?' asked Sally staring at Joyce.

She looked up at Elsie who herself was distracted by the arrival of the postman. 'Then don't bring it, Sally. What about a comic.'

'But my comics have been stolen.'

Joyce held her breath for a moment as she thought through the next challenge. 'Yes, I know but...I tell you Sally, let me bring you a comic. I'll get one on my way to court.'

Sally did not show she was pleased with the outcome. She had focussed on the end of the sentence.

'Will you be with me in Court?'

'I'll be at the court. I hope to sit alongside you but if not, you will see me in the gallery. It depends if the defence or the Judge lets me in,' she said crossing her legs.

'Now the accused will face you, they may smile at you but remember they are not on your side.'

'Yes.'

'You will be asked questions first by the prosecutor. Helen will be as helpful as possible. Then your evidence will be tested from the accused's side. You might find that difficult,' she said looking for signs of comprehension.

Joyce concluded the only appropriate way. 'I am sure you will be a good witness, Sally. Simply tell the truth. Answer the questions honestly. That's all you have to do.'

'Yes, tell the truth.'

Joyce stood up and shook Sally's hand. She smiled back at her but looked blankly into her eyes. Joyce knew this would be a challenging legal confrontation. She hoped the prosecutor would rely on other evidence. With that thought in mind she left as Elsie returned to the lounge.

'Did you understand what the lady was saying to you, Sally?' she asked.

Sally's eyebrows rose an inch. 'Not really,' she replied with shaking hands. Then she remembered. 'I must tell the truth.'

'Yes, and you have always done that haven't you, dear?'

'Yes, Mum. I always tell the truth.'

Elsie sighed, feeling sorry for what Sally was about to endure. She sat beside her and rubbed her knee.

'It will be alright. Now, here's is a letter addressed to you.'

She handed it to her. Sally took it and ripped it open. She handed it back to her mother as usual but mother always gave her daughter the right to open her letters on every occasion. It gave her ownership even although she could never follow the message a letter sent. Along with a letter was a cheque. It was from Coralee. It was her first royalty which had arrived. The cheque was for £2,947.75.

# 13

# The Trial

Monday 23rd August was an overcast day. It was a muggy, sticky day which promised a thunderstorm as the gods seemed angry. Sally was dressed in a new peppermint green striped blouse. Her yellow cardigan contrasted and her shoes had been polished for more than half an hour the previous evening. Sally knew this was the day, her day. Her citation, which had arrived a week earlier, had made that clear. In her pocket her fingers caressed her A key harmonica.

The County Court seemed very busy as Monday mornings often were. This was the court for the more serious cases. Other less serious cases such as disorderly behaviour were dealt with by the Magistrates' courts. Many initial Magistrate court cases which had been denied were now at the County court along with the more serious cases arriving for the first time. Frequently advised to deny their cases, their first time proceedings would be adjourned. By doing so the defence solicitors bought time for deals to be made at a future date. That future date had arrived for some of Wigan's defaulters. Bones and Donkey were in that category in the cells beneath the court hearing the falling rain on the high Perspex roof patter like a kettle drum.

Helen Regan entered the waiting room and found Sally and Elsie seated together at the far end of the room. She shook their hands warmly and advised them that their proceedings would follow after the cases of those now settled by agreement. Elsie stood up and ushered Helen to one side.

'Who will be defending? The Criminal Justice social worker Joyce told me that might be crucial,' she said holding on to Helen's sleeve.

'How true. I'll be up against Mr. Ralph Brown. I need say no more. I've got my work cut out for me today,' she said clutching the folder close to her chest.

At 10.45 a.m. Sally was led by Helen through the corridors to appear within Court No 2 and seated on the front row waiting to be called.

His Lordship Nigel Rotherham took up his position on the bench. A jury of twelve people took their seats at the side of the court room. The Judge then invited the Prosecutor to proceed with the next case and to cite the charges.

'Thank you my Lord. First may I say that that I am obliged to my friend for agreeing that the accused cases can be co-joined.'

'Is that so Mr. Brown?'

'It is indeed the case, your Lordship,' said Mr. Brown returning to his seat with a sneering smile of gratitude shown to Helen. It suited his clients as much as it did the prosecution. Court was pure theatre. The players enjoyed their roles, amid heightened concentration.

Helen returned to her feet holding a list of indictments. She peered over her black framed glasses at the accused on each count. 'Firstly, Ms. Donna Riley, also known as 'Donkey' and Mr. Barry Ritchie also known as 'Bones' are jointly charged as follows:

'That you, Mr. Barry Ritchie and you Ms. Donna Riley are jointly charged with the supply of Class A and B drugs on several dates within the last six months with intent to supply to others known. This being an offence under Section 14 of the Misuse of Drugs Act 1971.'

Secondly, Ms. Donna Riley and Mr. Barry Ritchie you are jointly charged with wounding or grievous bodily harm with intent to cause grievous bodily harm to Ms Sally Dunning in the Plantations Park grounds of Wigan on 24th May this year. This being contrary to Section 18 of the Offences against the Person Act 1861.

Thirdly, Ms. Donna Riley and Mr. Barry Ritchie you are jointly charged with Assault occasioning actual bodily harm to Ms Sally Dunning, on 24th May in the Plantations Park grounds of Wigan. This being contrary to Section 59 of the Offences against the Person Act 1861.

Fourthly, Ms. Donna Riley and Mr. Barry Ritchie known as Donkey and Bones are jointly charged with burglary from the premises of the Pines, Leyland Mill Lane, Wigan on a date between 12th April and 3rd May. This being an offence under the Theft Act of 1979 Section 9(3) a.

Fifthly, Ms. Donna Riley and Mr. Barry Ritchie are jointly charged with obtaining money by deception from Ms Sally Dunning between February 28th and May 24th this year. This being an offence under the Theft Act Section 1.

Sixthly, Ms. Donna Riley and Mr. Barry Ritchie are jointly accused of administering poison with intent to injure Ms Sally Dunning on 24th May in the Plantations Park grounds of Wigan. This being contrary to Section 24 of the Offences against the Person Act 1861.'

Thereafter Helen sat down as his Lordship continued to write. Her eyes crossed over to Mr. Brown's table but when she caught his eye he simply shook his head as if to say, you have thrown in the kitchen sink this time, you'll never get all these charges proved.

'Thank you Miss Regan, you may proceed,' his Lordship intoned.

Helen got to her feet again and pulled her gown over both shoulders. She had prepared the opening statement.

'Members of the jury, both accused face several charges and that may make you think that there was more than one victim in the events which will unfold. Well, you would be right. A burglary affects a whole family even if they do not live in that burgled relative's property. You will find there is a main victim and in this case before you today is a woman who has a restricted personality, if I may be as so bold to describe her that way. She is autistic and brain damaged. She has a very necessary and close relation with her mother and sister. This is a case I hope to prove has been devastating for this family and particularly Ms. Sally Dunning, a very vulnerable individual. The Crown will bring evidence of systematic and persistent grooming to the point at which abuse and violence took over. Make no mistake, this is a very serious collection of alleged charges which the alleged perpetrators face and the Crown wishes to prove.

I urge you not to place all your sympathies on the victim, as would be natural in this case, but to listen to the evidence presented and to decide accordingly. Thank you,' she said and took her seat graciously.

Mr. Brown?'

'Thank you my Lord,' said Mr. Brown getting to his feet and dropping his gown off his right shoulder. He opened his hands wide in an appealing manner. 'I don't deny my clients have known the police in the past. I suspect that, but for the Grace of God, we have not had such an unfortunate start to life. Born into drug consuming families, they did well to find a school which supported them and did much to give them a better start in life. They have tried hard to lead that life and they admit at times they have fallen short. But is that surprising? No, but what is surprising is the number of charges which my clients face. Don't be bamboozled by the amount of evidence which you will hear. It seems the Crown is throwing the book at my clients. It is for you to catch that book and read its pages. Let the evidence speak for itself. That will show a more caring and deserving couple of accused. I thank you.' Mr. Brown adjusted his gown and bowed to the jury theatrically as he returned to his seat.

The judge raised his eyes above his glasses and nodded to Miss Harper. She took the cue.

'I call my first witness, the alleged victim in this case, Ms. Sally Dunning. My Lord it is important for me to stress at the outset that my client is autistic and has through an accident at birth a mental age of a minor. The court must be aware of these facts and circumstances as she responds to questioning, from both sides,' she said looking across at Mr Brown whose sneer said it all.

'Very well,' his Lordship said while noticing Mr. Brown's intention to object. 'Mr. Brown?'

'My Lord will be familiar with proceedings in the Family courts where children of a very young age are able on occasions to provide crucial evidence which can lead to a parental prosecution and family convictions. While I accept Ms. Dunning may be on the autistic spectrum, I expect she will be able to answer with due ability. After all, it is a continuum and I am sure we are all somewhere on that sliding gauge ourselves.'

'That remains to be seen, Mr. Brown. However you are right to bring the matter to my attention. Nevertheless, I expect you to refrain from your usual robust enquiry for this vulnerable witness. Not so?'

Mr. Brown did not reply. He merely placed his hand on his writing pad and turned over a new leaf.

Helen then began the prosecutor's case. She had previously rehearsed the taking of the oath with Sally and so she obliged, holding the bible with both hands until Helen raised her right arm and Sally did the same. Sally then promised to tell the truth, a concept that was a very natural concept for her.

'Please tell me your full name,' she asked with a smile at her.

Sally gave a gulp before answering. 'Sally Dunning.'

'And where do you live, Sally?'

'I live at the Pines, Leyland Mill Lane, Wigan.'

'And your age?'

'Yes, and my age,' Sally replied instinctively repeating the question which she had failed to grasp.

Helen paused. It dawned on her that her questioning had to be more prosaic. 'Ms. Dunning, how old are you?'

'I am fifty-four.'

'Thank you. Now I ask you to look around the court. Can you see anyone you recognise?' Helen awaited the confirmation of Donkey and Bones but that was not what Sally had heard. Nevertheless Helen knew not to stop her in her tracks or criticise her for her ambiguous question.

'I see Mum, I see Mr. Brown, I see my social worker Joyce. I see the Judge over there, as well.'

The jury smiled, some of whom hid their smiles with the back of their hands.

'Is there anyone you missed, Sally?'

'Yes, I missed Donkey and Bones.'

'And where are they? Can you point to them?'

'Over there,' she said pointing at them and smiling. Both accused smiled back at Sally with wide and friendly smiles.

'How did you meet Donkey and Bones?' Helen asked as she flicked a stray strand of hair backwards.

'I was lost in the park and Donkey took me home.'

'That was kind of her. Wasn't it?' asked Helen eyeing Mr. Brown's surprise at the compliment to his client.

'Then she gave me a ticket to go to the cinema.'

'The cinema? And did you go to see a film?'

'Yes, she paid for my ticket. The film was called A Man Called Ove. It's a comedy about an old man who gets.....'

'Let me stop you there Sally, perhaps we can hear about the film at another time?'

'Okay, later?'

'Yes, that would be good. You were telling me about Donkey and Bones,' she smiled as did the Judge and most of the jury. In fact, almost everyone except Mr. Brown who was taking careful notes about Sally's interesting testimony.

'Yes, well then I met Bones, the accountant.'

Helen paused a moment giving his Lordship time to complete his writing. 'You said Bones is an accountant?'

'Yes, I brought money to him and he made it grow.'

'You brought money Ms. Dunning. Or were you asked to bring money?'

'Objection,' said Mr. Brown jumping up like a jack-in-the box. 'Leading the witness,' he said.

'Mr. Brown, Miss Regan asked a question with only two possibilities. Either Ms. Dunning brought the money on her own volition or she was asked to bring the money. From the evidence I have heard, so far, the money was received by your clients, or your accountant client, as I have noted. It is not a matter that the money was received, but how it was received is of significance to me. I wait to hear the response. Miss Regan, continue please.'

'Miss Dunning, were you asked to bring money?'

'Yes.'

Helen glanced at Mr Brown to make sure he was listening. He pouted his lips in response.

'I see, and have you received any money back?'

'Yes,' Sally said excitedly. 'I got £20 back.'

Mr Brown's eyebrows lifted in surprise. The prosecution was making his clients saints. Or that was his interpretation on the facts so far stated.

'Can you tell the court how much money you gave to Bones?'

Sally frowned. She did not like wrong answers but this was a wrong question.

'I didn't give him money. He asked for it.'

'I see, sorry,' Helen said biting her lip. 'But can you remember how much it was Bones asked for?' she said giving a mild grin at her adversary.

'No,' she said shaking her head vigorously from side to side, unable to remember the grand total.

Helen moved towards the table in the centre of the court holding a bank statement. 'This is Ms. Dunning's bank account from which, on a regular basis, the sum of £500 has been removed from the account. Does the sum of £500 ring a bell for you Ms. Dunning?'

'Yes, it rings a bell. £500. I gave him £500 each time.'

Mr. Brown got to his feet. 'Objection, leading evidence. Placing the sum of '£500' in her mouth. Like a parrot she replies just after not remembering how much she withdrew.'

'Noted Mr. Brown, for the time being. I look forward to reading exhibit 1 which will address this issue.'

Helen obliged. 'Production 1 is this bank statement in which £2,500 has been withdrawn in five equal amounts of £500 pounds.' She walked forward and placed the itemised bank statement on the table. She turned and looked at Sally.

'Why did you give Donkey and Bones these amounts of money?'

'Because Bones is a banker, an accountant and he can make money grow if you give him some.'

'Who told you Bones was a banker?' Helen asked drawing closer to Sally.

'Donkey told me.'

Helen let the moment swell in the minds of the jury.

'Now, you were away from home not so long ago on holiday weren't you?'

'Yes, I was in Malta. I met Tom.'

Helen looked at her papers. There was no mention of Tom. She had to either exclude this evidence or make use of it in support of Sally's case. First she needed confirmation. 'Who is Tom, Sally?'

Sally realised Helen had never met Tom and he was not in court. In truth she had difficulty in describing who he was and what he meant to her so she resorted to stare ahead and remain silent.

Professional eyes flew around the court for a moment but Helen did not pursue the enigma of Tom. 'Anyway, when you returned from holiday, was anything missing from your home?'

'My comics were missing.'

'To be more accurate Sally, these were not just comics were they?' she asked tilting her head.

'No.'

'What made them special?'

'I had lots of them in boxes. The boxes were empty.'

'Yes Sally, but what was special about the comics?'

'They were all mine.'

Mr. Brown looked at the bench who looked at the jury wondering where this line of questioning was heading, if not for the buffers.

'Were they not a collection of.... special comics....' Helen held her breath for a moment. She was going to annoy Mr. Brown but she did not hold back.

'Were they not the complete set from Edition number 1 to the most recent?'

'Yes.'

Mr. Brown got to his feet. 'My Lord, if my friend had asked if she had book markers in each comic, I suspect this witness would answer "Yes". In fact, this is an agreement exercise and I'd ask the court to take note that this is an unreliable witness.' Mr. Brown sat down his point having been made to his smug satisfaction.

The Judge looked at Mr. Brown with stern eyes piecing the lawyer's gaze.

'Evidence will be what it is, Mr. Brown. Be grateful you do not suffer from any affliction other than my wrath. We shall soon see if the Crown has produced a sequence of comics to redress the balance. Take note, Mr Brown. Miss Regan, please continue.'

Despite the frequent objections, Helen felt she had won the first round. 'Exhibit number 2 is a receipt. A receipt for the comics which were sent by Harper & Pierpoint to a special comic and toy auction in London. The receipt is signed by one Ms. Donna Riley.' Helen showed it to her opponent before lodging it on top of the comics on the desk.'

Helen approached the table and took a top copy

towards the jury for them to see the date of one of the early copies.

'Miss Regan, are you finished with this witness?'

'Not yet your Lordship.' She looked at Sally. It had been a damage limitation exercise in parts so far, but she had one final matter to deal with.

'You were badly beaten and ended up in hospital. Was that not so?'

'Yes, in hospital.'

'What were your injuries?'

Sally pointed first to her ribs then her face and finally her head. 'I had a head scan too.'

Helen took from the folder some medical X-rays and photographs.

'Have a look at these photographs. I warn you they don't look pretty. Is that you in them, Sally?'

Sally lifted the first of three photographs. She hesitated. She saw for the first time how badly beaten she was.

'Yes, I think that's me, but the photo of a bruised tummy? I'm not sure if that is my tummy.'

'Look at the back of the photo Ms. Dunning. Do you see your name on the back of the photo?'

'Yes, that's my name.'

'Indeed it is on the back of all three photos.' Helen took he photographs to the jury and then to Mr. Brown.

'Exhibits number 4, 5 and 6 my Lord,' she said laying out all three photographs facing the jury.

'These are some horrific photographs of you Ms. Dunning. Who attacked you like this?'

Sally looked round the court. She saw all eyes looking at her. It frightened her.

'I don't know,' she said bringing a beaming smile to Mr. Brown's lips.

'Think Sally. Why would anyone want to hurt you?'

'Because I did not bring the money?'

'What money do you mean?'

Sally looked up at the gallery and saw Joyce looking on. She smiled. She stared back. Then she looked at Helen again.

'I asked you, what money was this, Ms. Dunning?'

'It was £500. I did not have it to give to Bones that day.'

'And why was that?'

'Because Becky told me to give no more money to Bones.'

Helen gave an encouraging smile to Sally.'And Becky is your sister, Dr Becky Dunning, is that not so?'

'Yes, Becky is my sister.'

'Thank you Ms. Dunning I have no more questions to ask.'

'Before you rise to your feet Mr. Brown, I think we can resume after lunch at 2 p.m.' said the Judge prompting the large uniformed court official, who had been observing the proceedings, to play his part.

'Court rise,' the former Grenadier Guard shouted.

The Judge stood down from the bench and headed for his smoked salmon sandwich in the fridge in his chambers.

'I suggest you come with me to my office next door Sally and we can have some lunch.'

'What about my Mum?'

'Oh yes, she can come with you.'

145

Mr. Brown did not have lunch straight away. He went down to the bowels of the court, to the cells. He then spoke to both accused and told them that the productions looked grim but the prosecutor's first witness was their weakest link. The accused gave no ground. The case would not be settled or cave in that afternoon.

At 2 p.m. on the dot the Judge resumed his bench and the participants sat down once more. All except Mr. Brown who stood tall with his drooping black gown held down, as his hands grasped the material by his chest.

'Good afternoon Ms. Dunning, I just have a few questions for you, if you don't mind.'

Sally did not do small talk and said nothing.

'Let me call your friends by their nicknames. That's Donkey and Bones. Did Donkey actually find you lost in the park and brought you home safely?'

'Yes, she did.'

Mr. Brown let Sally's response linger in the ears of the jury. 'That was really a very kind gesture, wasn't it?'

'Yes, a kind gesture.'

A further pause for effect was made. 'Indeed, it was a kind gesture, Ms. Dunning. Was that what made you friends?'

'Yes.'

'And did Donkey not give you a ticket to see this film A Man Named Ove?'

'No, he didn't. It was a man called Ove.'

'I do apologise Ms Dunning, I have still to see the film. But you did receive a free ticket?'

'Yes, I did.'

'And did you enjoy the film?'

'Yes, I enjoyed the film. It was funny.'

'They chose a good film for you, it seems. So Bones and Donkey were very kind to you?'

'Yes, they were kind.'

'In fact, didn't Mrs Dunning send them a card to thank them for being so thoughtful, so concerned for you?'

'Yes, I took the card to them.'

A charming smile of the questioner now looked directly at her. 'Now, these are the actions of good friends. Not so?'

'Yes, good friends.'

'Friends unlikely to beat you up?'

'Yes.'

'Yes what, beat you up or not?'

'No, good friends don't beat me up.'

'Don't beat me up you say. But you did end up in hospital, didn't you? I mean you were injured weren't you?'

'Yes, I was.'

'And what happened to cause your injuries?'

'I don't know. I can't remember.'

'You can't remember. So it was not likely to be Donkey and it was not likely to be Bones, your friends, was it?'

Sally was panicking internally. She was not able to grasp Mr. Brown's question and she resorted to hide under the voice of silence. Conveniently Mr. Brown dropped the subject there and then.

'Now, about the comics. You say they were stolen, was that not the case?'

'Yes, that's what the police said.'

'So, you are suggesting someone came to your house and took the comics away?'

'Yes, took my comics away.'

'And you think they went missing when you were on holiday?'

'Yes, when we were on holiday in Malta. They were not there when I came back.'

'But Ms Dunning it is possible they were stolen, or went missing a month before you went on holiday. Would that be fair to say?'

Sally thought through his question. She tried to remember looking at the comics before the holiday. She concluded it was indeed some time ago.

'Yes, I had not seen them for quite a while.'

Mr. Brown paused. The doubt had been placed in the jury's mind. They could have been stolen a while ago. The pause was for effect as Helen knew and she wondered which line of attack was to follow.

'When you go on holiday, you make the house safe, don't you Sally?'

'Yes, make the house safe,' she said grabbing the witness box rail with both hands, turning her knuckles white.

Helen rose. 'Objection, there's too much leading the evidence from my friend. Make the house safe, indeed.'

'It seems I have given some latitude to both of you. Yet I accept there are some special circumstances required for this witness. I urge you both to keep your challenges in perspective,' he said.

'And you have a burglar alarm in your house?'

'Yes, we have one,' said Sally proudly.

'So, if anyone broke in to your home, the alarm would go off.'

'Yes.'

'Your neighbours would hear it?'

'The neighbours live down the road.'

'Yes, Sally, maybe they do, but sound travels and house alarms travel so that people can hear them. I don't think there were any reports of an alarm going off, were there?' Mr. Brown adjusted his gown with the panache of an actor.

'No, I don't know,' she replied casting her eyes around the court and shaking her head from side to side.

'I see you shaking your head. That implies a "No" to me. Anyway, Ms. Dunning, even if the house key was hidden in the garden and even if by chance the burglar found it, the alarm would go off until the code was silenced. Not so?'

Sally followed what was being said although felt the questions were going too quickly and were far too long.

'So, you can't tell me who entered the house when you were away, not so?'

'No, it was Donkey and Bones.'

It was not the reply Mr Brown had been suspecting. He cleared his voice. 'Ms. Dunning. I am not sure who told you it was Bones and Donkey that broke into your house but there is no evidence leading to my clients breaking into your home. Is there?'

Sally did not like his tone. She looked at him and raised her voice. 'Donkey knew the alarm code.'

Mr. Brown hesitated. He was on thin ice. There was

no need to repeat the question as it stood. He must try another tack. Helen scribbled furiously.

'Ms. Dunning, do you remember either Donkey or Bones ever being in your home?'

'No, they have not been to my home.'

'Exactly,' said Mr. Brown who strode across the court floor for effect; hopefully influencing the jury once more.

'I know Donkey's alarm code and she knows mine.'

Mr. Brown scratched his collar. 'Oh really, Ms. Dunning. I doubt very much if either of my clients have burglar alarms.'

Sally felt bullied. Her anger arose. 'Donkey's number is 9876 mine is 3629.'

Mr. Brown's mouth hung open as he turned towards his clients. His gaze cut through both of them. He had heard enough from this slippery witness. He simply said, 'No more questions.'

But there was some clarification required and Helen wanted the evidence confirmed.

'I have just a couple of questions, Ms. Dunning. So, I won't be long,' she said. 'Can you tell the court how the exchange of door codes came about?'

Sally gripped the witness box rail once more but with less tension and bent over it a little. She looked up at Joyce and her recollections came back.

'It was a game. They tried to guess mine but they couldn't so I told them what mine was. They told me Donkey's number too. It was 9876.'

'In that sequence?'

Sally did not understand.

'These exact numbers from 9 down to 6?'

'Yes, that's how I remember their code.'

'So you have no doubt that you gave Donkey your code 3629?' Helen asked in a slow clear delivery.

'Yes I gave it to Bones too. And they wanted to know where the spare key was left.'

Helen was taken aback. She had no notes about the key yet it seemed the missing link. She had to eek out this new evidence like picking out a winkle.

'You say Bones wanted to know where your spare key was. Did you tell him?'

'Yes.'

'And where was it?'

'It was behind a stone near the back door flowers. I use it when I forget my key.'

'Just to clarify, Ms. Dunning. You told Bones that the back door key to your house was under a stone in the back garden?'

'Yes,' she said and smiled as she saw Helen smiling at her.

'So Bones and Donkey not only had your back door key but also the code to enter your home?'

Sally realised that it was now possible for both Bones and Donkey to have been in her house. She had given them the means.

'Yes, I told them about the key and the code.'

'Thank you Ms. Dunning, I have no more questions. You may now leave the witness box.'

The Judge gave Miss Regan a moment to make her notes then his eyebrows were raised and Helen took the cue to proceed.

'My next witness is Mr. Brian Kinghorn.'

A man in his early forties came to the witness box in a light grey suit. His hair was cut short making him look rather bald. He took the oath.

'Mr. Kinghorn, your age and occupation please,' asked Helen as she gathered her papers in order.

'I am aged forty-one and I am a scene of crime officer of the Lancashire Police.'

'And how many years of Police service have you?'

'Er..that would be twenty-two years.'

'So a very experienced scenes of crime officer, I presume.' Helen raised her hand to prevent him agreeing to her assertion.

'I believe you attended a housebreaking report on 23rd of April this year. Is that correct?'

'Yes, it was at the home of the Dunning family, at Leyland Mill Lane on the outskirts of town.'

'What were your findings that day?'

'We did a thorough search of the house and ended up in the attic. There is a snooker table there. We noticed scores had appeared on the blackboard although an attempt had been made to rub the numbers out. We did however get a fingerprint sample from the chalk that was on the fingers of one of the accused. It was when the player had gripped the snooker table underneath its lip.'

'And what did that show?'

'It was a perfect match with the fingerprint taken of Ms. Donna Riley at the police station. It also matched our records of Ms Riley's past fingerprints.'

'Do you have that forensic report with you?'

'Yes, I have,' he said offering it to Helen to present to the court.

'Exhibit number seven,' she said and delivered it to the table moving a photograph to make room for this exhibit forming a jigsaw of productions.

'Did you encounter any other evidence?'

'There was a trace of blood on a fibre of the attic carpet. We managed to trace a further sample on a cushion which had recently been washed. Both samples were analysed.'

'What did the analysis show?'

'It showed a DNA sample identical to that of Ms. Riley.'

'Do you have that report to hand?'

'Yes, here it is,' he said holding it out.

Helen approached him and took hold of the document. In a flourish she approached the table.

'Exhibit number 8, I think, the blood DNA matching of carpet fibre and the cushion to that of Ms. Donna Riley.' She turned towards the jury and gave a contented smile. 'I have no further questions.'

'Mr. Brown?'

'Thank you my Lord,' he said rising and hitching up his suit trousers. 'Mr. Kirkwood, the attic you say, all evidence in the attic. You mean to say there was no other evidence relating to my clients anywhere in the house?'

'That is the case for the house, except the attic, sir.'

'Did you look for fingerprints, for example, on the alarm pad?'

'Yes sir. We left no stone unturned. We did examine the code pad but we suspected a gloved hand was used. The result was disappointing. The chalk fingerprint however was more than ample evidence in my opinion, that and the partial blood smear on carpet fibre and cushion which is matched to that of Donkey, Ms. Riley,' said Mr. Kirkwood in a smug fait accompli manner.

'So no fingerprints on the alarm,' he said to gain the upper hand. 'I have no other questions,' said Mr. Brown as he ran his fingers through his hair before sitting down. He gave a glance at his clients. They were chatting quietly to each other and grinning. They seemed to be enjoying the atmosphere, oblivious to the possible consequences. Most inappropriate he thought and his grim face pointed at them to show his anger.

'Miss Regan?'

'No questions my Lord. I call upon Mr. Ronald Pattison.'

A tweed-jacketed Ronald Pattison entered the witness box. His hair was brushed backwards and his forehead was tanned. He held the bible, raised his right hand and took the oath.

'You are Mr. Ronald Pattison? Please tell the court your age and profession.'

'I am aged sixty-five and I recently retired.'

'What may I ask did you do before retirement?'

'I was a veterinary surgeon with Kennedy and Marsham in town.'

'You have a dog of your own I believe. You walk it in Mesnes Park and also at the Plantations. Both dog walking parks in town. Not so?'

'Yes, I do. I have a Patterdale/Spaniel cross mongrel.'

'On the day in question you observed a fracas. Explain what happened.'

'Yes, I was walking Georgie, my dog, when I came across a woman on the ground being kicked relentlessly.'

'What did you do then? How did you react?'

'At first I shouted. That seemed to do little good. They just swore at me. But it eventually made them abandon the attack and then they scarpered off. At that point I phoned the emergency services.'

'And what else did you see?'

'The ambulance came quickly and assessed the victim. Then, after checking her breathing, they placed her in their vehicle and took her away. The police then asked my name and began taking a statement.'

'And I believe you were asked to come to the police station for an identity parade.'

'Yes, that's true.'

'Did you recognise the two individuals involved in the assault?'

'No, I recognised just one.' Then Mr. Pattison raised his arm and pointed to one of the alleged offenders. 'That's him there; he's the one on the left.'

'You are pointing to Mr. Barry Ritchie?'

'Yes, I believe that is his name. Mr. Ritchie was one of them.'

'And for clarification, although you only recognised one, both were engaged in attacking Ms. Dunning?'

'Oh yes, both were having a real good fight.'

'A fight, Mr. Pattison?

'Well, no, not a fight. Ms. Dunning put up no resistance. She was helpless on the ground.'

'Thank you. I have no further questions.'

'Mr. Brown, do you have any questions?' asked the

judge with a hint of an invitation to abandon the case now that his defence was becoming untenable.

Mr. Brown rose with his hands on the table in a slightly crouched position. 'Mr. Pattison, you were an experienced vet.' He took a deep breath. 'When a dog is old, what difficulties does it face?'

Mr. Pattison hesitated trying to see why this question arose. 'Er...no two dogs are the same. A larger dog may have hip difficulties and some go a little deaf.'

'Some dogs go deaf and what about their sight?'

Helen jumped to her feet. 'My Lord, my friend is being obtuse. We are getting a lecture on the canine health of older dogs. How can any of this be of any significance to the matter in hand?' asked Helen.

'I am inclined to agree,' said the Judge with an almighty sigh. 'Mr. Brown, I hope the lead is appropriate in this canine mystery.' Helen smiled at the Judge's dry humour.

'I ask you to bear with me, my Lord. Mr. Pattison, I was asking how frequent do older dogs lose their sight?'

'I think many do lose their sight or more likely their sight may be weakened. Rather like the sight of humans in their latter years. Dogs suffer the same ailments as humans.'

'So you are saying in our latter years we may lose our sight or have sight impairment perhaps?' but he left no time for him to reply. 'Mr. Pattison, you attended an identity parade at the police station and did not identify one person according to the report I have before me. You actually identified two people, not one. Not so?'

'Well, yes, I did think I spotted two people.'

'Oh, indeed you did. You incorrectly identified a police officer in civilian clothes as a suspect. Is that not the case?'

'Apparently so,' said Mr. Pattison with a shaky voice.

'I put it to you, as a retired professional, that your eyesight might be impaired. After all you saw both youths attack the victim in your evidence but you could not identify them both. Perhaps you are diabetic?'

There was a hesitation.

'Yes, I am diabetic.'

'And do you wear glasses?'

'Yes, I do.'

'Were you wearing them at the time of the alleged incident?'

'No, I don't need them when I am walking my dog.'

'Eyesight and diabetes have a close relationship. It would seem that this may have made recognition difficult. Would you agree?'

He felt his heart beat loudly. 'I identified Ms. Donna Riley. You must realise they ran away in a bent posture. In the identity parade their height was deceptive. But I assure you Ms. Riley was one of the attackers who assaulted Ms. Dunning. I remembered her face well.'

Mr. Brown returned to his papers. He scribbled some marks then accepting defeat, said 'I have no further questions.'

Helen was quick to go for the jugular.

'I call Inspector Mark Rawlings.'

The court official bellowed the Inspector's name and in he came standing erect and confident.

His hand was raised to take the oath as soon as he mounted the witness box.

'Mr. Rawlings, please tell us your length of police service and your position in the force.

'I have been a police officer for fifteen years. I am the lead Inspector of the drugs unit.'

'I believe you accompanied Sergeant Jim Boyd to the home of the accused. What did you find there?'

'It was not the first time I had been there. On this occasion we found a large amount of category A and B drugs in bags secreted around the house. A list of the drug recipients was also found and there were also stacks of money which could not be explained.'

'What happened next?'

'We then returned to the police station cells and charged both Mr. Ritchie and Ms. Riley for the possession and supplying of category A and B drugs.'

'Did you find anything else in the house?'

'Oh yes, I almost forgot. We took possession of their separate computers. They confirmed that they had tried to sell a necklace, an engagement ring and a broach over the eBay service.'

'From the list of stolen items from the Dunning home could you come to any conclusions?' Helen asked as she gathered her gown which had slipped down her shoulder and interfered with her writing hand.

'The items put up for auction on eBay were identical to the items stolen from the Dunning house.'

'You have a print-out of the eBay items?' asked Helen.

'Yes, all on the one page.'

'Then this list of eBay goods is production number 8,' she said taking it to Mr Brown before depositing it on the table.

'Thank you officer, I have no further questions.' Helen sat down pleased with this witness's confident evidence.

'Mr. Brown?' invited the Judge looking at his watch ostentatiously.

'Thank you my Lord. Yes, officer, and how do you link the eBay dealings with the stolen items beyond speculation, Mr. Rawlings?'

'I'm sorry? Speculation is not part of my work. I'd put the odds extremely high that these were the same items reported stolen from the Dunning residence. Fortunately the items were not sold.'

Mr. Brown's eyebrows arched and he pouted his lips. 'There must be some doubt surely? "extremely high" you said, but not definite,' Mr. Brown walked closer to the Inspector with anger in his face.

'Only a minimal doubt. I'd put it at 99% certain,' said the inspector.

'You want to put it at 99% because you want a conviction, don't you?' he growled.

'Indeed. I have known both of the accused for a number of years and the evidence which we have collated is before the court.'

'But never has either of my clients faced six charges before?'

'That is true.'

'In fact, it was usually one or two charges in the past. Understandable given their poor start in life. I put it to you that Bones and Donkey are not big time evil crooks. I suggest that you have thrown the book at my clients to bump up your police targets.'

'I find that outrageous, Mr. Brown. The Police do not do what you are suggesting. The evidence supports the charges which the Crown has brought to court,' he said, with his face and neck turning red as he spoke.

'So you are the Crown and the jury in this case? Thank you, Inspector Rawlings. I have no further questions,' Mr Brown turned his eyes away from the Inspector and sat down to scribble some more notes.

Mark strode off the witness box passing Mr. Brown as he did. He hesitated as he approached and gave him a stare which penetrated his eyes for a moment. Mr. Brown flinched first. The jury took note turning to each other with a look of astonishment. Then Helen rose to her feet.

'My final witness is Mr. Michael Harper.'

Mike Harper was the auctioneer. He strode into the witness box and smiled at Helen. He wore thick black framed glasses and appeared with a silver Christian fish on his lapel. He took the oath with his hand caressing the Holy Bible.

'Mr. Harper you are a senior partner at the auctioneers Harper and Pierpoint, is that not so?'

'Indeed I am.'

'You were approached by a customer offering comics to be auctioned. Do you remember that day?'

'Yes, I do indeed. Comics are rarely brought to us.'

'In the court room do you see the person that brought the comics to you?'

'Yes, over there Ms. Riley,' he said pointing to Donkey.

Helen then produced production number 2. She took it to Mr. Harper.

'Can you tell the court what this piece of paper is?'

'Yes, this is a copy of the receipt I gave to Ms. Riley on receiving the comics which I told her would be sold at a London Auction.'

Helen returned the receipt to the table in the centre of the court to join the other productions on the table.

'That is all Mr. Harper,' said Helen returning to her seat as Mr. Brown stood up.

He straightened his tie knot. 'Mr. Harper, did you not receive the comics from Wales?'

'That is what I was told, yes.'

'You see my client does not dispute she came to you and had comics to sell, but her deceased uncle in Wales collected them, not so?'

'That was the story she gave me.'

'Come, come Mr. Harper, it was not a story. Surely my client, with a minimal education, could not make that fabricated story up, a story worthy of a Coronation Street episode. Did you not believe her?' he asked with a circular turn making his gown's wings fly.

Mr. Harper took off his glasses and as he spoke jabbed them in the air. 'Then if I am to believe her, she told me she was going to give her aunt some of the proceeds she would get when the comics were sold.'

'Exactly. Not a thug, not a housebreaker but a caring niece.'

'The aunt had no name or address mentioned in Wales but I acted in good faith with a clear conscience.

It is an aspect of my profession to judge each submission with perspicacity,' he added returning his glasses to his nose with a grin informing all that his outburst placed the onus back on Donkey.

'I have no more questions,' he said ignoring the auctioneer's last comment.

'That is the case for the Crown my Lord, I have no more witnesses,' Helen said relieved that the battle with Mr. Brown was over from her side. She waited to see if Mr. Brown had any witnesses. If he had, she would object that she had not been notified of them or had not had sufficient time to precognose them. The trial had taken a lot out of her. Mr Brown had been up to his usual antics and theatrical roles which he loved to play, especially with the press in attendance. Helen was still very much on edge. She opened her handbag and looked down into it. Yes, it was a full packet of cigarettes she saw. She patted the box. It would soon be time for their appearance.

'Mr. Brown, are you ready to proceed?'

'One moment my Lord. May I have a brief word with my clients?'

'Make it brief Mr. Brown,' said Lord Rotherham.

Mr. Brown strode off to the accused like a half-time football goalie having let in a couple of goals. Three heads congregated in an inaudible murmur. There was a titter amongst the jury members and Helen tapped her pen on the table to a regular tempo.

Eight minutes later Mr. Brown arrived and the case continued.

'My Lord, I do not intend to call any witnesses.'

Helen relaxed. Mr. Brown seemed to have lost some of his confidence.

'Then, Miss Regan, are you ready to sum up the case for the prosecution?'

She nodded. 'Indeed, I am my Lord.'

Helen took the time to place her papers in order. It was appropriate preparation for the jury to see that she was a thorough professional.

'What this case is about is exploitation. Exploitation of the nastiest kind, carried out by two well-known locals with greed on their minds. So the grooming of Sally Dunning began, taking her home, giving her free cinema tickets. She received £20, not interest from her deposit, but to keep her from prying into their financial affairs and not forgetting their devious caring manner which bled Ms. Dunning's account to the sum of £2,500. Then we learned today of the banker, the accountant. The banker indeed. Would you use Banker Ritchie? I doubt it. Now I refer you to the fingerprint on the snooker table, the evidence of Mr. Kinghorn witnessing the attack. I remind you of what the computers of both accused showed. Stolen goods from the Dunning household being auctioned on eBay. And what can we say about the drugs? The reason they bullied and extorted Sally Dunning was to enable their drug kingdom to flourish in Wigan and beyond. And why could Sally Dunning not remember who attacked her? Was it because she did not want to offend them? No. Was it because they were friends? No. It was because they gave her Scopolamine a powerful drug which knocked her out before she was assaulted. Ladies and gentlemen of the jury, you have only one duty left to perform. It is for you to consider the evidence of what you have heard and the exhibits you have seen. Does the weight of facts tilt towards guilt or innocence? I put it to you that beyond reasonable doubt, the legal standard required in this case, Bones and Donkey, the aliases of Barry Ritchie and Donna Riley, did assault Sally Dunning, did defraud Sally Dunning's bank account, did break into the Dunning's home and did steal items of jewellery and comics, did deceive, did administer drugs to Sally Dunning and did trade in the supply of Class A and B drugs. If you agree then you must find Mr. Ritchie and Ms. Riley equally guilty of deception and exploitation in all of these charges. I await your verdict with patience and thank you for sitting through attentively to the trials of Sally Dunning.'

Helen returned to her seat and took a drink from a glass of water. She was dying for a cigarette. She would not have long to wait now.

'Mr. Brown, are you ready?' asked Lord Rotherham.

'Indeed, I am. Ladies and Gentlemen of the jury,' he began striding up and down the court close to the deciding members stalls. 'It is easier to drive a Mini than an E-type Jaguar with Turbo jets. I am sure you agree.'

Helen's eyes met the Judge's in disbelief at his opening gambit. Two of the jurors shook their heads in disbelief as well. It was a good sign, Helen thought.

'So, too, would it be easier to judge a Breach of the Peace case than a convoluted collection of half-baked charges as we have today. Ladies and gentlemen, you may think the evidence is cut and dried. But I ask you why the good vet was unable to identify both accused?

And was there any evidence, I mean the names, and not the list, of who my clients supplied the drugs to? Well possibly, but they were not productions of the Crown. Now, I crucially turn to the victim. I see and understand where your sympathies lie. Make no mistake, ladies and gentlemen, no one regrets the disadvantages in life which have befallen Ms. Sally Dunning more than I, but on her evidence we heard a woman anxious, indeed over anxious to please. Please the prosecutor of course, but please me too with her honest friendship with my clients. They are friends. It is, ladies and gentlemen, not a plain sailing case. At times it has been a muddled and confused story. If we have in the UK a system which stands up to scrutiny then it is the law of this land. I ask your consciences this. With the evidence you have heard, is there not sufficient doubt in your mind that Bones and Donkey have been set up in a system, out to catch them and return them to prison? We are, ladies and gentlemen above that temptation. If you agree with me, ladies and gentlemen, then you are duty bound to find my clients not guilty. I thank you,' he said gathering his black wings and perching on his seat to listen to the conclusion of the case.

Helen was still counting the times Mr. Brown had used the phrase 'ladies and gentlemen' in his summing up. She could admit he had charm but hoped that would not extend to the grim faced jurors.

Lord Rotherham then addressed the jury. He reminded them to make their decision on the facts of the case and not on the reputations of the accused, or either lawyer. He also urged them to consider Sally Dunning's evidence with care, particularly when she agreed with her questioners. Finally they could take as long as they wished to reach their conclusion. They were told to return to their room where tea and coffee would be served.

The court official rose up from a slouched position and loosened his black neck tie.

'Court rise!' he bawled like a football supporter and the proceedings ended. But for how long? Would it be a speedy decision? It could be, thought Helen, but not too soon she hoped. She was heading outside onto Darlington Street where she'd enjoy her cigarette watching the traffic flow by.

# 14

# The Verdict

At 4.45 p.m. the jury returned to take their seats. The accused appeared from the cells below and Mr. Brown returned to his desk shaking his head at them. Had his clients accepted his advice a deal might have reduced the sentence they now might face. But they wanted to have their day in court and it seemed to have backfired. Mr. Brown bore no grudge, it was unprofessional to do so, but his eyes now avoided them as if he were a blinkered horse.

Judge Rotherham mounted his bench. He called on the chairman of the jury.

'Have you reached a verdict?'

Mr. William Shankland stood in his sports jacket and orange tie. He cleared his throat. 'We have reached a unanimous verdict.'

'How do you find the accused in relation to the first charge: the charge of supplying class A and B drugs?'

'Both guilty.'

'On charge two: causing grievous bodily harm?'

'Both guilty.'

'On charge three: that of assault?'

'Both guilty.'

Bones shook his head while Donkey sat impassionedly as if a school master was reading out a poem.

'Charge four: burglary.'

'Both guilty.'

'Charge five: administering poison with intent to injury?'

'Both guilty.'

'Charge six: obtaining services by deception.'

'Both guilty, my Lord.'

'And you found them both guilty of all the charges, is that so?'

'Yes, my Lord both guilty of all the charges.'

'Thank you. You may be seated,' said his Lordship scribbling his last few lines should there be an appeal of the decision he was about to make.

The Judge gathered his papers together and bumped them on his table. He first turned to the jury on his left and addressed them.

'You have been chosen to represent your community and you have diligently followed this case. It has been a trying case and a challenge for all of you to make your decisions. I am grateful for your deliverances.'

The jurors nodded accepting the Judge's statement but none of them moved. They were almost impatient to hear the sentence.

'As I have said, this has been a distressing case in which the victim, because of her ailments, had been identified as vulnerable, set upon, groomed, deceived, robbed and treated cruelly and with distain. Her evidence was given bravely and she spoke with honesty, as best she could. Any sentence must reflect the cruel nature of the offenders' actions. They must be given time to reflect on the suffering and trials that Sally Dunning and her family have had to endure.'

A round peppermint sweet fell from the hands of a juror and rolled down two steps gathering speed and rolled past Mr. Brown. There was a pause as the object was identified but no response was forthcoming, nor was there anyone in pursuit of the errant sweet. Such was the concentration and desire to hear every word the Judge uttered. Helen put her fist over her smile. She would keep the moment of mirth for her colleagues back at the office when the laughter would be set free.

'Stand up both Ms. Donna Riley and Mr. Barry Ritchie.' Donkey got up, her head bowed but probably not out of respect for her surroundings. Bones nudged Donkey as he rose, looking through the eyes of the guilty.

His Lordship donned a serious expression. 'You have been found guilty of Supplying category A and B drugs, Assault to cause bodily injury, Burglary, Obtaining services by deception and Administering poison with intent to harm Ms. Riley it is by the grace of God that this was not a murder case. Mr. Ritchie you have not the brains to be an accountant. But you have the venom, to be an adder.'

Helen Regan and Mr. Brown chose to smile silently at the wit of the Judge as he continued his sentencing.

'I will now have a period of avizandum. In other words, I will take time to reflect and arrive at a suitable sentence for each of the guilty before me. The court will resume on July 2nd when I will have had access to psychiatric and social work reports. You will be detained as convicted criminals in the meantime.' The Judge then gathered his papers. He then stood up.

The court officer exercised his lungs once more.

'Court rise,' he screamed.

All did so, except Bones and Donkey who slouched to a vertical stance moments after everyone else.

It surprised Helen that both, like humble church mice, evaporated from the court to the cells beneath, without a murmur.

Sally arrived home at the end of Helen Regan's case for the prosecution and immediately Molly greeted her with enthusiasm. She decided to take her out for a walk on the lead and the fresh air cleared the pressures of the day which burned in her head. She looked at her small dog with its comical moustache. 'Now Molly if Bones and Donkey are set free and come back here, you must bark and let me know. Won't you?'

Molly looked up and gave a knowledgeable grunt. It satisfied its owner. It was not a long walk and Sally's pace quickened as she saw a police car in her drive. The policeman must be in the house already speaking to mum she realised, so she stepped up her pace with Molly who stopped every few feet for a sniff and the occasional widdle.

When she arrived back, she opened the door and Police Inspector Mark Rawlings was in the hall speaking to her mother.

'Good to see you Sally. Well, you did very well in court.'

'I don't know the result yet,' Sally said with sadness in her eyes.

'No, nobody does yet. But you are safe from Bones and Donkey. They are detained. We'll know their sentence on 2nd July. And because you are a vulnerable witness, we must make plans whether they get sentenced to jail for a long time or not. There even might be others trying to groom you. We have a duty to protect you. I was just showing your mother how this works,' he said dangling a circular bit of white plastic on a cord.

'What's that?' asked Sally.

'It's a personal alarm given to all our vulnerable adults.'

'Oh. Do I need one?'

'We think it's best. If you ever get frightened or if someone comes to the door at night or even day and you don't know them, then hit the centre of the button and we hear the alarm back at the Police station. Then we send out the nearest police officer to where you are. Understand?'

'And you wear it all the time, Sally,' said her mother.

Sally wondered about what all the time meant. Her eyes screwed up. 'All the time, even when I am sleeping?'

'No, Sally, you can place it by your bedside but know where it is in case you need it. Then wear it the next day and every day. You wear it out of sight, so nobody knows you have one. It's for your protection.'

'For my protection, yes, my protection,' confirmed Sally.

'Do I take it off in the shower?'

'It's waterproof. You don't need to,' he said.

Molly trotted in and sniffed the Inspector's leg. Sally picked her up in her arms. 'He's a good man Molly. No need to sniff him.'

The inspector smiled. 'Perhaps she'd make a good police sniffer,' he laughed.

Sally's expression was one of doubt.

# 15

# Payback Time

On the afternoon of 2nd July, the telephone rang in the Dunning home. It was Helen.

When Elsie answered the telephone it was the call she had been waiting for.

'Fourteen years each you said? That's a good result for us. And a clear message to all criminals exploiting vulnerable adults.'

'It is exactly Mrs Dunning but the case is not quite finished yet. Three matters remain.'

Elsie tilted her head in surprise. 'Three? Surely not three?' she said raising the voice a pitch or two higher than comfortable.

'Yes, of course they can appeal the decision but I am confident that will not arise. The second matter is that I will apply to the court for a seizure of goods. In other words to seize any money made from the illegal activities of the now convicted two, and for the stolen items to be returned to you. That way we should be able to refund the money Sally gave them and finally, I will also advocate for the Criminal Injuries Board to look at Sally's case.'

'Really? What does.... that....'

'What does that mean, you ask? It may mean a gratuity for what Sally has suffered physically and mentally. It is given to such cases.'

'I see,' said Elsie. 'Things are looking up for Sally.'

'Yes with them locked up they won't be troubling her anymore,' said Helen with a smile in her voice. 'And I hear Sally has her emergency button. That should be reassuring.'

'Yes, that's true. And there's the royalties she is receiving too.'

'Royalties? No, I mean gratuities, much the same I suppose,' clarified Helen.

'No, royalties from her record. Another cheque arrived today. It's for £4,500.'

Elsie placed the phone back down like an unexploded bomb. Gosh, she thought, Sally has found her feet at last. The number of times she had felt she had heard enough of her harmonica. She chided herself realising Sally had found her own golden goose. But more importantly she knew Sally's trials were over.

She left the lounge and entered the hall. She stopped. She listened. Sally was playing her harmonica in her bedroom once more. But whether it was Schuman or Schubert she was not sure. Sally would tell her which composer it was in a couple of hours when her evening meal would be on the table and her last note of her music had been played.

## The End ♪

# Sally's Music

Readers may wish to hear the music Sally played on harmonica on YouTube, record players, CDs or i-phones.

**Are You Going To Scarborough Fair**
Simon and Garfunkel

**Chasing Pavements**
Adele

**Rhapsody in Blue**
Gershwin

**The Elizabethan Serenade**
Ronald Binge

**Violin Concerto (Korngold)**
Erich Wolfgang Korngold

**The Lark Ascending**
Vaughan Williams

**Sailing By**
Heard as Radio 4 closes for the night. Also by Ronald Binge

**Shostakovich's Romance**
from the Gadfly

**Mozart's Clarinet (Harmonica) Concerto**
(Second Movement)

**Bist du Bei Mir**
J. S. Bach

**Spring** from **The Four Seasons**
Vivaldi

# Postscript

In talking about this book the most common question I have been asked is: what is the difference between Asperger's Syndrome and Autism. The answer is much more complicated.

Leo K. Tomer was the first person to describe the nature of Autism and its symptoms almost sixty years ago. Later, Hans Asperger wrote about a condition, which was first termed autistic psychopathology and is now known as Asperger's Syndrome. Though there were similarities in the two discoveries, Asperger claimed that his disorder was not a variation of the initial Autism discovery.

Both disorders are classified as Pervasive Developmental Disorders. Since 1994 Autistic Spectrum Disorder has been added as a separate disorder.

## Communication Differences
Individuals with more severe forms of autism are more likely to show symptoms of limited communication skills, both verbal and non-verbal.

## Diagnostic Differences
Autism can be detected early, usually at the age of five, while those with AS often remain undiagnosed until

eleven years old. The late onset of complex social skills explains how and why people with AS are diagnosed later than their counterparts with autism.

Studies conducted at Monash University conclude that children with Autism portray a particular style of walking. This will be fundamental in the diagnosis of Autism as children learn to walk before they develop social skills.

## Social, Motor & Cognitive Differences

Children with autism have limited interest in events, items and the people in their environment. They tend to favour repeated actions. Children with AS are less likely to show delays in age appropriate skills, such as self-help, curiosity and the ability to adapt.

Autistic children, in many instances, are characterized by having motor difficulties and tend to be preoccupied with parts of objects such as the wheels of a toy car; their limited and circumscribed interest consumes a great deal of their time. Individuals with AS are less likely to display these symptoms.

Children with autism usually have cognitive delays from early infancy. Children with AS do not tend to show this kind of delay; they might be quite talented in numeric abilities, learning to read, and being constructive in memory games.

Both individuals with autism and Autistic Spectrum Disorder have a similar behavioural profile; hence the same treatment methods can be effective for both groups. This is why some clinicians and researches suggest that it is inappropriate to talk about two separate conditions or different disorders. A dimensional rather than a categorical view of autism and Autistic Spectrum Disorder seems to be more reasonable.

## Important factors in Their Differences

The main worry in defining Asperger's as a lesser form of Autism is that it could imply that children with AS do not face as many difficulties as those with Autism, when in fact, they can suffer far more severe anxiety disorders and depression than those with Autism.

Parent's guidelines to assist their children to develop fulfilling social activities and a chance to lead successful career options can be provided.

Clinical psychologists describe the Autism – Asperger's continuum, as being the condition of Autistic Syndrome Disorder (ASD)


**The National Autistic Society** is recommended for further information. They have an informative website.

# Head Injuries

There are many causes for head injuries which may be congenital, tumour or disease-related or due to trauma. There are local head injury charities in most large communities.

**HEADWAY** is the Brain Injury Association Charity. See its website for case histories and information.

# Interview with the Author

**This is an interesting subject. What prompted you to write it?**

My neighbour informed me he had been robbed and assaulted. I knew he was on the autistic scale. I could see how those with this educational barrier could be manipulated and groomed and so I asked both him and his mother if I could write a story about autism. I got the green light from them both and so it is a novella. My proviso was that neither his name nor our town as the setting would be used. The Lancashire town of Wigan, which I know particularly well, was therefore chosen. The protagonist is also now a woman.

**How much of the story is true?**

Of course much of my neighbour's sad circumstances appear in the book but each scene prompts another and so the book takes off in many different directions. This is not a biography in any way, especially as I have made the protagonist, Sally, more ill than my neighbour. My 63-year-old cousin was born with too much oxygen and has been blind since birth. He also has the functionary brain of a 10-year-old child. Yet he is fascinated by cars and machinery. These two personalities with their ailments created Sally.

**Why is it only a novella?**

A book is not enhanced by writing more than is necessary. Did I know when I started if it would have been a novella? Yes, I knew the limitations of the subject and storyline and so it is a novella. But another novella now follows. So why not have two books for the price of one?

**Do you think this book could offend any autistic sufferer?**

I hope not. Rather this is an edifying story in which the protagonist finds her feet in music, is awarded damages and receives an award from the criminal injuries board. But it is also a warning that the courts must take offences against vulnerable victims very seriously.

**The longest chapter in the book is the trial. Was that the most difficult to write?**

It is crucial to gather all the evidence in sequence in this chapter to make it a plausible court case. I used to prosecute in Kilmarnock, Ayr and Dumfries Sheriff courts so I felt comfortable in that respect. Sheriffs do not often seek avizandum but as I had a complicated case once which went that way, I decided it would have been necessary for the Judge to reflect on the case before administering punishment. English law may not use the Scottish legal term avizandum but in practice in both legal jurisdictions it is undertaken when time is required before sentencing. Psychiatric and social work report requests, post-conviction, are frequently sought by the bench before pronouncing the sentence.

## What will be your next book be?

I can never tell but I know when I am inspired to write it.

My second novella, A Clerical Murder, follows this novella.

# A Clerical Murder

*For Procurator Fiscal Fiona Caldwell*
*and Clinical Psychologist Dr Laura Caldwell*

# Acknowledgements

This novella would not exist had I not been one of those notorious sons of the manse. There, I've said it. Yet that gave me an enquiring mind into denominational thinking. Religion has the power of good and the capacity for evil. That inspired me to write this unusual book. To Robin Wood, Venus Carew, Leslie Hecht, Farooq Ahmed, Kamran, Jehangeer and Sonia Malik, Malcolm Forest Charles Watt and Bill O'Carroll and Laura McKenna. To publisher Jeremy Thompson who never fails to impress me at Troubador and to Matador for publishing this unusual double novella. I cannot deny that on both the criminal side and the clinical side I can rely on my two daughters for advice and so this book is dedicated to them.

# Author's Disclaimer

This is a contemporary and controversial novel. If the novel offends you, please realise that offence may not be a universal perception and I do not write to offend. Dismiss the text as you wish but accept my right to write.

This disclaimer has two purposes. Firstly it keeps me one step ahead of a censure from angry clerics. Secondly, if after reading the book, it leads to further discussion of the issues raised, then the book has achieved even more than I expected. Do not forget, however, that this is a novella which my mind has actively urged me to write.

Send criticism, abuse, cheek or the occasional appreciative comments to me at:

netherholm6@yahoo.com

# Introduction

It is known beyond doubt that beavers do not have engineering degrees yet they build dams with expertise. Nor does the crime writer have to be a convicted criminal to write a crime novel. It should then follow that in this novella, I need not have knowledge of things supernatural or divine. This, however, is not the case. I have much baggage in this department. I should come clean from the start.

The UK is largely a post-Christian country if we gauge worship attendance figures. However I have been in the past, a son of the manse, a Jewish sympathiser, a West African Presbyterian missionary, a worker in a Roman Catholic school, a Humanist observer and a Baha'i supporter. I have lived with Sunni Muslims in the NWFP of Pakistan and I married an Anglican.

So how did this ecumenical boiling pot lead to me being, at this stage of my life, agnostic? This being a view that there is no proof of either the existence or non-existence of any deity, but since any deity that may exist appears unconcerned for the universe or the welfare of its inhabitants, the question is largely academic and that their existence therefore has little or no impact on personal human affairs and should be of little theological interest. Yet the Ghanaian Akan Twi proverb 'No state is permanent,' speaks to me. The future is an empty chapter at present.

I remind you this story is not just a book about faiths but a crime novella too.

# Prologue

At the age of eight I moved to Shawlands in Glasgow from Kirriemuir in rural Angus. My first day at primary school there was a seminal experience of considerable educational and religious magnitude.

Miss Dick demanded that we work out a sum on the board and proceeded to move unobtrusively up each row of pupils like a viper whose tongue was ready to dart out and pounce on an errant mathematician. The problem I had was I knew there was no long division in Kirriemuir. (I believe they have it now.) My ploy was to score out the sum and start to draw it in again as Miss Dick passed by. I knew if I could survive this day, then my older sister would be able to instruct me in this advanced mathematical mystery that night.

'We do not make a mess like that,' I heard. An eerie silence prepared the class for the day's ritual torture. I was dragged out to the front. The viper struck. Twice in fact with her Lochgelly manufactured leather belt, the likes of which I had never set eyes on before. I tried hard not to cry as my fingers tingled in red hot pain. I was sent back to my seat without any instruction in how to go about solving the sum and so anticipated another trashing that afternoon if we returned to this dark calculation. Morning break could not come quickly enough.

That was when I was approached by a caring pupil whose surname I had never encountered.

Leslie Hecht felt sorry for my morning difficulties and befriended me with a very strange question.

'Miller, are you a Jew?'

This was not the time to reject the kindly voice I was hearing. Somewhere in the make-up of my 'son of the manse' background, a phrase kept itching to be heard. Ah yes, Christ was King of the Jews. I could now reply with confidence.

'Yes, I am a Jew,' I said pleased with myself.

'Then bring your yarmulke on Friday. That's when we have Hebrew lessons.'

'My what?'

'Yarmulke. Your parents must be reformed Jews. Your school cap will do.'

The next couple of months were less traumatic than that first day at Shawlands Primary but my father, who was minister of Shawlands Old Parish Church, was also the school chaplain. He asked me what I was enjoying at school, probably to see if I had an arts leaning or a science preference.

'Hebrew,' I said.

'Hebrew?' clarified my father who had studied Greek and Hebrew at St. Andrews University as part of his divinity degree.

'Yes. Baruch hata Adonai. Elo-henu malech ho-olam, ha'tov, va-ha'me-tev,' I said.

'Why are you speaking Hebrew, Miller?'

'Because I am a Jew, Dad.'

'No, you are not.' he replied as my eyes fell to the ground. At that moment I realise no more bar mitzvah's of my friend's older brothers would come my way.

Several years later, when I was a student, I flew to the States with Camp America in the summer months. It happened to be a Jewish camp I travelled to. Beautiful Lake Onota, in the verdant Berkshire Hills of Massachusetts, nestled at this site which had served the New York Jewish community for three generations. There, they were not surprised that I spoke Hebrew. They assumed I was a Jew until we got ready to swim in the camp pool. I was certainly not a Jew after all.

Three months later I was working for the Presbyterian Church in Ghana. I was there from 1972 to1978. It was there I met my Anglican wife. Membership seemed open to all adherents in her mother church - except for us.

When my wife met the vicar of the church in Wigan, in preparation for our January wedding, he was somewhat concerned to find her fiancé was neither Anglican nor English, that he lived in West Africa and was not present. The Anglican Church did not open its doors to everyone it seemed, at that precise moment.

The Anglican Bishop of Liverpool was to be notified and consulted before progress could be made for our marriage. And so the famous cricketing Bishop, David Shepherd, gave his blessing on our marriage and the great personal event took place in January 1978.

The following year, we returned to the UK from Tema in Ghana. I enrolled to study a post graduate degree in West African traditional religions, geography and the history of colonial Africa. There I found a multitude of faiths mixed at the School of Oriental and African Studies of the University of London. Jews and Muslims, Hindu and Baptists mingled with Sanskrit poems and readings heard in the corridors. We drank coffee and smoked from Turkish Aykoc Meersham Sultan pipes and I made many friends of different faiths, in harmony with different belief systems.

After graduating, I was offered two jobs. One was in Surrey and the other in Stirling. With a family in mind, we preferred to head north and I found work as an educational social worker in St Modan's Roman Catholic Secondary School in Stirling. These were happy days in which I engaged in the rites of that denomination but when I left three years later, I was more than ever convinced that religion in schools should never be on a compulsory basis – as in France.

I became a reporter to the children's panels. Over the next twenty years, I was a reporter in Kilmarnock, Irvine, Ayr, and finally held the post of Regional and Authority Reporter for the south of Scotland. A Hearing meant that at every meeting there were three panel members. Robin Wood was an excellent member and held a high position on the Council for Secular Humanism. He gave me magazines and I attended some Humanist conferences, ironically some were back in Stirling. There were Jews, Baptists, Methodists, Atheists, Salvationists and Congregationalists – all caring panel members making decisions in the lives of children, influencing young lives in a positive manner and, in turn, influencing me to a significant degree.

After I retired, I knew a Policeman who also had a

restaurant. He was a Muslim. Farook Ahmed's niece was killed in the tragic earthquake in South Asia of October 2005. He met me in town. As he knew I had been the reporter, he asked if I would go to one of the camps to help the children who had lost parents and their dwellings in the disaster.

He had in mind that I would play with and teach the young children. Accordingly I travelled east with paper and crayons, several glove puppets and a mouth organ.

But there was trouble at the Mundihar camp in the Islamic Republic of the North West Frontier Province of Pakistan when I arrived. Aid had come flooding in from wealthy countries and the farmer and his wife, who had donated their land for the tents, could not cope. Some of the aid was taken by the farmer's wife to the local town's people who had not been affected by the tragedy. A meeting took place in the camp grounds. It was chaired by a Brigadier of the Pakistani Army. He was deciding if the farmer's wife should be prosecuted for her illegal distribution of aid.

I stood up and told the assembled circle of interested parties that when a major disaster occurred, the worldwide response was immediate. Money and goods were rushed to the area but so often, whether in Asia or Africa, the local networks were traumatised and understandably slow to get organised with a distribution plan. I had sympathy for the farmer's wife as she had faced this problem and then I sat down. The Brigadier stood up and pointed his finger at me.

'You are not a Muslim,' he said placing me on edge. 'You are independent. You will be the camp manager.'

And so I became responsible for the care, protection,

feeding and supply of the needs of 24,500 Sunni Muslim victims, of all ages, of the 2005 earthquake.

The camp had its own Imam. I regret my memory escapes me regarding his name but his English language was clear, educated and beautifully descriptive. But his wish was to make me realise Islam was the only way of life. Yes, Christ Jesus was a prophet but no more than that. He was persuasive and persistent. When I left, I did not reject his ranting but saw all religion as part of a human psyche trying to find the meaning of life.

Let each person use his or her senses to find that meaning but remember religion requires faith and faith is not fact. Nor should anyone be prevented from choosing their own vehicle of faith and certainly no one has the right to prevent individuals from abandoning their set of beliefs to acquire another, or none at all.

So these are my somewhat unusual, albeit unconventional, exposures to different religions over my lifetime. These encounters, I concede, must influence this novel, for writers rely on their experiences and what they know and have learned.

So why have I written this book?

There is a hunger to understand the forces of religion. They can drive both the politics of good and also the powers of evil. They can create acts of great kindness and acts of sheer evil, death and destruction. Religion is worn ostentatiously by some and covertly by others. Their way is the best way; the only way, if only that were true.

This novel looks behind the denominational beliefs to find the essence of a common human experience – the very values of what it is to be human.

# 1

# Overburdened

Dr Tony Scriven's marriage did not explode. It simply faded like an autumn dusk. His acrimony was negligible even after he learned his wife had a new partner. He was married to his work, a factor in the separation. Now city life was behind him. It no longer held its charms.

From a busy Manchester practice, he moved to a post in rural South West Scotland. Fewer cases pleased him. It gave him time to enjoy a weekly round of golf. An interest in ornithology had been resurrected too especially on his Rambling Club walks. These were the positive aspects of his new life. However there was a gap in his life and it was hard to fit into such a close-knit community. It became an increasing concern as he grew older. Could he find a partner before it was too late? Had he made the wrong decision to leave the city after all?

The Reverend Alan Barker reported to the desk secretary and took a seat in the square waiting room. The NHS could not afford a fresh coat of paint. So a flat screen stared at Alan. It fought to occupy his troubled mind with house purchasing in far-away warmer climes.

*"A mere quarter of a million would secure this view; twice as much with a pool and an extra bedroom,"* said the highly tanned, golden-haired and provocatively dressed presenter.

To Alan, this visual offering was pure Disneyland. His manse was large of course but it was on loan to each succeeding incumbent. It too had a good view. He had a glebe as well. But there was no swimming pool, just a damp patch at the bottom of the lawn supporting a few tadpoles this spring.

Dr Tony Scriven arrived extending his hand and projecting a warm smile.

'Mr Barker? Hi. This way please,' he said turning to take the lead. Tony had passed Alan's church on foot many times but he rolled out in his Volvo on Sundays to exercise his mind and body on the golf course. Easter and Christmas rituals with the occasional funeral had been his sole church visits in the past, making him a nominal Church adherent should anyone ask.

Alan felt a surge of relief. The process had begun. What lay ahead remained a mystery. This was a medical appointment of which he had no experience.

'Alan, the floor is yours,' said Tony the former GP turned psychiatrist.

Alan hung his coat on the peg behind the door. Should he state the over-arching problem with a monologue of gigantic proportions or produce make short sentences? He pulled out the wooden chair in front of the desk and sat down before the psychiatrist. He crossed his legs and rested his hands in a tight clasp over his right knee.

'Something's not right. I don't feel like.......well......'

'Burnt out? Sermon drought?' suggested Tony.

Alan nodded, briefly looking up at his inquisitor. He knew his recent sermons had been recovered from years gone by. He felt it safe to resurrect them, as few would remember a dust covered sermon or its message. But even those pulpit outings were of the past. He had not entered his very own church for over four weeks.

Tony flipped through his notes. He noted his wife was bedridden following a riding accident eight months ago.

'Your role must have changed considerably since your wife's accident.'

Was that a question he wondered? 'Of course it has, bloody difficult it is. What else would you expect?' he snapped.

Tony gave a supporting nod, surprised at the clerics mild swearing and anger.

'It's time consuming. I do everything now, everything. I clean, bathe, shop, garden, cook.........' He was cut short.

'It must leave little time to be a pastor.'

Alan gave a weird grin. It hadn't taken the psychiatrist long to confirm what he knew, but was that depression?

'Do you get enough sleep?'

'Disturbed, I'd say. But I try to go to bed early. We sleep apart – have to. Don't watch much TV these days either.'

'Does your wife read or watch telly?'

Alan looked across at the monitor behind Dr Scriven. It was either a television or heart or something else monitor. He wondered just what it was but did not ask.

'Your wife, Alan, I was asking....'

'She can't turn pages. The telly's in her room. Yes, it's her pal when I am out.'

Alan felt Dr Scriven had got a picture of his daily life. But there were still a few initial questions to overcome for the doctor's satisfaction. The interrogation continued.

'Does the congregation help in any way?'

Alan blew and sniffed into his handkerchief. 'No, not much,' he said in all honesty.

'And why's that?'

'Probably the nature of the disability. Possibly see me as the duty carer 24/7. Just no role for them, I suppose.' Alan sighed as the image of his daily drudgery was laid bare. He returned his handkerchief to his pocket.

'Not a very Christian lot I'd say. You mean no one to do the garden for example; ironing; making meals?'

Alan shifted from one buttock to the other. 'We occasionally get a few loaves and crumbles, that sort of thing.' He wondered if the psychiatrist was acting more like a social worker.

'Alcohol intake?'

'Teetotal,' he replied promptly then wondered if the Christmas drink or a birthday tipple constituted a light drinker. He was wondering whether to retract and amend his answer but his thoughts were cut short by a personal intrusion.

'Your sex life. Satisfying?'

God, sex always sex. Psychiatrists must be obsessed with the topic, he thought. I suppose he's heard everything, he concluded. He took a deep breath.

'The sin of Onan. Self-satisfying and sometimes mutual.'

'Good. I don't know how I'd cope in your situation Alan, especially as the change was so sudden. But you've not got depression. I can be sure of that. If anything you are too active, domestically. You are overburdened. You are doing the job of two people if not three and feeling guilty that you cannot serve your congregation. I can see why you feel you are losing the place. And you are.'

Alan knew he was certainly not functioning and was glad his own diagnosis had been wide of the mark.

'Just to clarify, it's not depression this thing I have?'

'No. Mind you, your GP was right to refer you to me. He must have suspected the dark dog. But there's none I'm pleased to say. Not a bark or a whimper,' smiled Tony.

Alan felt relieved but saw no further purpose in the examination. His eyes wandered round the room.

'So what happens now?'

Tony lifted his telephone. As it rang he focussed his eyes on Alan and smiled.

Tea perhaps? Yes, that's what he'll be arranging, the British solution to all aches of the mind and body. However his opening remark sent a shiver down Alan's spine.

'Can you come to my room? I've a client for you.'

# 2

# A Bridge Over Troubled Water

Shower-heads set on full. That's what the rain seemed like. Falling on roof tops sending gushes of bubbling water down into thirsty drains. The sky was dark. Streets were claustrophobic in busy home-time, wet-clothing time. It had been one of those life supporting necessary but so inconvenient miserable days. Coloured umbrellas identified female pedestrians while golf insignia and black ones kept the head and shoulders dry of the men as they headed, keeping their heads down, towards car parks, public transport and onward to their homes. Those in cars leaned forward, mesmerised by the full throttle of wiper blades out of time with Radio 2 and sometimes too fast for Classic FM.

Most pedestrians walked purposefully, watching for approaching puddles. Bus passengers looked down on them with some sympathy hoping the worst of the rain would have subsided when they alighted.

That was why police could find no witnesses or even an explanation why a man lay on a muddy reed bank beneath the town bridge. His life seemed to have ebbed away amid the constant ripples of water washing his face. None of the commuters glanced over the bridge. There was nothing to see but darkness, and the occasional effervescent ripple.

His hair moved, flowing backwards and forwards to the vagrancies of the tide and his bearded chin chattered in erratic bursts of nothingness.

The in-shore lifeboat stationed further down the river was alerted by one observant bus passenger's mobile. Yet another body in the river. Third this year but it was November. The average annual water death toll had just been achieved. Water always had its fascination; its alluring recreation and its death enticing moods. They sped towards the fatal casualty. They were certain to encounter a corpse. They were prepared as ever.

The location was fortunate. The body was under the bridge, not washed away. Reports of bodies in the water usually meant a search of the banks but this was an easy find.

The coxswain threw the dregs of his coffee flask into the river. His colleague threw his fag end into the dark ripples on the other side of the craft. The coxswain slowed down and approached the body with due reverence.

An ambulance stood by on the bridge with unnecessary flashing blue lights. The crew remained inside, dry, awaiting developments. Two policemen walked onto the bridge where the departing point of suicide began. But they knew the day's drenching would have washed away any possible evidence at that site. Perhaps the autopsy would determine whether he jumped or was pushed; whether he was drunk, depressed, deranged or drugged.

The boat hook secured a grip on the man's clothing. As he was dragged off the grassy reeds, a groan was heard.

'Easy, he's alive Mark, be prepared.'

Mark was the crew's first aid man. A paramedic in daytime, they always hoped he was available when life at sea was in danger.

The man was dragged over the rubber bulwark and placed in the recovery position. Some water trickled from his mouth. His right leg was clearly broken below the knee.

'Give me space,' said Mark straddling the body. 'He's unconscious.' There was certainly some life in him. 'Alert the ambulance.'

The inflatable craft sped towards the town slipway where the ambulance arrived. A crowd of passers-by forgot the rain to view some real life drama. Their second dose of drama awaited them at soap-time that night but this was certainly not acting. They sensed a different atmosphere, less paced than screen offerings.

Shiny survival foil was wrapped round the man who was transferred to a stretcher which was quickly secured inside the ambulance. The driver sped away with the siren screaming and blue flashing lights to the A&E department of the local hospital while his colleague fought to keep the patient alive in the swaying vehicle.

Alan welcomed medical social worker Lin Howie to his home. She was there to assess his wife's needs initially, and his, but before she could arrange all those identified to help, she spent three days getting the manse shipshape. He watched her settle in, like a sheep dog eyeing her every move.

'Right, now Alan. Off to your study. Coffee at 11 a.m. Skedaddle, on you go.'

Alan relaxed and raised his arms in the air.

'Yes....yes..yes,' he said. Menial jobs fell from his hands. His pen resumed its paper activity. The phone calls were now initiated by him. The Royal Volunteer Service provided Massie, a fun loving, book club enthusiast and recently retired pet shop manager, as a regular visitor to chat with his wife. Massie often brought some home baking. She read to Penny and opened her world to female companionship. On fair weather days she took Penny out in her personalised and motorised chair. Her collie dog Georgie accompanied them on such occasions. Alan was on the road to recovery as a result of this array of assistance.


Tony looked at the case notes of Major Risk and smiled. He hoped he would not live up to his name.

Major Paul Risk played the trombone. That piece of brass tubing which defies understanding to the uninitiated. A slide moves up and down making different notes. Sometimes it stays in the same place while a series of different sounds are heard. It has no keyboard or finger placing. It is the most mysterious of brass instruments. Paul had mastered this instrument to make its melodic tenor notes soft and warm or loud and harsh when the music dictated. Paul was the doyen of the Salvation band. His militaristic uniform was immaculate and his instrument polished to catch sunlight on its shaft and emit the glory of the Lord. Rotund like Santa, he had neither a white beard nor a constant smile.

Paul had a dark side. A decade ago he taught his instrument to a series of young music pupils. They came from different backgrounds and none were Salvationists. *The Moorov doctrine* was applied to the Police charge when evidence emerged of inappropriate touching of both boys and girls over a prolonged period. It was their collective evidence against his faltering words of defence that led to a three year prison sentence and a life on the sex offender's register.

That was ten years ago and the denomination had supported his resurrection, his seeking forgiveness and his firm faith. Music lessons were a thing of the dark past and no longer given. As a musician however, he was priceless. He was always on the front row when the Salvation Army Band was entertaining. After all, the movement of the trombone demanded space. That put him in the spotlight, which he devoured.

His wife Irene was also a Salvationist who supported her husband through thick and thin to all who knew her but the doubts about his past, although forgiven, were not forgotten and she would be first to admit not all was well within the marital home. She played cornet three rows behind her husband when on the march.

Tony made an appointment for the Major.

Ward 8 was for men who were recovering from medical treatments. One patient had all his rotten teeth removed yet he was anxious to communicate with his fellow bed companions. It was a struggle to hear him, let alone understand what his toothless gums were saying. It led to many misunderstandings, resolved by his inane smile.

There were no misunderstandings when the leg-plastered, head-bandaged Imam regained consciousness. He was propped up resting in the sitting position in bed.

He had not expected the approaching medic to stop in front of him.

'So it's Farook, isn't it? Farook Elahi?' asked Dr Tony Scriven.

Farook lifted his eyes to the psychiatrist whose tie sat over one collar. Failure was etched on his face but he managed a minimal nod.

Tony smiled as he put his hand on Farook's shoulder. 'Salaam Alaikum.'

'Alaikum Salaam,' Farook replied instantly.

Tony gave a smile of recognition.

'Taxi driver I think. That you?'

Farook was pleased to have been identified by profession. 'Yes, Ali's Taxis. Not running today.'

Tony's laugh came close to a snigger. His smile was not reciprocated. Farook was in a state of confusion. He had failed to end his life, like the unsuccessful bomber's unexploded suicide vest and yet he was being cared for and treated by those tasked to preserve his life. For what purpose? Tony ventured straight to the point.

'Well did you jump, or were you pushed?'

Farook shuffled around as much as he was able in the constricting bed sheets and set his dark eyes on the jug of water beside his bed.

'Pushed into jumping. That's what it was. The third option you didn't give me,' said Farook. He turned his eyes back to the doctor.

Tony thought for a moment. Perhaps this was a police matter more than what he had to offer but that was premature to conclude. 'So not a simple suicide attempt? You know, that was some height you fell. Many wouldn't have survived that bridge drop.'

'The lucky ones,' said Farook.

That statement determined Tony's response. 'I see. Perhaps we can arrange an appointment before you leave.'

'And when might that be?'

'The Physio will let me know. They'll get you ready for departure. It might be a week yet. Head injuries, you know, your plastered leg too....they take time.'

Farook nodded as if an apology for his failed suicide was necessary.

'Okay, stick in there, Farook. I might need your taxi one day.' He smiled and tapped his left shoulder a couple of times but the future seemed bleak for Farook.


Tony strolled back to his office. It was not far away. He enjoyed the light breeze, swaying branches and floating white clouds. They cleansed his thoughts to prepare for the next patient but the waiting room was empty. No apparent pressures made him more thoughtful than usual.

'Want a coffee?' he asked his receptionist Madge.

Madge stopped typing. What on earth did he say? Tony get the coffee? No way. 'I'll get it doctor,' she said instinctively rising from her computer screen to boil the kettle.

'No, no. Stay where you are. No patients waiting, I've got the time.'

Tony made his black coffee with a sensation of sugar, believing each day he stirred in one less grain.

'It's tea for you anyway, isn't it?'

'Redboosh tea bag, on the shelf. Just on its own, thanks,' said Madge keeping an eye on his unexpected domesticity.

Tony brought over her mug wishing he had not filled it to the brim. He moved with canny caution and managed to bring it to her desk. However when he lowered the mug to its coaster, he spilt some of her dark red hot liquid.

'Sorry about that.'

'That's fine, don't worry,' she said taking a tissue from her patterned paper hanky cube on her desk.

'Mail's on your desk sir,' Madge said dabbing away, annoyed that she had let him serve her.

The mail might take him comfortably through till lunchtime he thought as he kicked the door open with one eye on his coffee. Indeed there was a pile. But he was glad to see a couple of Journals in the mix. He sat down and took his first sip as he leafed through the collection. One brown envelope caught his eye. Pre-sentencing Court reports came every now and then. He opened the letter. He lifted the phone.

'Madge, this Court report. They have only given me a couple of weeks. Can you make an appointment for this patient, Lizzie Taylor?'

Farook arrived at the clinic three days later.

'A wheelchair I see, not your taxi?'

'No, not sure when I'll be back driving,' replied Farook.

Tony was pleased to see his patient seemed more optimistic, more mobile and less gloomy. It augured well for a better consultation. Farook wheeled his chair in front of Tony, prepared to face his mental daemons.

'So tell me about that day,' asked Tony crossing his legs and polishing his reading glasses.

'It was a build-up over many months. Pressures from my own people.'

Tony nodded, wondering, clarifying. 'What kind of pressures?' he asked not quite sure of who his 'own' people might be. Taxi colleagues perhaps or even Mosque attendees?

'I was asked to give an eighteen year old girl driving lessons. Of course her father had to sit in the back of the car. You know, traditional Muslim. I told the girl I could not teach her to drive if she was going to wear her burkah. She could not possibly be observant as a driver. She was putting lives at risk as well as her own. I was not going to teach her in a burkah, and that was final.'

'Eminently sensible I would have thought,' Tony frowned, as he put on his glasses again.

'Her father told me his daughter had a right to wear what she wished. I told him this was not Saudi Arabia. If he wanted to go there, then she could dress that way but she would not be allowed to drive at all then.'

'So, what happened?'

'The girl still does not drive but her father has influence in our Mosque and doesn't like the way I am running it.'

'Surely not because of the driving incident?'

Farook retied his left shoe lace. His head dipped under the desk for a moment. 'No that was the tipping point. You see, I'm trying to make the Muslim British more British. Of course they say they are but they are clearly not.'

Tony wondered how able he was to cope with this developing scenario; he was way out of his comfort zone.

'You don't see Muslims playing at Wimbledon and not many play football or golf. Some mix at school although these new Academies have Muslim-only pupils. Even at university they gather with their own. There is no inter-marriage, which you can expect with other faiths. They really don't mix enough. They are certainly not encouraged to mix. They are not part of the general community.'

Tony agreed with his observation. 'So it's a traditional, conservative Mosque you run.'

'Traditional? Isn't it the same in the Church of England? You have the traditional church attendees all set in their ways. They don't like the guitar playing or youthful pop choirs. There's friction, just like we have.

The elders have the voting powers. In our Mosque I am only their religious leader.'

Tony had never been in a Mosque but it was certainly not the time to ask to visit when there was ill feeling around. Farook's shoulders were tight, his hands clasped.

'You all right?' asked Tony.

'Yes, but you want to know about that bridge don't you?' Tony nodded without saying another word. He was in no rush. It was good to get back on track.

'I really want to bring my people with me. So I did a twelve week course at the Charmley Muslim College.'

'Where's that?'

'East Midlands. It's a course to empower British Muslims to feel confident in their faith while drawing on the traditions and the values they see around them in Britain, their adopted home.'

'I see. Like the Monarchy for example, they are big on that aren't they?'

'Yes, the Queen and the Houses of Parliament with all its faults. At least it's more democratic than the governments of most of the former colonial countries. The course had visitors from the Police, the Catholic Bishop of Birmingham and even a Rabbi. I had to keep that information from my Mosque because they don't want influence from other faiths.'

Good on him, thought Tony, taking a lead. 'So you were away for twelve weeks? Did another Imam take your place?'

'No, I came back every Friday but the atmosphere was not good any longer. They did not want to hear my new ideas of a better outward approach. They started to make life awkward for me. You see Islamaphobia is growing but not as bad as in France or in America where the press stoke the flames of hatred. But recent extreme events in France, The Netherlands, Denmark and Belgium make us nervous. People don't realise that ISIS kill Sufis and established Sunni Muslims in Iraq and Syria.'

'And don't forget the persecuted Christian minorities in the Middle East,' added Tony to complete the picture.

'Exactly. There are many victims. I agree. But also young unemployed Muslims from my own Mosque have been setting out to join Isis. They had the backing of the elders and I had no power and no permission to stop them or report them.'

Farook shook his head from side to side in despair. 'I could only silently pray that they would be caught before they left the country. That was the way our Mosque was being run. Run with a knife at my back. I saw no way out and I was not only losing influence but losing friends too. ....I needed to get away...get out.... out of this life and that is why I tried to end it. End it at the bridge.'

Tony sucked a pencil end and nodded as Farook spoke. Hearing yes, but not fully understanding the cultural divide he had been given by his patient.

'So what plans do you have now?'

'I've had a few visitors from the Mosque. They are quick to forgive and grateful that Allah - blessings upon His Name - saved me. So I suppose I can return there and I'll see if they will sack me as their Imam. It's within their power to appoint a new Imam. So taxi driving and the Mosque ....I'll give it another go.'

'Good. I hope it goes well for you Farook. But I want to see you again. Perhaps in a few weeks. I'll drop you a line. Are you comfortable with that?'

Farook smiled through his beard. 'That's what I like about the British. Are you comfortable with that? It does not translate well in my native tongue. It's why we should be more British. I'll be pleased to see you again.'

# 3

# Happy Clappy Lizzie

Lizzie Taylor paced up and down the waiting room like a hungry caged lioness. Her eyes fixed on the closed door handle. When opened, she would find someone whose attention would be tested. That was how she worked when she was high. Today was one of those days. She was approaching the peak of her parabolic mental health problem.

Tony found the woman to be in her early forties when he opened the waiting room door. She wore an open coat showing a glimpse of her cobalt blue jersey and its internal contours and a patchwork skirt with woollen brown stockings and a pair of well-polished brown leather boots with solid block heels. Her face etched agitated concentration.

'Lizzie Taylor, please. This way.'

'Tell me, are you a doctor or a psychologist?' she asked clinging to her overcoat, rolled up in a ball.

'I am a specialist in mental health. I am a psychiatrist but also a psychoanalyst.'

'So I am mad? That's what the Court said.

Wasn't it? Tell me, wasn't it?'

'Lizzie let me take your coat and hang it up. You have a seat over there, opposite my desk,' said Tony in a slow methodical instruction. It had no effect on his patient.

'Do I lie on the couch? I mean that's what psycho... psychotherapists want don't they. I'll take my boots off.'

'No need. Have a seat. So this incident took place on Good Friday I see. Tell me about it.'

Lizzie was glad to be given full control of her reply. 'I've never been charged by the Police before you know,' she began.

'That does not matter. I just want you to tell me what happened that morning around midday.'

'Glory be to God. Was it not the most sacred day of the year, Good Friday?'

Tony scrutinised the charge paper.

'It was, yes 12.07 p.m. on Good Friday.'

'Yes, I was driving a van. Not my van of course. I don't have a van. It's Billy Craig's van. He let me use it. It's a nippy little thing. Guzzles through the petrol mind you. Oh no, diesel it was. Mine's petrol. Yes, mustn't get them muddled. That would be a problem, not so? A really big problem. I've got a Golf Polo. Nippier to drive than a van. Good for the town, when it's busy.'

'Lizzie, let me stop you there. I want you to concentrate on what happened. Tell me what happened immediately before the Police arrived.'

'Oh yes. Well, I had an accident, you know. But the police did not come for at least another eight minutes, I think it.....'

'Lizzie take a breath. Yes, I mean take a breath, a deep breath. Now stand up, I'll show you.'

Tony stood in front of Lizzie and closed his eyes.

'Now you close yours too.'

'Oh don't do anything I won't like,' she intoned.

'Quiet Lizzie, concentrate. Now a deep breath. Fill your lungs and hold it......hold it...now breathe out. Now again, a deep breath.....'

Every time Lizzie pursed her lips ready to let out another uncontrollable outburst, Tony silenced her with his ram-rod index finger. The exercise went on for about another two minutes. A short interval for most events but it had a calming effect on Lizzie and Tony too.

'Now sit down. I want you to tell me how the accident occurred and nothing else, at this moment in time. Only the accident. Understand?'

Lizzie nodded briefly, then continued to take a deep breath, held it in, then exploded it out. 'Shall I start to tell you now?'

'Yes. Now Lizzie. Take your time and tell me only about the accident.'

'Well, it was Easter. You know, the day Christ was hung on the cross then rose to the heavens?'

Tony gave a nodding approval but kept his thoughts to himself. Was this the start of another outburst?

'In the past, we walked around town holding the wooden cross we made. But I felt we were not converting as many as we should so I suggested we had a larger cross and if someone could donate a van, then we'd be able to tour the town with the cross on the back of the vehicle. Be seen by more people that way, not so? Getting the message across, that's what I was doing.'

Tony followed her narrative like a shadow reluctant

to be following her laboured progress. But he persisted and just nodded. He was following.

'So I got to drive a blue van with the cross secured upright in the back of the van. But oh dear, I'm afraid that's what led to the accident.'

'An accident? So it wasn't a deliberate act? One that led you to a Court appearance?'

'I've not told you yet. Oh yes, it was really serious you know. I've never been in a situation like this before. I have always trusted God to keep me on the straight and narrow.'

'I see,' said Tony glancing at his wrist watch.

'Yes, it was quite silly of me. I did not remember how low the bridge was. I heard a snapping crack and slowed down immediately of course. Too quickly in fact. That's when the following car bumped into me. It was my fault I know but unfortunately the cross snapped and it broke the other driver's windscreen.'

'How injured was he?'

'Oh, not at all. But I had to reprimand him, quite severely.'

'You did?'

'Yes. His mouth should have been washed out with soap there and then. His language was quite unforgiveable, certainly not Christian. I had to tell him, you know. We can't encourage such foul mouthed swearing, can we now? It's such a bad influence on the young.'

Tony's eyes narrowed and stared at Lizzie. 'I must say I'd have some sympathy for a driver who has to brake suddenly and have his windscreen penetrated by a wooden cross,' suggested Tony. 'If it were me in the following car I'd let out a few expletives too. The driver must have been in a state of shock.'

Lizzie pooh-poohed his suggestion. 'He couldn't have been in shock. Otherwise he wouldn't have sworn so much. I really had to show him that God was loving and caring for him in his misfortune as well as mine.'

Then Lizzie stopped talking. And neither did Tony talk. It seemed he was playing a game to see how long it would take before the verbal deluge continued. Yet the silence continued. Lizzie looked down at her feet avoiding eye contact. Tony saw her machine gun eye blinking. Inevitably it was Lizzie who cracked first.

'So what will you tell the Court?'

'I'm not sure yet Lizzie. Tell me, have you been given any medication from your GP?'

'Well, there was some ibu..ibule...something when I had a pain in my leg.'

'Ibuleve?'

'Yes, that's the one,' Lizzie laughed. 'I believe, yes I believe, do you?'

Tony's lips parted slightly in recognition of her manic humour. He was not going to be drawn in to her evangelical world. 'I mean any regular medication?'

'Lamotrigine, I take that morning and night. My GP gave me that a few days ago. 250 mg in the morning and 200 mg at night.'

'Good, that's right.'

'Yes, I take Vitamin F every day too.'

'Vitamin F? There's no such thing.'

'Oh yes Doctor, Vitamin F is essential. For the believer, it is at the very heart of the matter. Vitamin F for Faith.'

'I see. So how long have you been an evangelical Christian?'

'Since the day I was born. Some forty two years ago.'

'I find that hard to believe. Presumably your parents are Christians?'

'Of course. My father is now in the realms of Glory while my mother is a hand servant here on earth just as I am. She's in her late seventies. Not so active physically but mentally she's right at His side. A faithful servant, if ever there was one.'

'Being evangelical, does that make you excitable, I mean are you always full of the Spirit?'

Lizzie's face was suddenly vacant. Gone was the certainty with which she proudly wore her faith on her face.

'No, not always. Some days I don't leave the house. I get exhausted. I just stay in bed and speak to Ginge and he comes to sleep on my bed.'

'Ginge?'

'My cat, well obvious isn't it, my ginger cat.'

Tony could have kicked himself. It was so bloody obvious she would have a cat. Dogs respond; cats ignore.

'And how long do these quiet days last for?'

'Sometimes as much as a week.'

'And would you say you are happier when these quiet days are gone?'

'Oh yes. Then I get so much more done.'

'Is there a regular pattern of feeling down, then high?'

'I'm never high as you say. I'm not on drugs. Good heavens no, I don't smoke either. My body is a temple of God's creation. It is as pure as I can make it.'

'I didn't mean drugs. Moods if I can call them that. Do they come and go?

'Ummm not exactly. I can go for long periods when all is calm. But then I realise I'm heading up or down as the moment takes me.'

Tony paused to take a breath before continuing.

'And today how do you feel?'

'Well I'd say returning to normal. Wouldn't you? Of course normal is hard to describe but normal, yes I'd say a sort of normal. Not a sort of normal. No, just normal.' She stood up briefly then sat down again. She got up once more and walked over to the window while washing her hands in thin air.

'Lizzie, you are here because I have a report to make to the court. That must have caused you some trepidation.'

'Yes of course. Surely for everyone who has to go through this process. It is the uncertainty of waiting to see if its prison, a fine or goodness knows what.'

Tony opened a new file on his computer and typed Lizzie into his list of clients. As he continued to type he informed her of her illness.

'As your GP has rightly prescribed, you are suffering from what we call a Bi-Polar condition Lizzie. I suspect your general practitioner told you that.'

'Bi-Polar? Something to do with the North Pole? I've never been north of Aberdeen. The only Polars I've seen are in the zoo.'

Tony smiled. 'You know that's possibly the best way to describe it. You travel from the North Pole to the South Pole with a few rests in between. You are high up north with no brakes to slow you down and then you have no more petrol in the tank and you are frozen on the South Pole. That's what we call Bi-Polar. But the treatment will help.'

'You mean, I am ill?'

'It's not an uncommon phenomenon. You might know others who have this but you don't recognise it. What the medication will do is reduce the highs and inhibit the lows. Make sure you always take your prescribed 250 mg of Lamotrigine tablets; one in the morning and one 50 mg at night.'

'Will this be in my Court report?'

'Yes, because your state of mind is part of my report to the Court.'

'Hmmm I see. Do you think it will help me to avoid prison?'

'I hope so. As you are a first time offender, that will count in your favour but it was your fault the man's car was damaged so I suspect the court will fine you but I'm out of my depth here. I presume you have a good solicitor to represent you?'

'I've an exceptionally good solicitor, one of the very best, yes I'd say the most educated and charming lawyer there is around,' she said smiling from ear to ear.

'He gets a copy of my report too. Let me know who he is.'

'Glad to.'

You rate him very highly, don't you?' asked Tony feeling more relaxed as the session came towards its end.

'Oh yes, of course I do. He's a born again Christian too.'

Tony had noted three of his last five referrals came from the clerical or faith community. It was a committed outlook each had. It was a dynamic he felt required special attention and he would have to put his mind to its influences. He was in unchartered territory.

# 4

# A Flat Note

Ivan Ross was out of tune. Something was holding him back and it showed in his clarinet playing for the local town's symphony orchestra. His was a very exacting instrument. His fingers and his tongue had to be in unison to craft the perfect note but his posture was that of a soggy scone. His glissando was straying beyond its comfort zone.

Ricky, the orchestra leader, felt it uncomfortable to enquire, yet he saw the elephant in the room. So too did the symphony conductor who took the bull by the horns to break the impasse.

'Ivan dear, what's the matter,' she asked laying her hand on his forearm.

Ivan looked up but his eyes could not engage Ruth Hollings. She was perhaps not the right person to hear his anguish.

'Just need a break,' he whispered to resolve her question.

'Okay. Let me fix it.'

So Ruth suggested Ivan have a two week break in the summer. No music practice. The next public concert was two months away. She suggested a break at his sister's home on the Yorkshire coast. It seemed the appropriate solution for him, with bracing sea waves, seagulls gliding and shrieking their news. Ruth conjured the idyll in her own mind. The thoughts, however, were not transferrable. Ivan considered the proposal with the appetite of a well fed alley cat. He would not move. There was no way he would go out of his way.

'Perhaps you should see your GP,' said Ruth with concern.

Ivan put down his clarinet on the wooden floor. He stood up, placed his foot on the instrument, bent down and pulled at the instrument hard. In seconds the instrument's reed, metal finger holes, pads and the bell were damaged beyond repair. It was distorted, rendered completely unplayable. He picked the remains up and threw it against the hall wall and stormed out of the door.

There was a moment of silence from the open-mouthed musicians.

'My, that's not like him,' was all Ruth could say to the symphony members. They all had that same thought, in much stronger terms.

Tony received Ivan's referral from his GP three days later.

The quiet morning announced it was Sunday. Those who attended church were seated in their pews, standing or kneeling as convention required for prayer. It was time for Tony Scriven to reverse out of his garage and honour his more active membership.

The Golf Club had few cars in the car park and

that did not auger well. Tony sauntered round the clubhouse and encountered the chalked board. The course was waterlogged. Unplayable until advised otherwise. Of course it was unplayable. He recalled the last thirty five hours of lashing rain assaulting his surgery windows since Friday morning. He recalled the dashes he made to his car at the end of the working day and the early switching on of room lights under the oppressive clouds.

He took the boundary path along the first tee and let his thoughts roam as his feet crunched the twigs beneath his weight.

Tony's freedom on the course meant so much to him. A selfish streak had grown within his independence. His new home was minimal, denuded of the clutter marriage had entrapped him by over seventeen years. There was none to share and appreciate his abode and that situation showed no signs of improving. Of course it couldn't without an effort on his part.
He progressed down the tee, counting the divots while his trousers attracted burrs like a magnet. Then his thoughts turned to his recent cleric clients.

Never before had he had a spate of clergy come to his attention. He may have had a handful of school teachers and council workers bending under the pressures of punishing government cuts, but clerics! No not even one.

Was not the clergy the backbone of the community serving the rites of passage? Christenings where sprinkled water disturbed silent babes, where the sanctified water hushed the screams of other babies being christened.

It brought back some memories for him. The sherry and christening cake to follow amid well-dressed aunts and uncles, parents and siblings. Clerics with their partners regularly attended such happy occasions. Cake too at the weddings bringing couples together with a spiritual blessing and to top it off, at the close of life, a reassuring funeral was the cleric's remit. There was much to do each week for every cleric and the ringing telephone would announce great joy or deep sadness. It was a life or death occupation and that made it a respected profession. But it seemed that the mental health of these figures in society was coming to the fore and not before time he thought. His caseload certainly reflected their sudden appearance. Mental health conditions were ubiquitous and the isolation of clerics in their communities seemed to contribute to the malaise of their ministries.

Tony began to wonder if his diagnoses would benefit from a stronger personal faith. Other medics had strong beliefs but his religious experiences to date drained through a sieve. He could not grasp the tenants of faith enough to ground anchors. It was easier for him to say he was agnostic or ......sometimes... he was an atheist. He was not sure. He looked in his Google box on his phone to clarify what he really was. Yes, he was agnostic. He was sceptical too. It was part of his medical training. He could see God as a concept but could see him no other way. Yet atheism went too far for him. An outright rejection of a god seemed wrong.

There were so many cultures all over the world that accepted what we term God that it did not feel right to be an atheist and reject that very same concept.

He stopped. He looked up at the alto-cumulus sky. He had no idea how it had all come to be in the first place and did not spend time on the thought but somehow this diverse group of clerics challenged him. Could they co-operate? Would they participate? Would it lead to conflict or cohesion? Could it change his perspective?

Such a diverse group of clergy, he recalled. A musical Methodist, presumably so, for Wesley had given Methodists those triumphant and well-loved hymns. Lizzie Taylor the bi-polar evangelical would be a challenge, especially for the Imam, for Farook would have a place in mind for women and an excited female Christian might be too much for him to stomach. Tony decided on a plan as he turned to return up the side of the fairway to his car.

On his return to work on Monday he sent out letters to the clerics inviting them to a group meeting to assist in their therapy. He made two provisions. Firstly if they attended it would be at their own free will. Secondly he told them that all had their faith.

The telephone rang. Tony lifted it from its cradle.

'Hello Dr Scriven speaking.'

Tony turned a new sheet over and started to write on his lined pad.

'And where is he now.......in the hospital? I'll be over in five minutes. Ward 3 you said?'

Tony read the case notes as he walked to the ward. The patient was found in St. Mary's Church in a broom cupboard. Found by the church cleaner. Found with a razor blade and some blood stains on his shirt.

There, sitting in a well-lit rest room was Ivan. Tony approached him and shook his hand.

'There's a smaller room behind you. Shall we go there?'

Ivan rose and followed through the door to find a stark room with only two chairs and a table.

'Perhaps I can order two teas?'

Ivan nodded and Tony phoned reception.

'So tell me about what happened?'

Ivan sat down and undid his jersey's central three buttons. 'There was a scene at the Symphony. I am the lead clarinettist.'

Tony nodded gently encouraging the story to emerge. Another musician, he thought.

'I lost it. Something snapped. I broke my instrument and stormed out in front of them all.'

The knock on the door stopped his initial flow.

A nurse entered with a flask of hot water, a bowl of tea bags and a small Nescafe jar. Tony lifted a tea bag and held it suspended to see which drink Ivan would prefer. Ivan tapped the coffee jar with his index finger.

'St Mary's Church? Tell me,' asked Tony measuring the coffee. 'How did that come about?'

'The next day after the orchestra scene I went to Boots and bought some razor blades. I wanted to be alone and I saw St Mary's on the opposite side of the road was open. I went in and no one was around. So I walked around and found the broom cupboard by chance and sat in there. It was claustrophobic.

It seemed the best place to end life. I took out the blades and started to cut my arm. See?'

Tony looked at his arm sporting some three parallel scars; none approached a vein.

'So when did this all start?'

'I don't know. It's been a long time coming. I've not been enjoying playing.'

'Do you think you have lost your tone, your embouchure, your...eh.....' Tony poured the milk still thinking what a clarinet's properties might be or require.

'Lost it? No the exact opposite. Note perfect I've always been. I read music like enjoying a Dostoevsky novel.'

'I see.'

'But something told me it was time to give way to the feelings I was experiencing. It was dramatic I know but I had to tell them I'd no longer play the damn instrument.'

'How long have you been playing it?'

'All my life, since I was a kid.' Tony scribbled away.

'Tell me about your parents. Did they play?'

'No, neither of them was musical. I was an only child. Spoiled me, I suppose. How would I know any differently? I whistled a lot. At primary school the teacher had me in the choir. She said I was musical, had an ear for that sort of thing. My parents encouraged me needless to say. So I guess I was about ten when they wanted to take me into the junior orchestra. I started with a trumpet but I really liked the clarinet. I was good and I knew it, too bloody good. That's the issue.'

Ivan put on a high pitched female voice. 'Isn't he good? I've never heard the clarinet played so well. Is that Ivan playing? You must be very proud of your son.'

And my parents always said I played perfectly. Perfectly, bloody perfectly every time.

'A lot of pressure,' said Tony.

'Yeah.'

'And what happened yesterday?'

Ivan had difficulty relating his childhood to what had happened the day before, but it was becoming very clear to Tony.

Praise for children was a double-edged sword he knew. It had been encouraged over the last few decades but on closer inspection it was creating in a child's mind their need for constant perfection. In adulthood it continued for Ivan and when he realised he was at the cutting edge of perfection, he had nowhere else to go. His musical journey had reached the buffers.

When Ruth told him that no one could ever better his playing, he did not take it as a compliment. He knew complements ratchet up the praise. His music knew no restrictive bounds. Never again would he play. His perfect notes would never improve. They would never be heard again. Tony felt sure of that.

# 5

# It Takes a Worried Imam

Tony enjoyed his weekend. It was the third time, every second week, he had gone with a group of walkers. He had joined the local Active Ramblers club only two months before and if he was not golfing, he loved the great outdoors without a sliced swing or an errant golf ball. There was a group of ten sometimes more meeting at an arranged spot with haversacks full of high energy biscuits and bananas. Bottles of water too saw them through the day. And at the end of the walk, a pub was always nearby where they enjoyed their glass before returning home. Tony could then look forward to a long warm soaking bath to unwind and prepare for the week ahead.

Major Paul Risk's referral came via the Relate organisation. He and his wife had sought sexual counselling advice as their marriage had been torn apart by his sexual conviction and now abstinence was the constant feature of their relationship. The sessions had been initially positive with tasks taken home to employ then report at the next session. But the tasks were not enjoyed. There was little commitment shown by Paul to his wife Irene. He was beginning to look elsewhere. Divorce was on the cards although it had never been Irene's wish to separate from her husband. Paul stormed out of the session making threats of a sordid nature and case worker Margaret reported the matter to the police.

They in turn saw no evidence to charge him but suggested he make an appointment at Tony's practice and he did.

Major Paul Risk was no longer a shining light in the Salvation movement. Shunned by some members as a bad example of married bliss, he had drifted from the very group that had rescued him after prison. He felt isolated and in search of his true identity, in search of a meaningful life.

Tony had another session with Farook in his diary. He was not familiar with the ways and culture of Islam but he knew mental health had universality about it. It was not like an influenza epidemic, arriving abruptly then disappearing. It was more selective. It permeated life from an early age increasing with age, often rejecting the help it cried out for. Farook was one such example. But so too were those in the isolated professions but the clerics had begun to surface from his clients list, as a group in particular need of treatment.

Tony's pen fell from behind his ear when his secretary announced Farook's arrival. He came in like a sheep eyeing the collie. He was offered a seat. The inevitable open question began the session.

'So how have you been Farook?'

Farook's eyes gave more information than his voice.

They were downcast, revealing he was deep in thought as how to respond. When he did, it was not a particularly unusual disclosure he heard.

'I've been having a recurring dream,' he said in a guilty tone.

'A daytime or night time dream?' His clients often deflected their situations by interpreting their conditions as dreams. This seemed to be another of those experiences Tony thought.

'Both. It happens a lot. It's about a thick wall. It's in front of me. I can't see over and I can't break it down.'

'And you want to destroy it?'

'I don't know. I want to see over but I can't. If it means breaking it, then that's what I'll do but the dream does not let me.'

Tony took a note of what he was being told. His pad showed not narrative but a picture, a drawing of the dream.

'And tell me does the wall have an end? Can you get around it that way?'

'No, I can't see the end of the wall. It bends round out of sight. I can never reach its end, if it has one.'

'What do you think is behind the wall?'

Farook found the question as hard as any theological riddle.

'I think I'd see a garden with many people. Sometimes walking round smelling the sweet scent of flowers and talking, yes talking. Too hard to hear exactly what they are saying but talking sometimes about me, I'm sure, I hear my name being discussed. There is a group of Muslims at the far side.'

Tony's drawing was starting to lack precision.

'Tell me Farook, pretend you are the wall. What would you feel, what might you hear and what can you see?'

Farook's posture changed. He looked away but not out of the window. It seemed he had created a wall beside him. He was seeing his dream another way.

'The wall is strong. It has firm foundations. But is it protecting me from the other side .......or the other side from me? I don't know but it's a broad wall. I could certainly walk on it.'

'And what's the wall made of Farook?'

Farook pursed his lips as if to ask if such a question mattered.

'It's solid. Solid stone. It's an old wall.'

'Now, try to imagine you are inside the garden. What are you doing?'

This question was tricky for Farook. Their faces were not clear. Had Tony got to the crux of the dream or what could he possibly deduce from all he had told him so far? Farook struggled to reply. His hands were tight together, his knuckles grew whiter deprived of a steady flow of blood. His knuckles clicked. He jerked.

'I don't like being inside the garden,' was all Farook could muster. A few seconds passed in silence. The room stood still. The rough-edged rasping of a rook outside was all Farook could hear. He wished he could be that bird no matter how demonic it sounded.

'Inside the wall...' continued Tony.

Farook took out his handkerchief. He wiped his perspiring brow.

'They are chasing me. They have angry faces....'

'The Mosque members?'

Farook simply nodded.

Tony went over to his coffee machine and offered Farook a cup.

'Tea please, thanks.'

'So you are not attending the Mosque as often?'

'No, not at all for the time being.'

'No Imam. No prayers?'

'Oh no, many can step in for me. It is as if I am ill, you see.'

'And are you?'

'To them I am...and...I suppose I am too.'

'Tell me, why?' the doctor asked.

'I can't cope. Maybe something is going to happen and I feel I am the cause. So I avoid them. I go for walks. I dress in a western fashion. I am searching for something. An explanation perhaps.'

'Those are the thoughts and behaviours you are telling me. What about your feelings, Farook?'

'Feelings', he pondered. A moment of reflection was required to move on from his heart-felt thoughts and behaviours.

'Feelings...well.. anxious ...I think... perhaps fearful.'

'And can you cope with these feelings?

'No, you don't understand my culture. No matter what good or bad befalls a Muslim person, it is the Will of God, Insha'Allah.'

Tony loosened his tie and yawned. He had little idea how to take forward the growing number of his clerical clients. Group therapy was no panacea for such an ingrained set of beliefs. He took the rest of the day off.

And he hit his golf ball with great venom. He felt the tension escape from his shoulders as he breathed in fresh air. He strode down the fairway with no cares in the world. It was perhaps not his best round. Too many bogies when a par was achievable but a birdie at the par four hole of the backward nine gave him a moment of smug satisfaction. As his limbs exercised, unknown to him, his psyche was at work untangling the future of his disparate collection of clerics.

# 6

# The Open Door

Tony filtered his mail, making a stack of some of the prepaid reply letters he was anticipating. The other letter which took priority was a hospital referral. Actually it stemmed from a hospital assessment. Priority was always given to such referrals. They had potential to be serious and/or demanding. Quick intervention for effectiveness was of paramount importance. Yet he could not prevent his inquisitiveness. The first letter was from Farook.

> *'Salaam Alaikum.*
> *'Yes, I like the idea. It would be good to meet other clerics. It is what I really want, you know, achieving better integration of the Muslim community. A good way to start. Put me down for the group.'*

Tony spread the letter on his desk and weighed it down with a polished stone. The paperweight came from the beach at Nolton in St Bride's bay in south Wales where a short break last year refuelled his mind and body. His family heir loom, an ivory paper knife, sliced open the second letter. He tugged at the last moment, ripping the final corner and tearing the stamp. It disappointed him.

He was not a perfectionist by far but accidents should not happen if they need not happen, he thought. The second letter was less formal.

'Hi Tony.
*What a super idea. Yes, that would be a real ecumenical scream. Can't wait to put in my oar. The group meeting sounds a real treat. Super, yup it's for me.'*
*Signed Lizzie.*

Tony smiled, shaking his head. Such a letter could only come from Lizzie. A scream, an oar and a treat, all in one short letter. Life seemed to be so colourful for Lizzie. He thought it would not have been out of place for her to have signed off, Love Lizzie even with three kisses. No, that was an improper professional thought. He chided himself.

The third letter was from Ivan.

'Dear Dr Scriven.
*I am grateful to you for your advice and support and feel I am in a much more stable frame of mind. I feel a group meeting with other clerics would be a negative experience for me bringing me back to face my daemons amid my growing atheist outlook. I wish you well with the group's activities.'*
*Signed Ivan.*

This letter was a disappointment. Ivan was perhaps potentially his most worrying patient, a man at an anxious crossroad in his life. He decided to continue with his individual sessions and hope he could persuade him to join the others at a later date.

Tony placed his clerical class aside, under the stone. The hospital referral was opened as a cup of coffee came his way at 11am. He looked at his watch.

'You need not look at your watch, Dr Scriven,' said his Madge opening his door. 'As long as you are not consulting, you know your coffee will appear at this very moment every morning.'

He grinned at her. 'You don't strike me as the fastidious perfectionist.'

'I'm not. I have Radio 2 on quietly. When they announce the 11 o'clock news will follow the record playing, I boil the kettle. I make your coffee as the headlines begin. If you notice, I actually arrive at 11.02 a.m.' she said turning, waving her skirt in an arc as she did so.

'Hope you catch the news too,' he said playfully as she held the door handle. She did not reply. Of course she did.

Tony consulted his watch again. She was right it was 11.02 a.m. as he crunched his custard cream.

The referral he opened was about Miss Karen Kane.

Karen Kane was not a cleric. She was however a church organist. Her world had caved in over the course of two days. One Sunday and the following day at school on Monday morning she lost control of reality.

When the hard-backed book flew across the classroom causing a dent in the plaster, it shocked the pupils. None could have foretold the event having observed no irritation to cause Miss Kane to have such an outburst. However one pupil put one and one together and at break time knocked on the headmaster's door.

'Come in,' shouted Colin Martin, the school head teacher.

Peter Anderson took a gulp. Reporting a teacher was a brave move. He was in unchartered territory. Would the teachers close rank on him?

'Well, what have you to say,' urged the Head, sorting his desk papers.

'Miss Kane, sir. She threw a book.'

Colin Martin put down his papers. After a brief silence he looked up at Peter and enquired further.

'Was anyone injured?'

'No sir. It hit the wall.'

'I'm a busy man Peter. You must realise teaching is not an easy profession. There are stresses. Children have more energy than adults. From what you are saying, I think this is a mountain made out of a molehill.'

'But sir, I was at church yesterday when she went loopy.'

'Loopy?'

'Yes, it was the final organ piece of the service.'

'The recessional, you mean Peter,' Colin wondered. How could this out of school report be relevant to a book throwing incident?

'Er..yes. She was playing Jesu, Joy of Man's Desiring....'

'Ahh....the Bach favourite.'

'Yes, but half way through the classical piece she changed her tune and played the Entertainer followed by that...that piece...you know.... the piece....the Stripper tune.'

The Head pondered what he was now hearing. Two unconnected incidents over twenty four hours. Something was not right.

'Thank you Peter, you did the right thing to tell me. That is all. Now, run along.'

Colin Martin thought about confronting Karen. A denial would prove awkward. No, instead he called in Mrs Grace Brown, the head of guidance and of course female. He urged her to keep a close eye on Karen after the incidents were shared.

Then as the pupils left the school at 4.10 p.m. Karen opened her class window and yelled as loud as her lungs would permit, the most vile and uncensored language ever heard from a teaching member of staff. The words could not be misinterpreted and were heard by teachers and pupils alike. Colin Martin telephoned the police, who arrived promptly. They took a statement from Colin Martin and made their way in his company to Miss Kane's room.

They did not knock. They had a view of her through the frosted glass. They entered and found Karen with her head in her hands and tears flowing down her cheeks splashing her desk.

'I'm very sorry, really sorry. I don't know why this is happening to me. I didn't mean to swear. I don't know...I didn't...' But her tears were now accompanied with cries of sorrow drowning her explanation.

Constable Amy Stevenson stepped forward and placed her hand round Karen's shoulder.

'Not been a good day for you,' she said.

Karen looked up and acquiesced nodding her head.

'Let's go, come along with us.'

'Where to?'

'Hospital. That's the best place to go just now.'

Karen looked at the uniformed police and reflected on the decision to go to hospital. 'So, no charge?'

'No Karen. I suspect you are ill.'

The hospital detected a first episode of schizophrenia and released her two days later with an instruction to attend treatment from her GP and then with Dr Tony Scriven. Prompt intervention with the patient was essential and Tony knew group sessions were crucial to aid Karen's recovery. The treatment of schizophrenia often required a combination of antipsychotic, antidepressant, and anti-anxiety medication. Dozes and ratios would have to be tried and monitored. But so too was a need for Karen to be integrated. It was a tenuous link but a church organist might add a certain interest to the clerical minds about to meet.

When Tony had his first consultation with Karen Kane, he realised she was a very special patient. A warm feeling drained through his veins. He was unable to prevent the feeling and suddenly the restraining collar of professional ethics encroached on his mind. Karen appeared as a woman in her prime. A woman who took care about her appearance and a dimpled smile greeted him. But she was anxious to inform him that the events over the last four days were not recognisable to her.

Voices in her head made her throw that book.

And as for the music, she felt it was someone else who took over the keys of the organ. It could not have just been her playing inappropriate music. It was just not like her.

'Yes, hearing voices ...' Tony said nodding his head.

'You are under 45 years aren't you?'

'Yes 37, three weeks ago. Why?'

Tony had not anticipated her questioning. He scratched his neck. 'First onset is significant and usually before 45.'

'So I will have many episodes?'

'No, not if we can agree a medicinal plan. One that gets you out and about, circulating in society. Doing things you enjoy doing, while not forgetting your medication. Will that be difficult?'

Karen looked lost. She was studying the artex ceiling thinking about what activities she enjoyed. 'I've not got many interests outside work. I don't play bridge, don't go to the gym. I spend time playing the piano of course,' said Karen.

'Dedicated to work, I am sure you are. Musicians are known for that. Not a bad thing but perhaps you should concentrate on people for a change. They can effect change. You should find a new outlet to meet non colleagues.'

'And keep up the medication?' she asked.

'I should keep an eye on that. Cures are not an exact science despite society knowing about schizophrenia for centuries. We fine-tune your medication, make it suit your requirements. It can take time. But with this ailment, you are in good company.'

'Really?' asked Karen with eyes lit up.

Tony nodded. 'You are among many creative people. Vaslov Nijinsky, Jack Keronac, Pete Green of Fleetwood Mac, Syd Barrett of Pink Floyd so you see some pretty smart folk.'

'Are you suggesting creative people have mental health problems?' she asked in surprise.

'As I say, many do. Beethoven and Dusty Springfield were bi-polar as are both Russell Brand and Britney Spears. I'm sure there is a doctorate in that statistic for someone. But there are many more not listed because they are unknown. Unknown because they are not really ill. They are by far the majority.'

'A doctorate? I don't make much of my doctorate.'

Tony looked at her case notes. He flipped through them.

'But you are known as Miss Karen Kane at school, not Dr Kane'

'Yes, I know. I find it's a bit pretentious. That's why I don't bother with it.'

'So what's your doctorate in, may I ask?'

'Doctor of medieval keyboard music.'

'Wow, that's a niche of its own. I mean there can't be many of you with that.'

'There are a few of us. Another girl in my year did a similar thesis on medieval song music.'

'I see. At which university was that?'

'King's College Cambridge. You see, I really don't want to be forward with that background.'

Tony smiled at her choice of words. 'That is an achievement not many can claim certainly, but no reason to hide your accomplishment.'

Karen gave a resigned sigh. 'You are right. Actually your advice has made me think. I should get out more.'

Tony smiled. She was prepared to take a step in the right direction towards her recovery.

'Yes, I have heard about a local ramblers group. Dumfries Ramblers they call themselves. I think I'll join that. Won't that be good for me?'

Tony shuddered in his shoes with a bolt from his heart. Of course it was good for her but ......honesty was required, the best solution.

'That's a group I'm in.'

Karen's dimples deepened as her smile grew. A natural chemistry was at play. Each was aware of the stirrings. But Tony had to keep his interest in check. It would be unprofessional to take one step further with this patient.

'So I should think of some other activity?'

Tony grinned. 'No, I think you will be in good company.'

Karen's face was split by a smile.

# 7

# Absent Minds

Tony's caseload fluctuated. Thirty five cases were as much as he could take on comfortably. Some cases required several sessions while others were over in a matter of half an hour, particularly if the GPs had proscribed appropriate medication and patients were returning home with support. Ages ranged from eighteen to eighty. The CAMHS service (Child and Adolescent Mental Health Services) attended to juveniles while the dementia clinics and geriatric counsellors attended to the over eighties. The demography was as distinct as the left from the right hand and it encompassed professionals as well as unemployed individuals and those in every kind of occupation and relationship, both established and transient. It was not surprising that Tony detected another case with a clerical perception when it came along.

Marty Mayvor fell into the Baha'i religion by chance. It was in her final year of university that she encountered this peace loving, understanding and all-embracing religion. She came from a sheltered Irish family drenched in Catholicism but found the harmonious and multi-ethnic tenets of the new faith rewarding. It welcomed her and she thought she had found her new home. Two months after her mathematics graduation, she began to work at a secondary school. Life was bringing its rewards and her mind began to focus on finding a husband and being a mother.

As the school Christmas Pantomime gave its last performance, Marty walked home to prepare a Christmas atmosphere in time for her parent's arrival from Brazil. But an unmarked police car approached her home. It turned into her drive, parked and the doors opened. Two police officers approached the front door.

'Miss Mayvor?' asked Sergeant Karen Scott.

'Yes, officer,' said Marty observing two nervous police officers.

'May we come in? We have some sad news for you.'

Marty fumbled with her front door latch. Her fingers shook uncontrollably. Her heart was racing. She could not accept that bad news could be coming. She invited the officers to enter her lounge. She put the light on and closed the curtains.

'Please have a seat,' she said as she herself sat down on a hard backed chair hardly placing any weight on it. It began to tip forward.

'Your parents, Owen and Hilary Mayvor were in Brazil?' asked Inspector Brian Fox.

'That's right. They work for the White Fathers in Brazil. They are responsible for all the financial side of their work,' said Marty in staccato words as a veil seemed to descend and reality hit her.

'It's my parents. They have been killed haven't they? Haven't they, well?'

Both officers nodded simultaneously.

'I am sorry. It seems that they were flying in a two-seater Albatross L60 monoplane,' said the Inspector as Constable Karen Scott approached Marty and placed her hands on her shoulders.

'Yes, I know that's how they travel between stations, but....what else...'

'Last Friday there was a storm, lightening too, apparently. It seems they came down in the Mato Grosso between Guiratinga and Diamantino. That was where they left from and .....were heading for,' said the police officer in a quiet responsible voice.

'But it's just that the plane is missing perhaps?' Marty said with hope in her voice.

'I'm afraid not. Wreckage was sighted and there was no sign of life. I am truly sorry Miss Mayvor, both your parents died.'

That was two years ago. Since then she had travelled to Brazil and met many of her parent's former colleagues. They flew her to where the plane came down and Marty saw the remains of the wreckage. She walked through the fuselage and turned over some of the wreckage which had never been removed. She bent down and found a sandal she recognised as her mother's. She placed it in her bag. She spent a total of seventeen days in Brazil before returning home.

That Christmas no decorations were on display in her house. Marty descended into a deep depression lasting the five days of the Christmas holiday until the first few days of the New Year. The very same thing happened the following year and found her in a far deeper place from which she had no energy to escape. Her deputy head called to see her and met her in a slurred daze. He wasted no time. His assessment was of meeting a very ill colleague. He suspected alcoholism. He called for an ambulance.

And so in due time, Marty appeared at Tony's surgery. When they met, there was no sign of either depression or alcoholism.

'The two episodes, they are seasonal, not so?' he asked.

'Yes that's right,' she agreed clinging on to her orange handbag.

'No illness throughout the year?'

'Nope, just at Christmas.'

Tony contemplated her defensive Nope as unexpected, out of character so far. 'It was a terrible time to lose your parents.'

'I know. I had been so much looking forward to seeing them that year. I had not seen them for three years.'

'What will you do next Christmas?'

'Next Christmas? That seems so far away. I cannot say if this will be a recurring depression,' she said smiling with optimism in her cheeks.

'I think I can. Unless we break this cycle, the pattern will be established. Tell me, your notes show you are a Baha'i follower. Is that right?'

'Yes, that's true.'

'They don't celebrate Christmas do they?'

'No, nor the New Year. We have a different calendar.'

'I see,' said Tony. 'Perhaps if you spent some time with them over the Christmas week it might help.'

'Yes, that's true.'

'I think you might also benefit from a group session I am organising. It is yet to get off the ground but I think you would be a good candidate.'

'Oh, you think so?'

'Yes, they are all known to me and all have a clerical background,' said Tony looking for a flicker of reaction to his proposal.

'I'm a busy teacher. I might not make all the meetings.'

'I think a Monday night for an hour and a half each week should be adequate. Would you care to join the group?'

'A self-help group?'

'Yes, I think that is what it is becoming. You see clerics are all figures in their communities. They have a persona to show but an interior which is under strain. It's good to know that others feel the same and if they don't do anything about it, it leads to a referral after what I might call a breakdown or an incident.'

'So it's a crash course?'

Tony smiled. 'Crash? No. I hope it's a course for winners.'

# 8

# The Ramblers Gather

Tony's car was the twelfth and last car to park at the Overton village car park. Counting him, there was a good turnout of eighteen of the ramblers' club members. Stuart, the leader of the group, announced he was expecting no more turning up that Saturday morning. That made Tony feel he was the naughty late comer. As the grey clouds gathered above them, he welcomed a new member to the group. Karen Kane. He pointed to her.

'You can get to know her on the walk. Don't all come at her at once or she'll never turn up again,' he laughed.

A few voiced some guffaws. Tony looked at his patient. Confident, she was wearing a tricoloured wool knitted toorie on her head, wine cords and, under a warm navy anorak, a powder blue sweater. By far she seemed the youngest of the group and she was. He chose not to walk too near her.

It was Pam who accompanied her. Pam, the retired dentist who's silky silvery black hair was neatly cut but not styled or tinted. She had an air of confidence and seniority.

'I've seen you in town. Have you been here long?' asked Pam.

'About seven years now. I'm a teacher.'

'No, I seem to remember you somewhere else.'

Karen chose not to rise to the church organist bait and manoeuvred her way out of the tricky questioning.

Loch Kindar emerged over a hillock's horizon and the downward approach was both exhilarating and interesting as each step seemed to enlarge the loch.

'I thought we were climbing Tannoch Hill today,' said Karen.

'We've done Criffel a few times and it's now a tradition we open our flasks for morning coffee by the water's edge. We'll be climbing soon enough,' said Pam striding forth with her two walking sticks.

Alex, the educational social worker, was talkative. As the steam rose skyward from opened flasks, he asked if anyone knew where was Santa Fe?

'New Mexico,' said Karen confidently answering as Tony thought South America somewhere but both were wrong.

'No. Santa's fae Finland.'

A few got the joke straight away. Pam, who originated from Kent, took a little longer to get an ear for the Scots tongue. When it was realised, her laugh was as loud as any. It created a friendly atmosphere.

'I've got a joke,' said Karen hoping this was a good opportunity to break into the group and be heartily welcomed.

'If you meet a bear in the woods, how do you coax him out?'

The assembled thought for a moment but blank stares ensured no answer was forthcoming.

'Give it French cheese,' she said but silence continued. Karen flexed a coaching index finger towards herself. 'Come on Bear,' she said.

'Ah I get it. Camembert,' said Pam and the whole group got the joke.

'The two of you should be on stage,' suggested Alex. Tony was pleased his patient's medication was working well. Very pleased.

Before they reached the summit of Criffel, the overburdened clouds burst. It fell straight down onto the waterproofed ramblers. They walked closer and Tony's thoughts turned to his patient. She had humour, intelligence, beauty and was active. It was just what his dreams created in his sleeping moments. If only she was not his patient. If only he had met her for the very first time on this walk. How different that might have been, especially as she wore no ring. His dreams created the perfect image and encouraged him in her acquaintance but his thoughts turned to the dark suited fraternity of his professional association wagging a finger over the client relationship. He had to get her off his books as soon as he could safely do so. That had to be his goal.

# 9

# They Heed the Call

The first meeting took place on Monday evening shortly after 7.30 p.m. It was a windswept night, most suitable for ensuring animosity in the approaching streets. They began to arrive at the brightly lit consulting room. Not all of them, but enough to get off to a hesitant start.

Tony sauntered into the centre of the room. 'Good evening. Well, all of you know me as your psychoanalyst and so I have met you all professionally. You don't know what health matter brought each other to this meeting but let me say one thing. All mental health is on a continuum. Like a length of string. Some of us have strayed from the centre where all is calm and in order. That's where we are heading and to get there, we need each other's support. But first, some refreshment.'

A table supported a real coffee trembling brew, its odours permeating every atom of air. The kettle was more selective. Tea bags and bags of infusions stood in drunken lines on the tablecloth and a solitary Ovaltine tub guarded over them. Lizzie levelled two spoonfuls of Ovaltine into a mug which made her smile. She raised the mug to her eyes.

'Typical. I dream of a world where a chicken can cross the road without having its motives questioned.'

Those present heard but were unsure if a smile, a guffaw or a nod was an appropriate response.

'Typical of what?' asked Tony.

'Perhaps typical of a psychotherapist's set of work mugs. My mug at home doesn't have sayings except for one. Its message is simple. "This is my Mug" and that's not thought-provoking.'

Tony laughed quietly and raised his eyebrows an inch. 'It certainly is, Lizzie. It's a very strong statement. It says, hands-off this is mine.'

Lizzie smiled at the thought that Tony could see through other's minds.

'I had a mug like these ones. I broke it,' said Karen keeping her eyes to the floor realising it was her first disclosure to the group.

'Accident?' asked Lizzie.

She grinned. 'Hmm...no, a fit of rage, last month.'

A moment's silence followed as the group imagined the anger this apparently gentle woman must possess. Another raised his mug.

'What's written on your mug, Alan?' asked Tony.

'Er... Too blessed to be stressed.'

There was a murmur more than a laugh but it did ease the group's anxiety and led to more word play.

'You think being blessed is not a blessing?'

'Depends, Tony. Depends who is blessing you and why.'

'But surely a blessing is by nature just that. It can't be negative. A blessing must lead to destressing. That's what I think,' said Alan.

'Good point. Remember the mugs may read as profound statements but some are just humorous even if we can't see the joke,' Tony said.

Karen perused the other mugs. She lifted hers. 'There's a bit of me I recognise yet I don't, on this mug. I'm not arguing. I'm just explaining why I'm right.'

The group let off an appreciative grunt then Karen explained. 'You see I'm usually the last to pick an argument yet recently I've been more controversial, questioning things, seeing different points of view.' The nodding heads not only seemed to acknowledge what she had said but also assessed her as a fellow group member, starting to reveal her medical issues perhaps.

They began to take their seats coddling their hot mugs, not sure how the evening would progress.

'So it's just us for this group therapy?' asked Alan.

'There are a couple more. Perhaps late arrivals or perhaps they will not take up this offer. I don't know. It's voluntary but I am pleased to see so many of you. I feel I can give you all a fresh start.'

'Fresh start in Life?' asked Karen.

'If that's what you want, why not? We can get out of our boxes and explore if you wish. Remember what happens in this room, stays in this room. Let's make a start. So, I have this woollen ball in my hand. I'll throw it. When you catch it you have the floor to tell the group something interesting about yourself. Say as much as you feel comfortable in disclosing. I'll give you a moment to think.'

Some heads looked up for inspiration; others sought the powers of eloquence from their stare at the floor before them. Many must have thought it too early to be speaking to strangers. How the session should have started was not on their minds either. But there was no time to retract or complain. Tony threw the ball from one hand to the other in a parabolic arc. It was hypnotic, a distraction for some. It prepared itself for a higher trajectory.

'Okay.' The ball was thrown to Alan. He caught it in both hands.

'Well, I'm Alan. I'm 56 years of age. Gave up a career as a professional footballer and became a Methodist preacher. Given up scoring; now saving, as it were.' The group laughed at his humour. 'I write poetry too. Well doggerel and verses I make into songs.'

'Do you sing the songs,' asked Tony who then slapped his thigh. 'Of course you would. How else could they be songs? Silly of me.' The group relaxed with broad smiles recognising that even the psychiatrist could make a mistake.

'Well yes, I play the guitar and sing them. Sometimes lead the congregation in singing the choruses.....but not recently.'

'I see so are all the verses, sort of...well...sort of church songs?' asked Karen.

'I used to play in a folk group before I was ordained.' Alan's eyes looked for approval. Had he said enough? Tony nodded with a relaxed smile and Alan was relieved to launch the ball to Lizzie. Karen wondered what his songs were about.

'Oh, well, I could tell you I was capped for England twice. Table tennis. Quick reflexes I've got. By training, I'm a computer analyst.' Lizzie took a deep breath.

'I'm a Christian. Some would say evangelical. I don't mind what they call me. I am one of His hand servants, heeding his call.' She had had her say. She threw the ball to Marty. Some felt Lizzie's contribution stepped over the mark. Was she out to convert them? It was a natural concern. She must have been nervous, they imagined. Only Tony was pleased that it was curtailed. That was an achievement for Lizzie. The ball came to Marty in surprise. It fell off her lap. She bent down to retrieve it.

'I'm a maths teacher. Brought up as a staunch Roman Catholic in County Mayo. I found the Baha'i religion answered more of my questions than any other so, that's why, I guess, I'm here, well that and my illness.' Marty threw the ball to Karen. Karen was not ready to speak. Marty's contribution had been too short. She felt short changed. She threw the ball back to Marty.

'I'd like to hear more about you Marty, something outside religion. What makes you tick?'

Marty caught the ball. 'I'm sorry. I was too brief wasn't I?' Her comment was received with smiles. 'Drums I played. Started off in an Irish Pipe band but when I was a student I became the fourth member of a group. The Bactrian View we called ourselves. I play mouthorgan too.'

'Bactrian View, that's profound. Tolstoy?' questioned Karen.

Marty smiled. 'Took it from a camel I saw in a weekend magazine. A Bactrian camel, standing on its own. I wondered what you would see from such a height. That's when the View came to us.'

'That's cool,' Karen remarked, her eyes still in the hot desert somewhere watering a camel.

'So that's me. Well, if you add in my dog Smarty. He's a collie.'

Marty had disclosed enough. She threw the ball again to Karen. She kept it this time.

'I'm not a cleric. My religion is token more than an actual practice, but I am a church organist, one that's a little out of tune at present.' The polite company smiled more than laughed at her answer. She hinted she had almost no faith, the first to do so. 'I teach music in school and am the annual musical director of the Christmas pantomime. Oh and I've just joined the local Ramblers.'

Karen threw the ball back to Tony, with a charming grin.

'Thanks. I hope that broke the ice a bit. Now I think we will now......'

'But I threw the ball to you. Which is your God Tony? How does it work for you?' asked Karen.

Tony was taken aback but tried not show it. Instead he steadied himself. He uncrossed his legs. He took a sigh as he gathered his thoughts. Then there was a knock on the door. Tony went to open it instantly, giving him a moment longer to compose his answer.

'Come in Farook. Help yourself to a tea or coffee and come and join us.'

'I'm sorry I was late,' he said bringing his hands together before him in a clasp of forgiveness.

'Not at all. You are not too late. We've only just started. Observing prayer time delay you?'

He nodded. Then he shook his head. 'That would have been a good excuse. But the truth is I was not too sure about coming here. It took some persuading ......of myself. Yes, I do speak to myself. Anyway carry on. I'll join you in a moment.'

Tony returned to his seat.

'You were about to tell us about your God, Tony.'

'Yes Karen I was. You see I am an agnostic. I see God, if He exists, and He may well do so, as the Random Process Generator showering some with favours while ignoring others who need help. A sort of insurance policy provider bringing calm and order to anxious minds. An insurance policy which is stubborn to pay out.' He felt relieved to have owned up to his disbelief although he had let himself down by playing into their hands. He had to retain professional distance from now on, no matter how difficult it might be with this diverse group.

'So you're the odd man out Tony, a non-believer?' asked Alan.

'Don't you think that's a bit hard? I mean I am not denying the possibility of there being a God, but until I am satisfied that there is one, I remain agnostic to the idea.'

'So no faith at all? No God? Not an easy concept for me to accept,' said Farook as he approached, stirring his well-sugared tea.

Tony pointed at Farook's mug. 'Go on read it out.'

Farook looked around the room. Smiles met his eyes to encourage him. He raised the mug to focus and his lips smiled through his beard. It seemed they had already read the ceramic text of his mug.

'Worry works! 90% of the things I worry about never happen.'

'Very true. To those who worry too much, take note,' suggested Tony.

'I worry about God, perhaps he's not a man?' teased Lizzie.

'The Christian Church has always had a bit of a problem with God's gender. He doesn't have one. But to talk about him is impossible without giving him a gender,' said Alan.

'I see what you mean. Calling God 'it' seems a bit rude, talking as if God was an impersonal force like gravity or inflation. So God has to be "He" or "She" and in a patriarchal society there's no contest. As The Catechism of the Catholic Church says: God is neither man nor woman: he is God,' said Alan with clarity.

'I think we can all accept that,' said Tony.

Two empty coffee mugs were placed on the floor.

The silence was awkward for a moment. As if headlights had made them freeze. Karen moved uncomfortably in her seat.

'I think...I mean...I'm not sure what we'll get out of these meetings. Er... what I'll get out of them. How will this group develop, how will it benefit me or what will we be talking about in the weeks ahead?' she asked.

Alert eyes looked at Tony for clarification.

'From my perspective, we've got off to a good start. I see a relaxed group being able to speak to one another which in turn relieves tensions and instils confidence, the latter being the very tools of socialisation.'

'But where's it all going?' asked Marty.

'How would you like it to proceed?' asked Tony somewhat provocatively.

'If this was the last meeting, I'd go away feeling it was a lost opportunity,' said Alan.

'Yes I can understand that. But at the back of my mind is the fact that we all had mental issues and we've all got some religious background. Are we addressing both or either?' said Marty.

'That will be for you to decide.'

'Come on Tony, that's not fair.'

'I want it to continue. I need it,' said Farook.

Eyes turned towards him for a fuller explanation but it was not forthcoming.

'I need to pass you the ball, Farook. We've all held the ball. When you have it you can tell the group something about yourself.'

Farook took on board what had been said. He caught the ball in one hand. He smiled. 'We love our cricket in Pakistan.' His comment brought happy smiles to the fore. 'I came to Britain when I was five years of age. My parents were ambitious for me, not so much my sisters. They wanted me to live out their dreams. British schooled, university trained ...you know the drill. But my father in his last few years felt the education I had received should serve to lay a firm foundation in our Mosque. So instead of finding a profession, I became the Imam. That was in the late 90s.'

The group felt a privileged insight into Muslim life was well under way. Their interest was perceptible from their forward seated positions.

'In August 2001 I visited a cousin, Sahil, in Florida. I had not seen him for ages and so it was a welcome break and I was relaxed. I had a wonderful time. Although I still had my daily prayers to attend to, Sahil paid little attention to his faith. We discussed this for some time. I was not angry with him. I saw young men leaving the Mosque and not saying their prayers but worshipping their mobiles. Times were changing for some Muslims in the West.'

'I didn't think that could happen, Farook,' said Alan.

'It happens in all religions does it not?' Heads acknowledged that it did but were surprised that Farook had mentioned the fact at all.

'From Florida I went to New York where there is a sizeable Muslim population. I wanted to see the city so took a bus down town to the centre. I planned to see the Empire State building. A building I had heard of as a very young boy in Pakistan.'

Farook stopped. It was if he was there again or perhaps thinking why he was mentioning his travels.

'Then it happened. I heard the aircraft's engines whine as if it was directly overhead. I looked up. It went straight into the side of one of the Tower buildings. I froze looking at what I was seeing. What an accident, not more than a few hundred yards from where I stood. Others were frozen to the spot too. As if a starter gun had sounded, we all headed towards the building. In my mind there may have been many dead but many injured too. Perhaps some prayers for the injured, the deceased and the dying were my duty.

I got to the base of the burning Tower and saw the final seconds of life for the bodies falling to the ground from the affected floors above. I knew this was a very serious accident.'

'Gosh 9/11. You were there Farook?' The question need not have been asked but Farook lifted his eyes and nodded to Marty.

'Then another explosion occurred. I presumed the noise had come from a collapsed floor not far above me. But the shrieks and sobs, the shouts and the curses began and I realised a second plane had hit the other tower.'

Farook's account created a silence as each relived the horror and terror of 11th September 2001 in their own minds.

'That was when I realised, only one faith, one corrupted faith was responsible. Mine. Yes, thousands were killed that day but also too many Muslims. This was not the faith I knew nor did it represent my feelings. It was a watershed in my thinking. We had to live in a peaceful world and that meant change. But change was not on the minds of my fellow worshipers. They were at a loss to explain how this could come about. They saw it as a fresh generation fighting against traditional conservative Western values.'

Farook's account brought him great sympathy. It was heartfelt.

Mugs were then returned to the table amid muddled comments but all present were amazed that one of their fold had been at the centre of a horrific worldwide televised crime.

Tony brought the gathering back to the present.

'Then let's meet next Monday night.'

A few heads nodded making their views apparent.

'I'm up for it,' said Lizzie.

A show of hands suddenly sprung up like fir trees. 'Yes, I'll definitely be here,' said Farook.

'Er...it seems to me ....that there are quite a few of us ....who play music. I wonder...' said a hesitant Alan instantly feeling he had swerved the group away from its original purpose.

Eyes looked at each other. It was hard to gauge if it was a lukewarm response or a lit taper about to explode.

'I mean, I play guitar; Marty drums and mouth organ and Karen has the keyboard. Lizzie you sing don't you?' asked Alan.

'Sing? Of course, every day I sing and in my bath too.'

'Good. Tony, am I speaking out of turn?'

Tony saw where Alan's thoughts were going and this seemed an ideal bonding opportunity he felt he could encourage. Just what they needed in fact and he told them so.

'Tony, do you play any instrument?' asked Alan.

'It's not my group activity. I'll be more of an observer.'

'No, I mean, do you play any instrument?'

'Well Alan, I can't deny I play a mean saxophone.'

'Great, just what we need.'

'Farook do you play anything?' asked Lizzie with an encouraging smile.

Farook twiddled his thumbs. 'I listen to Radio 2 when I can. It's not encouraged. But I'd like to listen... make tea? I'm good at that.'

'Right, instruments to the fore, next Monday?' Tony could see by the smiles that the group saw a purpose in meeting again.

# 10

# Out of Class

A loose gathering formed outside as the group headed for their cars that night.

'Must say I had expected individual sessions from a psychiatrist, not group therapy,' said Marty to no one in particular.

'Therapy or drugs? Much the same I recon,' said Farook.

'I'm okay with it. It's just unexpected. That's all I am saying. I think we'll all get along,' Marty skipped a couple of steps.

'Seems to have done you some good Marty,' said Alan. 'I wish I had your athleticism.'

'It's the athleticism of the mind I need. I guess we all do.' Marty flipped her mauve scarf around her neck.

'Then mind games it is,' said Farook fumbling for his car keys.

'Mind over matter,' said Lizzie cocking her head.'

'Mind the gap,' said Alan and they all laughed. It was on that optimistic note the car doors were opened. After hand waves and smiles the group dispersed both ways along the main road.

# 11

# Getting in Tune

Harmony prevailed as they gathered the following Monday and took their hot drinks.

'I see it's a 12 string model, Alan,' said Marty.

'Yes, Echo Ranger 12. I've had it a long time as you can see.'

Alan played a three chord strum for her benefit.

Karen was setting up a portable keyboard's stand.

'Can I lend a hand?' asked Farook.

Karen looked round at the bearded Imam and wondered if he knew anything about the instrument.

'Thanks. Can you take the keyboard out of its cover please.'

Farook eased the black and white notes from its case and brought it to the stand. His gaze lingered on the portable organ's option buttons and slide volume controls.

'Does it sit on top here?'

'Yes, it will. But depends on where the electric socket is. Can you see one?'

Farook bent as he walked around the room, running his eyes along the skirting board.

'Over here,' he called out.

Then the door opened and eyes turned towards a man, a visitor. He was a man of excessive obesity.

A round face with a jet black brushed back coiffure and a neat short black moustache too. His eyes scanned the group until he saw Tony.

'Paul, glad to see you. Have you come to join us?'

He shuffled forward and nodded.

'Ladies and gentlemen. May I introduce Paul Risk, Salvationist without his trombone, right?'

'Yea, but I got a new one. It's in the car.'

Tony looked at Paul's slightly unkempt appearance.

'Paul, a minute, over here.'

Tony led him to the end of the room where they sat down. 'So second thoughts?'

'You could say that. I wanted to speak to you and I saw there was a light on here. Chance meeting I suppose. Coincidence I have a new instrument in the car.'

'Not easy to hold a consultation here with everyone around setting their things up. Make an appointment. I can see you on Tuesday.'

'Don't need an appointment. I'm no longer a Salvationist. I've gained a freedom. Play when I want to. Play what I want to. I'm in recovery and pleased to be at peace with myself. That's what I came to tell you.'

'Good to hear it Paul. You know we have found some of us can play instruments so it's a music night. They've never played together before. You could be a good tutor for us.'

Paul looked round the room. If music was the night's theme, he was in a safe zone. 'The Muslim, what does he play?'

'He's helping out. I suspect he won't be playing.'

Paul nodded. He thought as much. 'So who has the sax?'

'Look no further,' Tony replied.

'You on sax? Well, brass is looking good.'

'Play your trombone loudly, hide my mistakes. Go bring yours in.'

Paul needed no further encouragement and he walked smartly towards the exit door. Some saw it as an abrupt departure and looked at Tony.

'He'll be back in a minute.'

The room swelled with the A note tuning each instrument. Karen's fingers ran up and down the keyboard in an arpeggio but could only just be heard as her volume was set low.

'Okay, finish your coffees then take a pencil and a piece of paper. Write down in order of preference your type of music you like to play. Mark then 1,2,3.'

Tony deposited the paper on the desk.

Tongues were peeking out of bottom lips as concentration gripped their thoughts. All, except Farook, who twiddled his pencil and stared blankly at the sheet.

Tony collated the papers and sorted the categories. 'Three for folk; three for Jazz modern and traditional. Glad to see there's no Hip Bop or whatever the youngsters jive to.' The group laughed.

'Alan , can you suggest a folk song start?'

Alan opened his blue, hard backed jotter collection of songs and flipped through from back to front.

'He's got the whole world, in His hands,' he said feeling everybody should know the tune.

'Bit churchy, isn't it?' asked Karen.

Alan sat back abruptly. 'Only a suggestion. Have you got one?'

Karen had not an instant reply. Her ponderings took her eyes to the ceiling.

'Dylan, The times are a-changin', she said looking around for support.

And that was their first harmonious effort. Thereafter, the traditional jazz took over with Sweet Georgia Brown and Midnight in Moscow. The group gained in confidence as they played and Tony came in with his saxophone to give a solo spot in each song. His confidence grew too.

Tony knew he had been able to bring these patients out of their shells; out of their secluded environments and, despite their doctrinal differences, had them socialising beyond his wildest dreams. They had gelled. It was just what Tony had wished for. Times were indeed changing.

# 12

# A Change Afoot

The following week the clients or musicians as they now saw themselves were anxious to return. Each wondered where their music might take them. Practice was the vehicle and they were enthusiastic. It seemed to bond them and make them forget about their illnesses.

That night a man dressed in jeans and a T-shirt sporting a moon symbol against a dark star-lit sky background arrived. He had black hair and an almost dark complexion. Nobody seemed to have any idea who this man was.

'Can I help you?' Tony asked.

The man smiled. He approached Tony and held his hand out.

'You don't recognise me, do you?'

Tony thought for a moment, his size, his voice, could only mean one thing.

'Farook?'

'I was Farook. I'm now Frank.'

'Frank?'

'Yes, changed by deed poll through my lawyer. Frank Armour, joining you, sir. Time to amend your files.'

'I see. So your Muslim faith, er...where are you with that?'

Frank smiled raising his shoulders. 'I've thrown in the towel. I've started to go to Alan's church.'

'And how will your Mosque see that?' Tony enquired.

'That's why I changed my look. But this is the UK. I suspect they will leave me alone. God help me if they don't.'

Tony looked across the room at Alan. He caught his eye. Alan put his thumb up as if announcing one convert had arrived in his fold.

'I'm not a musician but with my larger taxi I can take the players around if they want to play for an old folks home or something like that.'

The idea caught on and they sat down to prepare a musical evening for the local home for the elderly, the Edendale Citizens Retreat.

Tony rang them that night and a date was arranged. They wished them to come one Friday evening and that meant two consecutive days practice. But each had found their voice through their instruments as Marty gave the drum kit a good whacking to keep their timing in order.

'If we are going to a Home, then I think we should call ourselves something. Any ideas?' asked Lizzie.

Heads nodded indicating it was a good idea then their silence put them into thinking mode.

'The Singing Clerics?' offered Karen.

'I think we want to get away from our church anchors. What brought us together? Are we making progress? Sink or Swim is my offering.'

Some interest appeared to be shown for Lizzie's suggestion. In fact after a few more suggestions were made, they came back to hers. Sink or Swim it became.

Tony did not see his clients in such a light but he was not going to interfere.

'Then on Friday, we meet here at 7 p.m. Farook, I mean Frank, can then pack his taxi with keyboard, drum kit and he says you will all fit in. The home's not more than three miles away anyway. Are you all able to come to our first concert?' asked Tony.

There were no dissenters, just keen musicians who seemed to have found their calling through folk and traditional jazz music. Frank revelled in what he heard at the music practices through the tapping of his feet.

# 13

# A Clerical Murder

Tony's first patient on Friday morning had just left his surgery when the time honoured 11 a.m. coffee arrived with the local newspaper. Tony read the headline. It made him catch his breath. He opened out the tabloid and brushed it flat with his arm. His mouth was agape and his fingers ran through his hair. The headline was unambiguous. The former Imam was found dead last night. Police have cordoned off the area around his home and are making their door-to-door enquiries.

A murder inquiry. The report did not say how he had died, but a police statement would follow at midday. He had to hear that.

Tony's hand was on the phone cradle. He was thinking through the consequence of what he might say. Farook was dead; Frank was dead. Anything said would no longer be in breach of his rights. The call was answered promptly.

'Hello, police?

'Yes sir. How may we help?'

'It's about Farook, the Imam's murder. Who can I speak to about it?'

'You need to speak to Superintendent Graham. I'll put you through, now.'

Tony's knuckles turned white on the phone, matching his face.

'Hello, Dr Scriven?'

'Yes. Er...I should say Farook, or Frank as he recently became, was one of my patients. I knew his background as I am sure you know too...you know...the bridge and river incident?'

'Yes, we have a lot of intelligence from that day but this was not a cry for help this time. This was pure murder possibly by someone who knew him.'

'You are certain about that?'

'As certain as I can be at this stage. Mind you it's early still. Don't be repeating what I've said. The statement should clarify these details. Farook, or Frank as you say, was stabbed nine times on his bed.'

'Good grief. I see what you mean,' Tony said as the scene dominated his mind. The thought frightened him. Nine times he considered. God, how he must have suffered.

'Anyway, you have some information to share?'

'Yes, I think so. My case notes are complete. They may assist you.'

'Then can I call to see you, today?'

Tony looked at his diary on line. 'Last patient is at three. I'll be free by four if that's okay for you?'

'Four it is then Dr Scriven. By then we will have issued a statement.'


They met for three hours that afternoon. The reason for Farook's referral was analysed; his failing to return as the Imam; his disputes with the elders; his enthusiasm for the musical group finding a role in transporting the musicians; his change to western clothes and looks, his becoming a Methodist and finally his name change. It all pointed to one thing. Killed by apostate intolerance.

'Yes, the dominating factor. But I fear the Islamic community will close ranks.'

'I am sure they will but this is the UK not the North West Frontier Provence. They ought to respect the police enquiry.'

Superintendent Graham nodded. 'After we find the murder weapon, that's my next port of call.'

'And what was the weapon used to murder Frank, may I ask?'

'Dr Scriven, you will appreciate I cannot give you police intelligence at this stage, other than he was knifed to death. That is in the public domain. That's all I can say.'

'I see.'

# 14

# Taking Stock

## ALAN

It was time for Tony to review his mentally ill musical patients individually. He was particularly keen to hear from Alan. Appointments were made.

Alan arrived in good time for his meeting. He was a much more relaxed individual and felt he probably did not need any more counselling or medical intervention, but his guitar practices had resumed and he liked being part of a musical group.

'How are you coping now, Alan?'

'It's not a cure I'm after, because that's a solution. It's more of a recovery. That's a process.'

'Good point. Is the recovery on track?'

'Derailed by what happened to Frank.'

Tony nodded like a back-ledge car dog. 'How do you see it?'

'His murder?'

'Yea.'

'Open and closed I should think. It all lies in his past surely.'

'I suppose so. I think that's Superintendent Graham's view too. Difficult to break down.'

Alan strode over to the window. His hands rested on his hips. He half turned round.

'You know he began to attend my church?'

'Yes he told me, remember?'

'He sat with Paul. Two new members. They stood out of course. Paul led Frank in the singing as only a Salvationist can and Frank was making a grand effort to absorb his new faith.'

'So Paul and Frank hit it off then?'

'I should say so. Similar ages, I think.'

Tony stood up and placed his hands in his pockets. He walked round his office with Alan's eyes watching his progress.

'You know Alan, this murder ...perhaps it was overdue.'

'What. You mean someone planned it sometime ago?'

'If the murderer was from his own community, then there have been many opportunities before yesterday to cause him harm.'

Alan nodded wisely. 'But the changes were all of a sudden more radical.'

Tony nodded. 'Well Supt Graham seems to be getting to the bottom of it. Perhaps we should leave it at that.'

'I wish I could.'

'What do you mean?' Tony asked showing concern.

'If Farook died a Muslim, then his funeral should be underway. if Frank died a Christian, well, I will hold the service next week but it might be a difficult service.'

'You mean doctrinally?'

'Yes, but also security will be necessary, just in case.'

'I see what you mean. Superintendent Graham should be kept informed. I can let him know if you like. And I'll leave you to consider an appropriate service.'

'Thanks.'

'But you, still on the tracks?'

'Yes, I can say I'm almost back to normal. Sermons in good time and all the other parts of the job going well too.'

'Almost?' asked Tony raising his eyebrows.

'Yup, it will always be now. Marriage I don't treat lightly. I'm getting the balance right at last.'

## LIZZIE

'So probation it was. No prison. First time offender and a period of time to reflect on how your life should be. Not so?' asked Tony wiping his nose.

'A fine to compensate the driver and his car, £600 that was. But a year's probation? That's too long, far too long,' she said throwing her hands into the air.

'Shorter than a prison sentence you must agree when you consider probation is only once a week.'

'Twice a month actually, providing I fully cooperate with the social worker. He's a man, Colin something. You know what these social workers are like, all on first name terms on first meeting.'

'And you are still taking the proscribed medication?'

'Well actually my GP and I had a sort of contretemps over the Lomotrogine.'

Tony could imagine the scenario but enquired further. 'Why?'

'My body is God's creation. A pill is like alcohol or drugs. They are not natural.'

'You are sounding like a Christian Science member. They don't go for treatment either.'

'No, I'm not like them. It's simple. Put into your mouth what God has approved.'

'So does God approve of an obese person having a chocolate bar?'

'God gives us a free will to do as we wish. It's the thinking behind the action that determines the outcome.'

'I see,' said Tony having difficulty digesting what he had heard.

'Well I think some very clever people have worked out how to make medication that works for specific individuals and that to me is a work of God.'

A moment of silence ensued as minds worked out the conversation.

'My GP won the argument. I am still taking the pills you will be pleased to know.'

Tony relaxed. Thank God she was taking her medication. But her mind had already travelled in a different direction.

'Frank, you know the former Farook; what a shock. Do you know who could have possibly killed him?'

'No, but possibly from his own community.'

'I never really knew him. I mean really knew him,' said Lizzie pulling her cardigan zip up and down.

'Yes, he was quite quiet.'

'I don't think he was married. Quite a lonely life perhaps.'

'Yes, I believe so. I never heard of him speak about any partner.'

'Will you be going to his funeral?' asked Lizzie leaning her head forward.

'Yes, I think I should. I was part of his life at its close. Will you attend?'

'Of course I'll attend. We want him to reach heaven don't we?'

## KAREN

Dr Karen Kane arrived for her appointment a little out of breath.

'Relax Karen, you are not late.'

'I am you know, seven minutes late. I am sorry.'

'Don't worry.' Tony recalled her forwardness and wished to stay aloof as much as he could despite the warm feeling he had for her.

'So how have you been?'

'Probation for one year.'

Tony was surprised she had not confided in him about a court appearance. It disappointed him. 'So it was a court case?'

'A court case? Oh no, not that. The General Teaching Council gave me a year off. Subject to medical reports I will be able to return as a teacher in eleven months now. A bit less when you consider the long holidays we get at Christmas, Easter and summer.'

'Ah then that's promising.'

'Yes,' she said crossing her legs. 'And it's on full pay.'
Tony's eyebrows arched in surprise.

'Are you taking your Proloxin?'

'No, not now. Loxapine, better on my stomach. I had issues with Proloxin.'

'Some do,' said Tony without enquiring any further. The moments passed seeking further conversation.

'Terrible tragedy, you know, Farook.'

'Yes, a big job for the police.'

'I suppose the culprit came from his community.'

'Yes, which community though? He had recently thrown in his weight to the Methodists and taken on a British identity.'

Karen's stare fixed on the coconut shell on Tony's desk. She ruffled her hair.

'What's in the shell?'

Tony followed her gaze to her desk. 'Paper clips. Perhaps the odd elastic band.'

'Very ethnic.'

Tony smiled gently. It had been an arts and crafts present from the ten year old who lived next door to him in Manchester. He had been a friend of his daughter.

'The funeral. Will you be going?' she asked.

'Not sure when it will be. I suspect I should give it priority.'

'That's good.'

'How do you mean?'

'I'll be there too. Alan asked me to play the church organ. His usual organist will be on holiday.'

'Karen, you are taking your medication. You have a year to relax from work and you are responding well.

Perhaps I can conclude our medical appointments as long as you keep your medication under review at your GP surgery. How does that sound?'

Karen showed no delight in the suggestion. Worry was the look on her face. Tony was disappointed having satisfied himself he could take the premature risk.

'Don't you think you could manage on your own? With your keyboard playing with Sink or Swim, of course? I'm seeing you swim,' he said hoping she might bite this bait.

'I think you are a good psychiatrist. I'd miss my appointments.'

'Don't forget I play sax in the group. So you can contact me any time if you think an appointment is needed.'

Karen wondered if she was being snubbed but there was something in Tony's smile which was comforting. 'Should I read anything into your wish to see less of me, professionally?'

God, she's on to me, thought Tony. I'm trapped.

'Less of you professionally, yes. That's my goal.'

There was a silence which seemed to last forever. Karen stood up. 'Well, if this is the last consultation, I must thank you for seeing me through my trauma.'

She thrust her hand forward across the table. Tony stood up and shook it firmly and held on a few moments longer. Karen felt the connection made.

'Then I look forward to our playing, together.'

Tony smiled. 'Not as much as I do. I look forward to being with you again.'

It was an awkward moment for them both. Tony had implied a new relation had been launched and

Karen, having shaken his hand, went to the door, a little confused.

She opened the door and turned round. She smiled and slightly opened her mouth but no words came out. The door shut and the moment was over as Tony sank back into his chair.

## PAUL

Paul declared that his life was on a new footing. He was freed from a loveless marriage and left the Salvation Army to break from the restrictions he had felt. The waiting room was however empty.

Tony waited for him as Paul's first priority was the loo. By the time Paul returned, Tony had his questions ready and in order.

'But the Sally Ann was there for you when you needed them most,' stated Tony.

'That was a long time ago.'

'Yes, but you were indebted to them, surely, weren't you?'

Paul checked his i-Phone. He looked up and Tony had gone. A metallic rumble came from behind. Tony had gone to pull down the blinds as dusk was falling and in response he replied curtly.

'Are you really in a better place as you say, Paul?'

Paul put his phone away. He sighed. 'I should never have married.'

'Surely you wanted your marriage to last a lifetime when you got married.'

'I fell into marriage. Pretty girl, fellow musician in

the army.' He sniggered. 'Didn't like the bows on her bonnet mind you.'

Tony smiled as the picture appeared to him in his mind.

'So what went wrong?'

'It wasn't just the court case. Bottom line is I am gay. She could not handle that.'

'You just come out?'

'I guess you are the first I've really told.'

Tony wondered if the other Salvationists had come to that conclusion. Perhaps that was also a stumbling block.

'So do you have a partner, a support?'

Paul scratched his arm. 'Not yet. I'm going online to find someone my age.'

'That takes time. I wish you success. Your health, any other problems?'

Paul uncrossed his legs and placed his hands on his thighs. 'Mind if I go to the loo again?'

Tony was crouched looking for a book in his bookshelf when Paul returned. 'How often are you up in the night, Paul?'

Paul looked towards the ceiling as Tony returned his chair. 'I think four or five times.'

'Have you mentioned that to your doctor?'

'No, should I? Isn't it just aging?'

'Maybe, but get it checked anyway. Looks like you may have an enlarged prostate.'

Tony straightened his tie with a tug.

'Will you be coming to Farook's funeral?'

Paul's response was quick. 'Hardly knew him.'

'Well, it's up to you.'

Paul drew in his cheeks and took a deep breath.

'Then count me out. Religion is less of an attraction these days. I want to wean off it for a while.'

## MARTY

Marty appeared in a warm orange heavy jumper wearing jodhpurs. She carried her helmet and a whip in her left hand.

'Just come from a pony hack,' she said stating the obvious.

'You are a keen rider?'

'Yes, four hours this morning. I should have made it less. I nearly forgot the appointment.'

Tony threw his sport jacket on to his desk chair. 'Drums still sounding?'

'They certainly are, but not at night. The neighbours are not back till seven most nights so, I've got an hour or two to practise. Harmonica then takes over.'

Tony saw Marty as a woman ready to accept her parent's untimely death, as long as she had support.

'Is it a large Baha'i community here in town?'

'Twenty six strong with many sympathisers in attendance.'

'A good support group?'

'Yes, I'd say all of them. They are an all embracing religion with respect for every religion and every person.'

'You'll be with them on the run up to Christmas, then?'

'I could, I want to.'

'Marty, I think you should take the lead in making that happen.'

Tony caught a whiff of perfume. He was not sure if it was an expensive concoction or the sweet smell of some horse sweat but it was neither off-putting nor unpleasant.

'About Farook,....' she ventured. 'Such a shock. We were only getting to know him. I simply cannot imagine what happened.'

'There's still no word about who did it. Police are frustrated, I hear. They've got nothing to say to calm the general public's fears,' said Tony.

'You mean the murderer might do it again?'

'No, not very likely but he or she remains loose in the town perhaps and that worries folk. With no concrete evidence the mind sometimes creates worry and unrealistic and sordid expectations.'

'I would think the Muslim community would have more to fear.'

'Why?'

'Because the police will think one of them did it, surely?'

'That's the way most people see it,' said Tony.

Marty cleared her throat.

'Frank was not musical. Yet I feel he was looking forward to being the roadie.'

'Yes, he was becoming more westernised by the day,' said Tony scratching his elbow through his shirt.

'That was his downfall. Pity that. A dreadful way to go,' she said with her eyes fixed on the wall behind Tony. 'The musical group will continue?'

'Oh I think so. I think we all get something good out of it.'

'Yes, we certainly do,' she said.

'Will you attend the funeral?'

'You know I hadn't thought about that. I suppose I should, shouldn't I.'

'I leave that to you. I'll be there. After all he was one of my clients.'

The telephone rang the next day as Tony drank a glass of water. He placed the glass down on his desk and lifted the phone. It was the Methodist pastor.

'Hello, Alan.'

'Thought I'd tell you about Frank's funeral. It will be next Friday.'

'Next week Friday? How will that go down with his community?'

'His community? Farook was Frank to us. He died on the cusp of becoming a Methodist. He loved singing the hymns. He's not a Muslim anymore.'

'No, he's not. Not to you and me but what about his community?'

'I did have one threatening call.'

'Really?'

'Yes, he did not leave a name but his accent gave it away. He talked of us stealing their brother. I simply thanked him for his call and placed the receiver down.'

'Did you tell anyone?'

'I phoned the police. Superintendent Graham took the message and told me he and some other plain-clothed policemen would attend the funeral, on duty.'

# IVAN

Ivan's appointment was early. 9 a.m. early. It rarely suited Tony for such an early consultation but Ivan was an early bird and insisted that was when he'd attend.

'So Ivan, tell me how you've been over the last week or two.'

Ivan took a deep sigh. Then he smiled at Tony.

'You will hardly believe it. I've gone and bought myself a new clarinet.'

'Really?'

'As real as I am before you now.'

'So what's brought about the change?'

'Reflection. You don't know what you have until you lose it.'

Tony looked at Ivan. He seemed to have lost some weight or perhaps his peppermint longitudinal striped shirt made him look more lanky. His clothes looked fresh and his shoes had been polished that day. He had made an effort.

'You know some of my clients have formed a musical group. Sink or Swim we call ourselves. All amateurs like me with the sax.'

'You play the saxophone? Well, I'd never have guessed.'

'Why not? Even a medic has to relax sometime. The point is we have no high expectations. We gladly welcome the bum notes and no one blushes,' Tony said with a degree of optimism in his smile. 'You know Ivan a clarinet would be greatly welcomed to steady the ship. We have no prima donnas. Are you interested?'

'You know I am. That's the standard I need. No need to prove myself. Just turn up and play,' Ivan said at a hurried pace. 'When does the group meet next?'

'We've hardly got off the ground. You may have heard about the recent murder.'

'That Muslim guy, you mean?'

'Yes, that Muslim guy we knew as Frank. He was to be our road manager, carting instruments and some folk to our playing venues. He was really looking forward to that. So we won't meet up till after the funeral.'

'Is he not buried yet? The murder was about five days ago.'

'Ivan, Frank was not a Muslim at death. He was a Methodist.'

'Wow, big change there. What's the difference anyway? They are all searching for God, aren't they?'

'Big difference Ivan. Methodists say it in music; Muslims in a chant in unison.'

Ivan bit his bottom lip. 'I don't know much about their faith but they do say Inshallah a lot, as if anything done seeks God's approval.'

'You know Ivan, sometimes I feel music is the real religion. It's a sound that speaks to us, interprets our thoughts and delivers moods and feelings. So good in its own way. That's what I like in religion,' said Tony leaning back.

'I've still to find a church home. I'm in no rush. The Salvationists are a lifestyle. I just want to be a church member.'

'You can meet some of the band at Frank's funeral Ivan.'

'No I won't be there. Don't like funerals. Not the place to meet folk in my opinion.'

'Okay, then I'll phone you and let you know when the next practice will be, after the funeral.'

'Suits me.'

'I'm glad you are back on board with your music. It's as good as medicine.'

'It certainly is.'

# 15

# The Funeral

Frank's cremation took place three days short of two weeks after his death. On several counts this annoyed the Muslim community. They sought a funeral as quickly as possible and immediate announcement of his death to his family. This ruling stemmed from the Middle East where a corpse would decompose rapidly in the heat of the desert but took no account of the refrigerated offerings of a western undertaker. The other matter was the crematorium. Burial was required for a Muslim funeral. Furthermore he had presumably not been offered the final ritual wash. This information was conveyed to Tony by Alan by telephone.

'No, these are not my fears. It's what they are saying.'

'Who is saying this, Alan?'

'Amed Aziz is one of my neighbours. I know him well. He told me what they are saying.'

'And is Amed not one of the Mosque attendees?'

'No, his prayers are said in his house, in a very sparse room. Only a carpet I remember.'

'And why not prayers at the Mosque?'

'The Sunnis attend the Mosque here in this town. Amed and his wife are Alevis, a cut off sect not recognised by orthodox Muslims. He knows many of course but through business and not the Mosque.'

'I see.'

'It worries me that they still think he was a Muslim. Perhaps I should go and see them to calm things down.'

'I'd advise against that Alan.' A moment elapsed as he thought through his response.

'I suppose so. The timing about informing his family seems strange though. What family he had would have known he was no longer the Imam and he was not married. He lived alone, did you know that?'

'I was aware he lived alone. I had thought that was because of his position in the Mosque. He never spoke of his family members.'

'Mmmm.....probably. But Tony I suspect there will be a few of them coming to his funeral tomorrow.'

'Yes, maybe. Perhaps I should alert the police about that.'

'Good idea. Will you do that for me?'

'Yes, I'll do that right now.'

'Okay see you tomorrow 11 a.m. Bye.'

Tony had not been at Alan's church since last Christmas. He could not remember the service of carols and lessons but he remembered the mulled wine and mince pies. He was familiar with the church premises and had attended some funerals there too. This funeral however would be different for the obvious circumstances but a concern for possible disruption was on Tony's mind too when he lifted the phone.

'Superintendent Graham? Hi, Tony Scriven here.'

'Hello, hope you are well?'

'Well, health wise I'm fine. Mentally I feel I'm slipping on the ice rink. Murder of a client is pretty rare. You feel the pressure too?'

'Sure. So what's the matter?' he said looking at his wristwatch.

'Frank's funeral tomorrow, there is tension around from the Muslim community as you can imagine.'

'Yes, I've got cover for that.'

'Perhaps a few plain clothes police at the funeral won't go amiss. Would put my mind at ease.'

'Don't I know that? The killer could be among them and so I can assure you there will be several officers in plain clothes deployed as eyes and ears tomorrow.'

'Huh..... I must be thinking like a policeman. Anyway, that's what I was hoping you might say. I hear there will be a short service before heading to the crematorium.'

'Yes, we've got both covered.'

'Good. That's reassuring. Can I ask, are there any leads yet?'

'Sorry, intelligence is following several leads but that's all I can tell you.'

Tony thought about replacing the handset but he could not help himself dive deeper. 'Mr Wright, Dan Wright my consultant pathologist colleague, confirmed the knife wounds. Unusual blade he thought.'

'As I said, we are following several leads.'

'Of course and I suppose there's a pressure to give the public some reassurance and information. There will be no quick solution unless something unexpected and dramatic surfaces, I suppose.'

Tony thought he heard the officer tap his pen against his writing pad. 'Then I hope tomorrow I'll get some good leads.'

It was raining. Not the proverbial cats and dogs rain, more of a grey damp air, creating sheen on the pavements and drizzle on car windows. Tony parked in the Tesco car park and crossed the road to the church. He joined the mourners nodding to his clients as they arrived.

Paul Risk was first to catch his eye. He was two rows in front of Tony. Paul held a handkerchief in his hand, occasionally wiping his eyes, as Karen began to play Vater Unser, a melody from Geistliche Lieder 1539 arranged by Johann Sebastian Bach 1685-1750. The pipe organ sounded like a whispering call around the aisles. Dressed in a black dress and heavy black coat, Lizzie stood up to accompany the music. Her soprano voice pierced the air and cleansed it as it did so.

*God of the living in whose eyes*
*Unveiled thy whole creation lies,*
*All souls are thine; we must not say*
*That those are dead who pass away;*
*From this our world of flesh set free.*
*We know them living unto thee.*

Tony was impressed with Lizzie's singing. Her expression and tone were exemplary; befitting the client whose acts of perfection dominated her life.

Tony noticed three men enter. All wore dark Shalwar Kameez and sat together mid aisle. It gave him a shudder as the stereotype influenced his senses. He also seemed to identify the male and female police officers present and wondered if, despite the sanctified venue, they were armed. He hoped so, just in case. Lizzie held the music before her once again.

*Released from early toil and strife,*
*With thee is hidden still their life;*
*Thine are their thoughts, their works, their prayers,*
*All thine, and yet most truly ours;*
*For well we know, where'er they be,*
*Our dead are living unto thee.*

Frank's coffin was simple, not ornate just as all Muslim coffins are. On top of it lay two flags, the Green and White flag of Pakistan with its Muslim Crescent and Star and the Union Jack.

Alan entered his pulpit in his black gown and stood to acknowledge the attendees come to pay their last respects to Farook Elahi, lately known as Frank Armour. A titter of quiet comments could be detected.

'We stand to sing Hymn 604. Go, happy soul, thy days are ended, thy pilgrimage on earth below; Go by angelic guard attended, to God's own Paradise now go.'

Karen got us to our feet playing the first two lines in preparation for our lungs to fill and burst open on the right note. But the singing was edgy. Eyes strayed from hymn books. There were three verses, possibly four. Such was the distraction on Tony's mind. He was glad to resume his seat while noticing Paul still held his handkerchief to his eyes.

A prayer followed and then Alan spoke of how Farook had arrived in the UK, how he had established himself as the town's Mosque Imam and how, towards the end of his life, he had adapted to the Methodist tradition, lavishly devouring Methodist hymns and the simple direct prayer which held no binding mantras. A further shorter prayer followed then a surprise development occurred which no one was expecting.

'And now I ask Sadar Zubaid to come forward.'

Alan made a gesture with his hand and Sadar stood up then made his way to the chancel step beside the coffin.

'Salaam Alaikum. Farook was our friend, he was our Imam. We learned from him as his devout prayers and examples carved out the lives of two generations in this town. We are grateful to Allah for his service.' Sadar then approached the coffin and took from it the Pakistani national flag. The plain-clothed officers could be seen exchanging glances to their colleagues and Alan leant forward from his pulpit to see what was about to transpire.

Sadar opened the flag and begged one of his Pakistani mourners, who he introduced as Kamran, to come forward and hold the other end, making the flag stretch to its full splendour.

'What do you see?' he asked. But there was no response. 'Yes, it's our national Pakistani flag. But look closer. It is not a green flag with a crescent and a star. It is a green flag with a crescent and star and a white vertical stripe down one side. You see it?'

Heads nodded. His speech so far was not controversial. It seemed to be almost educational.

'Since 1947 this flag has not changed. The narrow white colour represents all in Pakistan who are not Muslim. Yes, that's what the white stands for. The Baha'is, the Christians and the Jews, and of course even those who have no religion. They are represented on this flag. Now we can say that Farook crossed from the green side to the white side, but retained his national identity. I do not know why but I am sure he did so with God's permission. I cannot make that move. Nor do I know whether Farook was settled with his new religion. So, whether he was or not, let me ask you to hear my prayer:

'O Allah, forgive Your servant, raise him to high rank among those who are rightly guided; make him as a guardian of his descendants who survive him. Forgive us and him, O Lord of the Universe, make his grave spacious and grant him light in it.'

Heads rose. The flag was replaced to fall over the coffin. Before sitting down, Sadar raised his hand to Alan to indicate he had one other matter to announce.

'I have never attended a crematorium. I will not and cannot either. It is not our tradition to burn a body. So this service may now continue and we will remain till its conclusion.'

Thereafter Sadar returned to sit with his two Muslim friends. Tony felt a relief that there had not been a demonstration or indeed much criticism of the funeral being delayed a week or being held in the Methodist church.

Alan concluded the service by announcing a hymn which Frank had enjoyed learning to sing. Inevitably it was a Charles Wesley hymn. And Can it Be with music by T. Campbell. It was a hymn of Affirmation. There was no doubt in Alan's mind, Frank was a Christian.

# 16

# The Cremation

As the mourners left the church, Paul Risk's shivering shoulders bore witness to his distress. Tony caught up with him.

'I'm sorry, I can't help it,' he said in a stuttering voice, wiping his tears from his eyes.

'Don't be. It's good to grieve. It releases the tension of the sad day,' said Tony.

Paul turned around. His face still etched in agonised pain.

'I had no idea how much I would miss Frank. I felt we were rowing in the same boat, away from our troubles. I can't believe he's no longer with us.'

Tony was touched to think Paul and Frank had found each other's company mutually beneficial. 'It was a brave route Farook took to become Frank. I admired him for that, although it cost him his life.'

'Yes, it must have riled his community. But why take revenge? It was evilly excessive to murder such a gentle man,' Paul whimpered again.

'The police are working on it, Paul. Perhaps one day we'll hear what happened. It might even raise the debate about the right to change one's religion,' said Tony.

A further sob led Paul to take Tony's sleeve.

'I don't think I can come to the cremation. It's still too raw for me and I don't want to make a scene. To be honest I couldn't last a half hour without a loo break either.'

'I understand. That's all right Paul. You made an appointment with your GP?'

'Yes, I did. I certainly did.'

Tony nodded then smiled offering his hand.

'Then I'll see you next week. Take care.'

The coffin bearing car passed them as they parted. Marti approached Tony in its wake.

'A touching service, wasn't it?'

Tony turned towards her and smiled. 'Yes, went off quite smoothly. Quite a relief.'

'I was not sure what that Sadar was going to say. I was actually quite apprehensive when he was asked to speak.'

'I was too, but in the end I was glad he did.'

'Yes, I had no idea what the white stripe stood for, why it was on their flag. He spoke well.'

'Are you going to the Crematorium?'

'Of course, aren't we all?'

Tony hesitated. He looked around to see Paul head away on the street towards town. 'Paul has decided not to go.'

'That's just as well. He could not control his grief. I had no idea they were so fond of each other.'

'It wasn't noticeable in our group musical practices,' said Tony.

'No, different focus there.'

The mourners made their way to the crematorium

and arrived in good time. The previous service was underway when they arrived. Supt Graham joined Tony as they waited in the forecourt for the mourners to leave and head out to their cars.

'Went quite well I thought, Superintendent.'

'So far so good. I've not stood my men down yet.'

'Are you expecting trouble here?'

'On the face of it, in our planning we felt this would present more of a difficulty if it was seen to be a Muslim cremated. But after Sadar's speech to the congregation, perhaps there will be no trouble. In fact ...' said the Superintendent looking around, 'I can't see anyone here yet from the Muslim community.'

'Then you could perhaps stand down your men.... and women officers of course?'

'No, I won't do that, not yet. A bit of spiritual exposure will do them no harm.'

The men laughed quietly as the Crematory doors opened. The previous grieving family left by the back of the chapel. Those attending Frank's cremation made their way in from the front.

Once more Karen Kane was on the organ stool playing Barber's Adagio for strings. Only three pipe stops were out, just the violins, violas and cellos which gave a peaceful aura around the chapel.

Farook's simple coffin, still covered in the national flags of Pakistan and the Union Jack, rested in the centre of the church on a catafalque in the centre of the chancel.

Tony sat beside Ivan on one side with Marti on the other. A moment later, Alan came out of the vestry and stood in the pulpit.

'We meet again, this time to say our final farewell to Farook or Frank as he became. Farook had taken a journey from Islam to Christianity and now takes the final journey to dwell in the presence of God in heaven. Let not your hearts be troubled; ye believe in God, believe also in me. In my Father's house are many mansions, if it were not so, I would not have told you. I go to prepare a place for you. Let us pray.'

Tony's mind wandered during the prayer. He did not believe in what he was hearing, more accepting the prayer as the opium of the people as Karl Marx had said of religion in general. The hypnotic effect of the prayer with eyes closed found Tony back at his office wondering what the day's referrals might bring. He was brought back to reality by the request for the congregation to stand and sing I To The Hills Will Lift Mine Eyes. Tony enjoyed singing such a familiar tune but briefly stopped singing when his throat turned hard.

Alan asked them once more to pray. A light touch of Karen's fingers played less of a melody, more of a dirge, a sombre piece. Tony noticed the curtain start to close. In no time at all, the coffin disappeared and the curtains closed. Frank was on his way to cremation.

Suddenly, a loud explosion came from the back of the crematorium. Heads ducked down as clouds of dust entered the Chapel of Rest. The closed doors took the brunt of the explosion as some of the glass shards flew into the backs of the last row of mourners. A few received cuts to their face and hands. Four police officers immediately responded.

'Lie low,' shouted one officer.

'Wait till we see the situation is clear,' shouted Supt Graham.

An officer pointed his Tazer gun as he proceeded while the others held truncheons at the ready. They left the chapel and entered the vestibule. Its walls remained intact but cracked. The male toilet door had disintegrated. Vases were on the floor, cracked and broken, their flowers scattered everywhere and a pool of water seeped into the hard wearing Triumph cut pile tiles. The toilet was the scene of most damage. Suspicion that the exploded device was lodged there surfaced. Despite the burst water pipes running around the broken urinal china, Superintendent Graham sealed off the site as a scene of a crime while a colleague requested the ambulance service. Then he alerted his command station.

Out of breath, the woman police officer returned to the vestibule to inform the Superintendent that there was no obvious terrorist in the area but the general public were approaching out of interest from the town.

Supt Graham returned to the chapel to see the frightened mourners, many holding an arm or hand of their seated neighbour.

'The crematorium has been made secure. Now has anyone got any injury of any kind?'

'Yes,' said Alan. 'There are two ladies with glass in their heads over there on the back row. They are both bleeding and I guess we are all in shock.'

'I am sure you are. Alan is there another male toilet here?'

'Yes, next to my vestry.'

'Then that's where the men should go if required. Fortunately as the ladies toilet is situated down the outside wing of the building, I can confirm it is not damaged. However to get there you will have to go through the back of the building.'

A siren was heard faintly at first and then it grew louder.

'That will be the ambulance. So those of you who have any cuts, the walking wounded, please go through the front of the chapel. Put your hand up if you can't manage to do that.'

One lady raised her hand. 'Then stay there till the medical staff arrive.'

Tony ran his hand through his hair. He had not been injured. Marty did so too and her finger bled as a shard of glass pierced her hand.

'You'd better go for a check-up too Marty,' said Lizzie. 'I'll go with you if you like.'

Tony stood up and left the pew. 'And I thought all was going well. I did not expect this.'

'No Tony, disappointing. No one expected this at all,' said Supt Graham.

'Perhaps the suspicion lies with the Muslim community for this as well. It seems so,' said Tony.

'If we catch who did it we might catch who murdered Frank.'

'I suppose so. So will that make it easier to find him?' asked Tony.

'Possibly, depends what these people can find,' he said pointing to his colleagues.

Tony looked towards the vestibule as a team of scenes of crime officers dressed in white overhauls entered. 'Yes, they might find the evidence.'

'Yes, evidence of attempted mass murder.'

'Mass Murder?' Tony realised this was indeed a very large police enquiry now. He saw an officer approach the Superintendent.

'That's the source of the device sealed off, sir. We've made it safe.'

# 17

# Suspicions

Superintendent Graham held a press conference the following day. The local Standard journalist Magdalene Smith began the questioning.

'Superintendent, with the local murder and this explosion, are the two crimes related?' A general nod of heads suggested the right question had been asked.

'That must be a factor but it is not conclusive. We must keep the options open at this stage. We are still combing the area for evidence and following up some leads.'

'With the murder of the former Imam and now the explosion at the crematorium where no Muslim is ever cremated, the suspects must stem from their own community,' suggested Magdalene lowering her microphone and brushing back a strand of hair from her eyes.

'Is that a question? I doubt it. Ms Smith that is merely your summation. Not mine. As I say I must remain open to the evidence which will emerge.'

'And what evidence will emerge and how will that link to my community?'

'You are sir?'

'Mohammad Waris, owner of The Orchard Restaurant.'

'You must understand no one is charged unless there is evidence against that person. To find the offender we must use whatever tactic is required and within the law.'

'Yes but will this mean interrogation of the Muslim community? We will resist such biased targeting, I assure you.'

'I urge you to think carefully. We will act with due care and have no intention of offending anyone. Now unless there are any other questions, I end this press conference.'

The silence which ensued gave those in attendance a moment to reflect on the tension which had emerged. Eyes flirted around the room but no further questions were put before the Superintendent left smartly.

'Mr Waris, before you go, can I have a word with you?' asked Magdalene rising from her seat with pen and pad in her hand.

Supt Graham returned to his office and unclipped his black tie. He laid it on his desk and took a long drink of water. He lifted a brown envelope marked urgent lying at an angle before him. He opened it with a sharp plastic date knife which stood erect in his pen pot. It was a report from the forensic team. He eased the report out and sat back in his desk.

A smile crossed his lips. The team had located a fingerprint on the device which had exploded. It was an amateur device, one which a third year pupil could easily have produced in a chemistry class. It had a battery with

310

a timer. It was however an Improvised Explosive Device, a so-called IED. A CO2 cartridge had been filled with an explosive powder and a slow burning wick.

Only by the grace of God had this device not made the building collapse thereby leading to multiple deaths. Had that been the intention, it had failed. Had it succeeded, then no Muslim would have been injured. Once more the elephant in the room came into sight. The Superintendent had to face the wrath of the Muslim community. He would have to interrogate each and every one.

Sadar Zubaid was the obvious link. He had spoken well at the church service. He was a level-headed man and Supt. Graham hoped an interview with him would take the cases forward. He phoned him.

'Salam Alaikum.'

'Alaikum Salaam,' replied Sadar.

'You appreciate we have two major incidents going on in our town at present, the death of Farook and the explosion at the cemetery.'

'Please, I accept Farook changed his mind. Let us refer to him as Frank, his chosen name.'

Supt. Graham acknowledged his statement with an unseen smile and a pleasing nod of his head.

'You see the Holy Qur'an is very clear that mankind has a free choice in the matter of religion. There should be no compulsion in religion. Surely, right has become distinct from wrong....Ch 2 V 257 of the Koran.'

'I hear what you say.'

'Do you?'

'Yes, but what about those who support ISIS,

as extremists, for these crimes in our town have been committed in a similar way?'

'No. Islam strongly and unreservedly rejects and condemns terrorism in any form, whether committed by an individual, group or government. In fact, according to Islam, no religion can sanction violence and bloodshed of innocent men, women and children in the name of God, since all religions came from God Who sent His prophets to establish peace in the world. Islam places an obligation on every Muslim to uphold peace. This concept is so rooted in Islam that the Holy Qur'an describes true Muslims as those who .....walk on the earth in a dignified manner. And when the ignorant address them, they say Peace. That is verse 64 Chapter 25 of the Holy Qur'an.'

'I do not doubt the wisdom you are imparting to me, not at all. But Sadar, I have a problem.'

'Then share it brother.'

'I have a fingerprint. I must match it to an individual.'

'Then you are well on the way to finding the culprit or culprits.'

'I hope so,' said Supt Graham wondering if the penny had dropped in his thinking. He waited a moment.

'I will have to obtain all the finger prints of your Mosque attendees and the wider Muslim community.'

Sadar's neck veins seemed to bulge. 'You select only one group to isolate the suspects? No Jewish, no known criminals who could have murdered or tried to murder others, Supt Graham? I do not like what you are insinuating. This is discriminatory.' Sadar's tone left no doubt about his feelings.

'Wait a moment Sadar. I'm not targeting anyone.'

'It's not the message you are giving out.'

'I assure you we have tested the prints with all known criminals. There is no match there. If only there was. I ask you if you were in my position, what would you have done?'

'How can you ask me that? I don't know your procedures.'

'I suggest each fingerprint I take eliminates one of your community. Does that not reassure you?'

'Superintendent, my community is unlikely to cooperate. Fingerprint everyone in the town and we will oblige but single us out to the ridicule of the local people then expect a reaction. Good day Superintendent.'

His phone returned to its holder with a bang. The Supt threw his pen down on his desk and shouted through to his secretary.

'A coffee please. Make it black today.'

# 18

# Soundings

Saturday mornings meant shopping for Tony. He was later than usual this Saturday. It had already past noon. He parked his six year old Volvo V70 in Morrisons car park and noticed Karen get out of her Volkswagen Passat nearby. He approached feeling his heart accelerate.

'Hi Karen.'

'Oh hello. Off duty today?'

'Well, you could say that, if I ever am.'

Karen lingered by her door. 'Why? Surely you need a complete break from work?'

'Yes, it should be like that but sometimes it's a call from the police about a patient or I bump into a client who needs my attention.'

Karen laughed loudly, her dimples imploding.

'You mean, like me?'

Tony smiled feeling a little awkward and dithering over how close his proximity should be.

'Oh sorry. I'm not thinking about you needing attention at all. I mean medical attention of course.'

'Just slipped out, did it?'

'Okay Karen. You caught me out. You'll never believe me now. Let me make it up. Can I invite you for a coffee then?'

Tony felt excited and on edge. He wondered just what Karen's feelings were at this moment.

'Okay, yes a coffee. I've loads of time this morning. Let's cross the road. The Bakehouse is more exclusive than the goldfish bowl here.'

They made their way across the superstore car park and crossed the road. Tony held the cafe door open as Karen entered and the freshly baked bread warmed their senses.

'That table, over there perhaps?' pointed Tony.

The waitress approached with pen and pad at the ready.

'A cappuccino, please and a...fruit scone.'

'Yes, I'll have a fruit scone too and a peppermint tea if you have one?' asked Karen

'Certainly. Jam and cream with the scones?' she asked.

'Like a Devon Cream?' inquired Tony.

'Yes, sort of,' she replied and with a grin and a smart twirl, she then disappeared heading towards the kitchen.

'Herbal teas, very healthy.'

'Yes,' said Karen, 'but I start the day with a coffee. It's the only one I have all day.'

Tony wanted to keep work from the conversation at all costs. He wanted to seem like a man who had a life outside work; a man with an ulterior motive to be played cautiously.

'So what has the rest of the week got in store?' he asked unbuttoning his sports jacket.

'Playing the organ at the morning and evening services.'

'Of course, how could I have forgotten? So that's Sunday covered.'

'You don't understand. There's a lot of preparation. The introit and the recessional require music and that's at my discretion, subject to the seasons. It was my downfall too,' she covered her lips with her right hand and giggled.

Tony's eyebrows gathered. He had forgotten the incident. Karen saw his eyes float upwards seeking the event.

'The Stripper, remember. First time heard in a service I bet.'

They laughed as the incident was remembered and enjoyed.

'All in the past then?'

'Yes, probably. Not possibly you hear. Yes probably as long as I take my medication.'

The waitress brought a tray with what they had requested.

Tony cut his scone in two and buttered each side liberally. Karen sipped her peppermint tea. As Tony layered the raspberry jam over the cream he became aware of a sound.

'Do you hear that?'

'What?'

'That sound. Listen.'

Karen suspended her scone half way to her mouth and cocked an ear. 'Sounds like voices,' she said with little interest in the disturbance and ate her first bite.

As the moments passed the noise became louder and both of them realised it was some sort of demonstration. It grew louder as the gathering approached the cafe. Tony rose and approached the window. Then he realised that the Muslim population were demonstrating. Some of the slogans read: 'Why Us?' and 'Muslims are Innocent.' A man held a drum before him and kept the pace going forward with his beat.

'Oh my God. This could cause problems.'

'But why?' asked Karen.

'The two recent crimes are pointing towards their community. This could set off a multicultural clash. We certainly don't need that.'

'Certainly not,' said Karen clearing the jam from her front teeth with her pinkie.


Superintendent Graham called in Constable Miraz Yusef to his office.

'You wish to see me, sir?'

'Yes, Miraz, have a seat.'

The Superintendent twiddled a pen between his fingers. 'These two crimes, you obviously know which ones I am referring to?'

'Yes sir. Farook's death and the crematorium explosion.'

'Yes. There is sensitivity around. It could frustrate the inquiry,' Mr Graham spoke at a slow deliberate rate.

'Yes, I am aware of that,' said Mirza crossing his legs.

'Until I get any other lead, I am concentrating on your people. You understand why?'

'Yes, but was there not a Luton factor sir?' Miraz asked holding his dark shaded chin with his right hand.

'That was an early inquiry. That was when one of your traditional Mosque leaders left here to go to Luton but he has a solid alibi. He could not have been here when either event occurred.'

'So the inquiry has run aground here in the town?'

'Not run aground. I have deployed a fairly large team but the evidence is just not coming out.'

There was a pause. Mirza clasped his hands tightly.

'You are wanting me to infiltrate the Muslim community?' he asked to relive the silence.

Mr Graham smiled. 'I can't see it any other way. Can you?'

Miraz shook his head. 'They don't exactly appreciate me being a policeman, you know,' he said narrowing his dark eyebrows.

'Miraz, we serve the whole community. Don't forget that.'

'I don't, sir. I don't, but we are not the whole community, are we?'


Magdalene Smith had been assigned by the local paper to follow the two crimes. She asked to see Superintendent Graham the next day.

'Thank you for taking the time so see me, Superintendent.'

'Miss Smith, sometimes I need the press to make my voice heard.'

'I can certainly do that but I must also tell the whole truth.'

The Superintendent smarted. 'And what do you mean by that?'

'The demonstration the other day. That had to be reported.'

He nodded, conceding her point.

'You know, Miss Smith everyone and I mean everyone is innocent until found guilty by the courts of this land. That's one message I'd like to get over. The other is that when each fingerprint is cleared, then that's one less suspect.'

'I don't suppose that's news to the Muslim community but I'll incorporate it in my report.' She placed her pen against her teeth. 'Can I ask one question, you may refuse to comment but, I'll ask anyway? Have you heard about the main demonstration for twelve noon next Saturday?'

The Superintendent tried to hide his lack of awareness of the demo.

'Who told you this?

'The community are talking about it. I mean the Muslim community. They are bussing demonstrators in from towns nearby, from over the border too. Not just Carlisle either, Newcastle and as far down as Bolton and Manchester.'

'As far as I am aware, I have not heard about this demonstration. It must go through the channels,' he said realising it was a serious matter which would have to command sufficient police coverage. But how on earth was the police intelligence unaware of this development?

'Is there anything else you might want to add?' she asked.

'No I don't want to hog your column. The main points I've covered. This will be no witch hunt.'

Miss Smith stood up to leave. Mr Graham approached to shake her hand. 'At times like this we need to support each other.'

'I assure you I am supporting everyone engaged in the detection of the crimes, Mr Graham.'

Magdalene Smith left the room closing the door behind her. As soon as she had left, Mr Graham seized the telephone and contacted his operations Inspector.

'Mark, no leave for operational units this weekend. We have a major Muslim march to police from 2.00 pm to 4.00 pm as well as the local derby match between Dundee United and our Queens lot at 3.00pm on Saturday.'

'You could get a ban on grounds of public safety. Get them to change their day.'

'No Mark, I can't move the match but I'd be loathed to ban the march. They would see that as a further imposition. I'll just have to take the risk and run with it.'

'So that means three days to plan for a potential perfect storm.'

# 19

# Things Boil Over

Tony was anxious to get the group back together again and concentrate on their musical initiative. He requested them to gather at his office at 7 p.m. the following Friday. By Friday he had heard of no development in either case. He wondered whether Superintendent Graham might have to involve other constabularies to increase his detective capabilities. Even the Standard had dropped the story to the letters page apart from a three line quote from Supt Graham.

Marti set up her drum kit while Ivan assembled his clarinet. Karen set her music on her keyboard's stand; Tony presented his reed-filled mouth piece to the saxophone as Paul blew down his trombone and opened the drain button.

They played a varied programme starting with Cym Rhondda played to the swell of the brass and keyboard organ instruments. Alan gave a solo of Red Sails in the Sunset and they all played Baker Street with Tony taking on the saxophone solo. Their break was well deserved.

'I think we have a programme we can deliver,' suggested Alan.

'Bit early isn't it?' questioned Paul.

'Why?' asked Lizzie in a curt manner.

Paul scratched his left calf. 'You know. Farook. He was our driver wasn't he?'

'Yes, but he's dead and buried. In the arms of the Lord and I don't for minute believe he is not with us in spirit,' said Lizzie.

'I used to think like that,' Paul replied in a down-hearted manner.

'It's not about thinking, it's faith Paul. Surely that was the practice of the Salvation Army?'

'Yes, it was but I've had a change of heart.'

The coffees arrived. Marti offered a coffee to Paul. 'You two are looking serious,' she said.

'Yes, Paul is having a crisis of faith.'

'Not a bad thing Lizzie. So did I. I left my church and joined the Baha'i faith. Never looked back. Give him time, there's no rush in such matters.'

Tony brought his tea over to the assembled trio.

'I sometimes think religion is for a certain type of personality.'

'What do you mean Tony?'

'Well, and I'm thinking this through as I speak. If I was born in southern Ireland, I'd probably be a Catholic. Likewise if I was born in Islamabad, I'd be Muslim. So there is a cultural element.'

'Maybe so but America has no traditional State religion and France has practically divorced itself from the church in a drive towards a secular state.'

'I don't get what you are saying.'

With an uncertain smile Lizzie said; 'Culture is only

part of it. The central tenants of religion are that there is one God and all accept that.'

'What if I don't? I mean, who is God; where can I find Him; will he speak to me? I tell you it was easy being a Salvationist. I held my faith in my instrument.'

'So Paul why the change of belief?' asked Lizzie.

'Because I had fallen out of the Salvationist tradition and could not find a new home for my beliefs.'

'Have you given up looking?'

'I suppose I have. Just waiting for the answers to fall into place.'

Lizzie's look was one of pity laced with frustration. 'You'll find your life with God if you try a bit harder Paul and pray, yes don't forget to pray.'

The Superintendent was up early on Saturday morning.

So too was Tony because he had had a poor night's sleep. Dogged by the memory of Farook and his demise and the lack of police progress in the case as confirmed in the local Friday paper, he stirred his morning tea without looking at it. His stare was focussed on the nuthatch eating his column of ground nuts in his upside down fashion in his back garden. If waking, eating and sleeping were his only chores he would not mind returning to this world again someday as a bird. Not a nuthatch however, working upside down was for Australians. He laughed at his surreal thoughts.

Supt Graham had no smile on his face. He was already in the control room monitoring the road traffic as it entered the town. Police intelligence was warning him of buses from Edinburgh in the north and Manchester in the south setting off for the town's Muslim demonstration. They would arrive at 2 p.m. an hour before kickoff at Palmerston Park.

As the hour struck noon, the skies darkened. The first of the Muslim demonstrators had gone to the Mosque for prayers while others searched for halal shop vendors. By word of mouth the Muslim brotherhood were fed spiritually and nourished to satisfaction. The early football supporters had also been fed at the cafes buying sausage rolls, pies and Tunnock's caramel wafers. Many washed their mobile lunch down with cans of beer. Other supporters were in the Lion's Head ensuring by kickoff time that they were sufficiently fired up to shout out support for their team.

Circulating around the town were police cars and police officers were in close communication as they took up strategic positions along the route. The Muslim brotherhood assembled and their umbrellas were opening.

Rain, thought Superintendent Graham, just what was needed to quell any confrontations. But voices were being raised and confrontation seemed to be in the football supporters' minds.

A bolt of thunder made the Superintendent think it was the starting gun. But the sky was heavy. It had an angry bruising colour. Its strength to retain the rain could not hold. A flash of lightning preceded the tremendous downfall which followed. It did not stop. Gutter water was running in retreat towards leaf-blocked drains and cars were pulling off the road as drivers struggled to see ahead. The Muslim demonstrators were made of sterner stuff. They had organised themselves to march through the centre of the town and congregate in the local Park at the southern side. That was near the venue of the football match.

Still the rain fell making the ink-stained letters of the banners run and eliminate their visual protest. This led to chants being heard. "Allah Akbar. Allah Akbar. Muslims Targeted, Muslims Together, Allah Akbar".

Through the empty town streets the procession slowly walked chanting while from shop fronts and shop windows the public looked on dismayed both at the weather and the marchers. A smile or two came the marchers' way out of pity for their right to march was not in question but the day was. They had not chosen well.

At Palmerston Park the referee made a pitch inspection as the terraces were filling. He consulted his two linesmen as they treaded over the green surface gingerly. Their boots sank gradually in the waterlogged penalty area. They returned to their dressing rooms with their decision to be made. Supporters of both teams looked on from under their covered terraces to the rain still falling heavily. Even they were beginning to accept the game was too dangerous in its current wet condition and not one silver lining could be seen around any cloud. Rain had set in for the afternoon, at least. It therefore came as no surprise when the Tannoy came to life and declared the game abandoned. Both set of supporters gave a groan of disappointment but without much further delay, they set off towards the pubs in the town.

Superintendent Graham heard the game was abandoned and that meant the supporters were leaving the ground in their droves and heading for town and a possible confrontation. He had to redeploy his officers to the centre of town and try to guide the Muslim marchers along a parallel road and out of the path of the supporters.

The disappointed supporters of both teams heard the chants and then the marchers came into focus. For a moment they stood still, taking stock. They might not be outnumbered but the Muslim marchers were six deep and progressing in an unhurried manner.

A police car arrived and instructed the march to turn left then right again to keep them on their circuitous way to their park. However the car had arrived too late. The front marchers were already beyond the exit route and were closing ranks as the supporters approached. The football supporters began to chant. "Integrate and speak English." "Ban Sharia law." The Muslim marchers continued to march ignoring the supporters. "Muslims together; Not to be targeted."

The away supporters were enlightened about the death of the Imam and the bomb at the crematorium by home supporters. Most had heard about the offences while others received the news for the first time. Fuelled by drink and bravado the first stone was thrown.

Soon the two forces mingled throwing punches, stones and hoardings at each other. Scuffles broke out. Some continued their wrestling on the damp ground.

Shouts of pain and injury from both sides were heard while the police used a loudspeaker ordering the combatants to desist. Police notified them that they were on CCTV and offenders would be identified and prosecuted.

That did not seem to matter. The fighting grew tenser as the younger members of each group tried to settle scores while protecting their elderly supporters.

Superintendent Graham knew his forces were stretched. He telephoned the Chief Fire and Rescue officer. A water cannon was requested. It seemed a strange request as the rain had not stopped and the foes were soaked to the bone.

Police reinforcements were summoned and the local TV crew arrived with their reporter who glided between the confrontational rivals to gauge the true feeling of the combatants.

For over an hour the volume of excited Urdu voices and aggressive mumblings of football supporters mingled. The fans were venting their abandoned afternoon field of conflict to the streets of confrontation. The sound of ambulances drew nearer as police strived to divide the adversaries. It was a thankless task. Neither enemy wished to give ground. Fists flew and blood ran down faces further accentuated by the streams of falling rain.

The water cannon arrived gushing between the rivals and arced its powerful spray equally causing the warring factions to part. Most away supporters made their way to the rail station after that. The Muslim demonstrators then called their protest off, blaming the weather as much as the unexpected opposition. The local support dwindled, trampling over the Muslim banners as they took to side streets to avoid police identification. The rain subsided. The demonstrations were over. The ambulances carried off a few bloodied combatants and the police were stood down shortly afterwards.

The Superintendent returned to his office to make a report of the afternoon events. He flung his luminous jacket over a wooden chair and looked at his watch. An hour should be enough he thought and took a pen from his tunic.

'Bugger it,' he shouted. His pen had leaked ink.

# 20

# The Repercussions

As Superintendent Graham poured himself a strong 4.8 % can of dark beer to the strains of his Saturday night Match of the Day opening theme, his thoughts returned to the day's events.

Had the weather only been drier, the game would not have been cancelled and the demonstration would have gone off without a hitch. It was a fine line between a peaceful Muslim demonstration and instant conflagration. The press and TV coverage took only one view. The conflagration. He stroked his black Labrador and took another sip. Watford had just scored the first goal and his focus was now on the televised match.

Tony spent that Saturday afternoon at his office all on his own, tidying up papers, sorting out his next week's cases and reports and binning, shredding and shelving other articles. He did so to the strains of Vivaldi's Four Seasons. Playing was La Primavera No 1 Spring in E major. Classic FM was his default station as he was a morning Radio 4 riser while Radio 2 quietly played in his waiting room for his clients.

Looking out of his office into the darkening skies,

he distinguished a car with lights on approaching and coming to a halt. The lights were extinguished. Footsteps approached. Tony was alerted to the visitor and made his way through from his room to the open reception area. Then Tony recognised who it was.

'I saw your light was on when I was passing. Didn't know you worked weekends.'

'I don't usually Paul. Come in.'

'To be honest I wanted to see you.'

'Well, grab a seat. I'm here,' Tony said waving his hand towards a rocking chair in his room.

'I've not been on one of these for a long time,' Paul said with a quiet chuckle.

'So what's on your mind?'

Paul took in a deep breath, held it for a moment then exhaled.

'It's not easy to say. I've lost my faith completely and I've been having pains.'

'You told me you had seen your GP?'

'Yes, I have.'

The hush filled the room. Tony waited a moment longer in silence.

'I'll have to give up playing in the group.'

'Are you sure?

'Yes, very sure. I was sent for tests. Testicular and rectal cancer and both are aggressive.'

Tony's eyebrows tightened. His expression was sincere. 'I'm very sorry Paul. How are you coping?'

'I need to simply my life. No band music, no church attendance, just reflection and getting my things in order.'

'Can I ask how long you have known about this?'

'Almost two weeks now.'

'Shortly after Farook's murder or around then?'

Paul hesitated. His mind was engaged.

'Yes, about a couple of days after his murder. I do hope they get who did it soon. It's taking the police so long.'

'Don't you worry about that Paul.'

'Well, there's not much more I can say.'

Tony nodded in agreement. 'Do you have more hospital appointments?

'Oh appointments, yes loads. I have to call the McMillan nurses whenever I want. The hospital can do nothing now.'

Tony stood up and went over to Paul placing his hand on his shoulder and tapping it a few times. 'I can see why Lizzie could not understand your position.'

Paul smiled. 'She is a well-meaning lass. I just could not tell her the truth.'

'Do you have close friends to be with you?'

'My friends were the Salvationists. We were a happy band. I married the movement not a woman.'

'So no one other than the McMillan nurses to tend you?'

'And when they say, it's hospital, that's the end.'

Tony went to his bookcase. He selected a book.

'I was tidying up the office when you arrived, sorting out things. I'm not always reading textbooks you know. Some are simply rib tickling. Here, have this book Paul. It's one of the funniest I have ever read,'

Paul received the book and read its back cover first.

He smiled. 'The General danced at Dawn. It sounds good, sounds prophetic too.'

Tony interpreted his remark as being dark. It was not the mood appropriate for departing.

'Do you want me to keep in touch?'

Paul looked up as if a light bulb had been switched on. He smiled. 'Yes, I'd like that. Come visit me in hospital won't you?'

'Of course I will Paul. I'll let the McMillan nurses know so they can keep me informed.'

Paul nodded his agreement and stood up. He looked at his book once more and smiled. He tapped it against his left hand palm and made for the door.

'Thanks Tony. For all you have done for me.'

Paul was out of the room and heading towards his car as Tony still could not find appropriate parting words.


Monday was a bright sunny morning. Superintendent Graham was reading through the police report of Saturday's incident when the phone rang. His secretary informed him that Chief Superintendent David Rae of the Scottish Police had arrived from Glasgow. He lay down his report. As he made for the door, it opened and C/Supt Rae made straight for the seat in front of the Superintendent's desk.

'It's more than two weeks since this murder investigation started and just over a week since the explosion at the crematorium. You have made no progress, have you?'

The Superintendent realised he was in for a toasting. He began his defence.

'I don't think you know how strong the Muslim feelings are around this case? They have not been very cooperative.'

'You'd be upset too if you were Muslim.'

'I don't think so. We have a fingerprint to go on in the explosion case and we are hoping that if we can make that match, we'll almost certainly get the murderer too.'

'Pie in the sky, Mr Graham. What you have done is alienate the Muslim community on a hunch and caused a demonstration and a mass disturbance.'

'I am here to relieve you of your post Mr Graham. From now on I will be in charge of this double investigation. You, Superintendent Graham are demoted to Inspector. I will make this a force announcement in ten minutes. I leave you to gather your things from this room. I will take over in half an hour when I will address all senior ranks. I suggest Mr Graham, you cover for them when I speak to them.'

The Superintendent was in shock. Could he accept his demotion? He resolved to utter one last volley at his superior.

'If the needle is in a haystack; there is no need to look in the field. We had identified the most likely source of the offender.'

'You just don't get it. Do you? You should have arranged to take the fingerprints of all men in the community from 18-30 years of age. That way you would not be targeting the Muslim community. That way you would have had no demonstration; no pitched battle as the press and TV are calling it.'

'Chief Superintendent Rae, you will find my investigation team top notch. They will be devastated to learn of this encounter but I can save your embarrassment if you have any. I tender my resignation forthwith.'

Mr Graham unclipped his black tie and threw it down on his desk. His thirty eight years of policing had come to an abrupt end.

C/Supt Rae lifted the self-clipping tie and threw it at him as he made for the door.

'Here, keep it. You might be going to a funeral one day.'

# 21

# Behind the Silver Cloud

The following Tuesday while Tony was leafing through his list of clients the telephone rang.

'Ah Superintendent, how are things,' asked Tony as he recognised the salutation.

'No longer Superintendent these days....'

'Ah Chief Superintendent now. Congratulations.'

'No, no, no. I'm leading you astray. I am retired or perhaps I should be more truthful, I was asked to retire.'

Tony rapidly tried to interpret what he had heard. 'Obliged to retire?'

'Taken over by the city. I've been replaced by Chief Superintendent David Rae. Says we are not making enough progress on the murder and explosion. Keeping our eggs all in one basket, as it were. Not throwing a wider net around the place.'

'Doesn't seem wrong to me. The answer is surely within the Muslim community.'

'Well, he's covering all possibilities. There will be a fingerprinting of all males between 18 and 40. It's bound to show we are not making any progress. I can see some officers giving it a wide berth.'

'So he's already decided it wasn't a female.'

'Frankly, when this matter is resolved I could not care less. My days in the police are over. No longer Superintendent Graham. Just plain Colin Graham.'

The weekly paper's headline read: City Cop Takes Over Murder Inquiry. Tony read further. Chief Superintendent Rae was scathing of Colin Graham and showed a determination to have the cases wound up within the next few weeks. All males over 18 and 40 years of age were to make themselves available at any of the town's four substations to have thumb prints taken.

The C/Supt insisted that if they had a clear conscience, then their prints would prove it. All innocent prints would be shredded on completion. Extra staff had been called into record the prints which would take each individual only a couple of minutes of their time. The C/Supt suggested they should come with passports or recent utility bills or any other irrefutable documentation of identification.

It was time to get the clerics musical group up and running again. Tony sent out e-mails for them to come to a practice the following Friday. There was a full turn out.

Tony began the meeting by explaining why Paul would no longer be attending.

'Oh dear. I was a bit harsh on him last time we met. I was only trying to get him to hold on to his or any other faith but he seemed, well, out of this world. I now know why, poor Paul,' said Lizzie.

'Perhaps I should call and see him. Do you think that would be appreciated?'

'Alan, the McMillan nurses are likely to be there. Perhaps take their advice first,' suggested Tony.

'McMillan nurses,' said Marti, 'he seems to be very ill indeed.'

'One trombone down then,' said Ivan assembling his clarinet.

That evening they played for almost two hours and after a general discussion, principally led by Lizzie, they decided to give a town hall charity evening. Alan agreed to create the programme and all were pleased to hear he had plans to add a spot for a local comedian as well as a local poet.


All police stations had a steady flow of young men coming to have their fingerprints taken. A team of four experienced officers stood by to examine them immediately after the attendee's identification was complete. The Muslim community were anxious to attend as they felt their demonstration had led to this more comprehensive exercise.


Magdalene Smith was following the C/Supt's intervention in the cases. She was persistent. She kept an ear out for the fingerprinting progress. Her weekly column commented on the fact that no females were under suspicion and neither were teenagers who were known to be responsible for acts of vandalism and other more serious anti-social activities in the community. It also precluded the over 40s of either sex. It was not a truly comprehensive trawl. Chief Superintendent Rae responded saying that the police knew how to target the probable offenders. His policy of restricted targeting would please the wider law-abiding public.

The following day Magdalene had a scoop. She learned that three of the Muslim volunteers who had come forward could not provide conclusive evidence that they were bone fide citizens of the United Kingdom. One had brought a gas bill with another householder's name on it. Another brought a Pakistani passport informing the police he was only a visitor. However it soon emerged that he had outstayed his visitor permit. The third man spoke no English at all. An interpreter was called. He brought no identification and was detailed to join the others. All three men were taken to the UK Border Force's detention centre.

The news did not endear itself to the Muslim community and Faisal Muhammad made an appointment with the Chief Superintendent. It came about two days later.

Faisal's eyes grew large as he was escorted into the Chief's room. He was not going to beat about the bush. 'Sir, first you target the Muslim Community to have their fingerprints taken. Then you climb down and now target our community by a snatch and grab policy. This is intolerable.'

'Mr Muhammad it is a universal right to travel but not to outstay a welcome.'

'You do not understand that these men are helping their elders. They do the shopping and cook meals and tidy houses for our elderly community. That saves the NHS time and money and keeps beds free for the more needy.'

'That may be so, but the law is the law. They can

appeal against their detention but they are in this country illegally. I said illegally.'

Faisal turned to leave the office. 'You come here and sack the Superintendent. Don't think you can do any better.' Then he left, slamming the door behind him in a moment of anger. The walls seemed to shudder. The wall calendar no longer hung perpendicularly and his glass of water on his desk rippled.

Chief Superintendent Rae lifted a desk folder and slammed it down. As a senior pen-pusher he had not been used to dealing with the public for some time. All he could hope for now was a fingerprint matching the suspect.


Dr Karen Kane's appointment was the last for the day. She had requested an appointment after the last musical practice. What would be her reason? Tony had no idea but he had subconsciously tidied his office before she arrived.

'Come in Karen. Take a seat.'

Karen brought a seat nearer to Tony's desk. He noticed she was wearing makeup, not something she did at music practice. He sensed some perfume in the air too.

'So I presume no incidents to tell me?'

'Tony, I'd like to thank you sincerely for all you have done. You have taken me from that dark place, organised the medication, and that's given me a more confident take on the world.'

'Hmmm on the world even,' Tony clarified.

'Well makes me feel more on top of life perhaps.'

Tony smiled taking in the beauty of her face. She did not speak and Tony struggled to find his words. The silence lasted almost ten seconds, a time in which eyes were moving all over the place in embarrassment, expectation, doubt and hope.

Karen's eyes dropped down to her lap. Then she looked up into Tony's eyes.

'Tony...I.....I'm not sure....I...' she smiled then relaxed defeated in sharing her thoughts.

'Karen, I think you have a spell on me and it's most efficacious.'

He looked to see what reaction his thoughts might have and she was clearly smiling so widely he could see her gleaming teeth.

'I was not aware I had the power to make spells but....if spells are about....Tony, I think I'm under a spell too.'

Tony came towards her and lifted her hand.

'I am divorced, have been for some time. In the past few years I've settled here in the south-west getting into golf, walks, Rotary and work. Thought my days ahead would be alone but wondering if it had to be that way.'

Karen opened her mouth but Tony placed his finger on her lips. 'Let me have my say first. I was beginning to think I'd live life alone from now on. Then through circumstances, you came onto my books as it were. I knew right from the start that you took my breath away. I realised if I ever settled down again with a partner it would be someone just like you. And the feeling grew. On our Rambling excursions I've seen you as a caring member, thoughtful, fun-loving and entertaining. What more could a man wish for? Karen, I think I've said enough. Have I offended you?'

Karen blushed a dark pink and her dimples produced deep shadows. Tony was pleased she had not run out of the room threatening him but what was on her mind?

She stood up a foot or two away from him. Her arms drooped by her side.

'Tony, will you kiss me?'

Tony smiled at her, raising his arms he stepped forward and held her close. He lowered his head and kissed both of her dimples. She closed her eyes. She pouted her lips and his met hers.

They parted, taking a step back.

'I have to be honest. I simply had to let you go. Had you stayed on my books my professional standing was in question. I could have lost my job. Dating a patient, it's a big no-no. But I could justify releasing you.'

'Oh I hope not releasing me, just after we have kissed?'

'I think we need to have time to talk. Get to know each other better. Are you free tomorrow night?'

'Of course I am,' she replied smiling from ear to ear.

'But what about your music preparation on a Saturday night?' he asked with concern etched on his brow.

'I can cope I assure you,' she said in a low sexy voice.

'Let me take you to Primo Piano.'

'The Italian restaurant?'

'Yes, in town. I know the manager. He'll give us some quiet discretion.'

'Very thoughtful,' she said.

Tony smiled relieved that his choice suited her. 'Then I'll pick you up from your home at 7.00pm?'

'Just in case the neighbours pry, will you be in disguise?' she teased.

'Oh yes certainly. I intend to drop my professional guard.'

# 22

# An Interrupted Meal

Tony had been on cloud nine all day. There had been a spring in his step. He polished his shoes and had a body cleansing thorough shower. He had ironed his new shirt the night before and had gone to bed wondering where this relationship might lead him. Was this to be a brief romance or something which might develop into something much more lasting? He just was not completely sure. Yet he knew he did not want to let her go. He certainly found Karen attractive. She was well educated and an expert in her musical sphere. He'd like to hear her play more. But was the keyboard a suitable suitor for the saxophone? He doubted that. The Belgian Adolphe Sax, who invented the saxophone, was generations in front of the middle aged baroque sonatas. He had not been in a relationship for some time. Was it too late for him to adjust his ways? The questions kept mounting to fill his grey matter. How much could it hold?

He wore a candy pink striped shirt and found a contrasting tie. Tie or no tie? Tie was for work; what image was he trying to create? He took off his tie and returned it to its rack. He found a lamb's wool jersey and wore that instead. Now, a jacket or not? No, his leather jacket would get him there and then he'd discard it. That would be his smart/casual sartorial option. He hoped Karen had not dressed to the hilt.

He drove up to her driveway to find her closing her front door. There was neither need nor time for him to get out of the car. That might flummox the neighbours he thought on this first occasion although there was no doubt about Karen's attire. She was going out on a date.

As they set off, Karen teased.

'Do you want me to hide my face and slide down the seat?'

Tony laughed. 'So you are in MI5?'

'Too scary for me.'

'Tell me; does music fill your head like words and images fill an author's mind?'

'Good question. I've not really thought about that. Do I hear music in my head? Yes, most of the time. Don't you, after all you play music too?'

Tony thought for a moment. 'Songs, tunes, yes a few times a day but not usually at work.'

'So you don't play Classic FM at lunchtime?

'Lunchtime is Radio 4, the news,' said Tony realising that was such a conservative response.

They spoke of music, naturally, sought out mutual friends or acquaintances and even tackled some doctrinal views before the car parked opposite Prima Piano.

'Dr Scriven?' inquired the head waiter.

'Yes,' replied Tony.

'This way please, your table is over here, in the far corner.'

The waiter ensured they were comfortably seated and gave Tony the wine list and menu.

'Here, have the menu. Meanwhile, can I interest you in a red, white or rosé wine?'

'Do you drink yourself?'

'Never when I'm driving. It means a whisky some nights and a beer with an evening meal sometimes. But you are not driving so enjoy a wine, why don't you?'

'Then this Beaujolais 2013 St Pierre de Vances, they do it in glasses as well as half bottles.'

'Then a half bottle?'

'Goodness no, that would make me sing! A glass will be more than sufficient.'

Orders were taken and Tony raised his ginger beer to her glass.

'A toast. To a pleasant evening ....and an adventure begun.'

'To a pleasant evening and ...what? An adventure begun?' she laughed.

'Yes, aren't all new situations an adventure waiting to unravel?' asked Tony.

Soon they had discovered Tony was her senior by three years. By the time the main course arrived they had learned each other's backgrounds from birth to student days, first loves and what had brought them to the same town. There was only one other matter to investigate.

'So divorce and no family?'

Tony wiped his mouth with his serviette.

'Or why did I leave general practice to become a psychiatrist? It's the same question for me. We had a daughter.....'

'Had a daughter?'

Tony raised his hand gently to signal he had the floor. 'Yes, had a daughter, Carole. She was a Christmas baby. Of course she was. A smart girl who had a satisfying childhood but the teenage years got to her. Anorexic she became. And two years later, we lost her. She slipped from our life; aged fourteen on the cusp of what should have been her best years. Absolutely devastated me.

Getting into her mind became my obsession and so I retrained to understand the condition better for the sake of others suffering with this dreadful disease. And that's why I am a psychiatrist.'

'Tony, I am so very sorry for you losing a daughter. It must be particularly hard for a father.'

Tony felt a tear gather, forming a congregation of sorrow but the waiter arrived with the profiteroles. They breathed under a lair of melted chocolate on Karen's plate while Tony's Eton Mess was served in a conical glass with a long spoon. They discovered they both had a sweet tooth.

Karen spoke of boyfriends in the past but none stood up to the mark when it came to her musical interests and her love of outdoor activities. She accepted marriage would slip by until one last chance came her way.

The waiter then escorted them over to the roaring fireplace and a twin seated alcove where coffee was served.

'I see you like your coffee black,' said Tony.

'Yes milk takes away the flavour of the coffee. Do you usually have hot chocolate after dinner?'

Tony dropped his left hand onto Karen's knee and lightly rubbed it. 'Actually I quite like Horlicks, though it is not appropriate to reveal that on this first date.'

'Why ever not? I do want to know the real Tony,' she said playfully. Just as Tony was raising the romantic stakes his mobile phone went off.

'Damn, I should have had that on silent mode. Do you mind?'

'As long as it's not a threesome you have in mind,' she laughed but Tony already had the mobile to his ear.

'Yes, okay. Then I should come over tonight?'

Karen saw the gravity on Tony's face. A client needing his expertise at the hospital or clinic, Karen thought. Well, how could she complain, after all that was how they first met all those weeks ago. Tony switched off his mobile and returned it to his pocket.

'Karen, that was a McMillan nurse. Paul has been taken into hospital. It's looking grim. I promised I'd see him before...well...before he died. Do you mind?'

'Oh, I knew Paul well too. Can I come with you?'

'Of course, I'd like you to.'


On the way to the hospital, they spoke of Paul's departure from the Salvationists. Karen recalled donating to them for Christmas gifts for deprived children. She remembered Paul holding onto his trombone as he held a bucket. 'He's not very old is he?'

'I think he's fifty nine. Cancer comes to all ages. It makes him look older too.'

'So you think he's near death?'

'We cannot be sure. The will to live is strong in some but I don't think he'll get home again.'

'Do you think a strong faith can make a dying patient hold out?'

'I am sure it can. But what's the point. We all die.'

It seemed a practical reply. She liked Tony's clear thinking.

They made their way to the town's general hospital at the end of the by-pass. Tony was on home territory. They made their way to the cancer unit and the control desk.

'Dr Scriven. It is good to see you, I haven't seen you for a while,' said the middle-aged desk nurse. Is it a relative or patient you have come to visit?' she asked noting Dr Scriven's casual attire.

'A patient, Paul Risk. Is he able to take visitors?'

'Yes, he's under an anaesthetic you understand. His speech may be a bit slurred.'

'I don't think I've met your wife Dr Scriven,' she said smiling at Karen.

Tony turned round, 'No, Dr Kane has joined me this evening.'

'Oh I am sorry. Jumping to wrong conclusions, do forgive me,' said the nurse blushing. 'Please follow me and I will lead you to him.'

They walked along the dimly lit corridor to a single room where they entered and saw Paul with his eyes closed lying propped up on his back.

'I'll leave you with him,' said the nurse drawing a second chair up for Dr Kane. 'Let me know if you need anything else Doctor,' she said looking first at Tony and then Karen with an apologetic misunderstanding look. She left closing the door behind her.

They sat together on either side of his bed in silence for a few moments then Tony stretched out his hand and held Paul's wrist.

Paul opened his eyes a few seconds later and tried to focus.

'Tony?' Paul said in a whisper.

'Yes, Paul and I've also brought Karen Kane.'

Paul turned his head and tried to focus on Karen.

'Oh, I thought you'd come alone.'

Karen jolted. 'Then perhaps I should be excused?'

'No, Karen. I'm glad you are both here. Yes, very glad you are both here.'

'It's okay Paul don't exhaust yourself,' said Tony

Paul nodded and turned his head towards his travel clock.

'It's late. I've been sleeping a lot so I'm quite alert. How about you both?'

Karen wanted to say where they had been but thought that inappropriate. Tony was less reserved.

'We went out for a meal, that's when I got the message from the nurses.'

'Sorry I spoiled your night,' said Paul trying to raise the white sheet further up. Karen did it for him.

'You have nothing to be sorry about, Paul.'

Paul's eyes fell down to the bed covers. He tried to clear his throat. He coughed a few times.

'Paul....and Karen, I have a lot to be sorry about.'

'Don't you worry. You must not talk like this.

Just relax. Don't get bothered,' said Karen.

'But I must be honest with you. I...killed Farook.'

The atmosphere froze.

'What?' said Tony who raised his voice as Karen's lips said the same silently.

'Yes, if you go down to my back garden and look under the green hut, you will find the Islamic Kindjal. It's a traditional Afghan warrior's knife. It will be there. I put it there after I killed Farook.'

'You Paul, killed Farook? But why?'

Paul tried to sit up. Tony helped him.

'You did not know Farook completely, did you? I mean, you knew he was gay?'

Tony had no knowledge of what he was saying.

'Yes the Mosque knew he wanted to modernise their worship and be more multicultural but they got rid of him because they found out he was gay. That depressed him and so he tried to take his life, but that I am sure you knew.'

'Okay,' said Tony realising he had missed a very important side to Farook. 'But what's that got to do with you?'

'You have my file. You know I had difficulty dealing with my sexuality. A paedophile no less. But that was a long time ago. My identity remained in question. But I got to know Farook and wondered if we could live together. I went to his house and tried to have sex with him. He was not as keen as I was and I was too forceful, I know I was. That's when Farook took the decorative

Kindjal from the wall. I knew he wanted to kill me. I saw it in his eyes, so I fought with him and managed to get it from him. I should have stopped there.' Paul's eyes were watering. They were not crocodile tears.

'You mean you stabbed him to death?'

Paul nodded. 'Yes, Tony. God knows how many times I did it but once I started I knew I had to go through with it.

If only it hadn't been that way. If he had not displayed that knife on the wall, it would not have ended as it did.'

The ward fell silent for a moment as the reality sank in. Before them was the man who murdered Frank. God how the trail led to him no one could have imagined.

Then Tony remembered what Superintendent Graham had said about catch one and he'd solve the other offence.

'Paul, did you have anything to do with the explosion at the cemetery?' asked Tony.

Paul nodded for a while before informing them.

'The murder focussed on the Muslim community because Farook had been exiled from them but I felt it would not find an accused there, no matter how long they tried. After his funeral service there would be a cremation. I knew Muslims did not cremate and so that would strengthen the conclusion that a Muslim had been behind the explosion. With both incidents leaning towards the Muslim community, I felt I would not be found out.'

'But Paul, why are you telling us this now?' asked Karen.

'You might not believe me, but I wanted to meet my Maker with guilt yes, but also with the knowledge that no one else can be sought for these offences. Does that make sense?'

'Yes Paul. But having told us, we must relay this evidence to the police.'

'Yes, I accept that. I accept that.'

The nurse came in at that point and checked his blood pressure. 'Dr Scriven, I think Mr Risk has had a long enough chat. You may wish to come tomorrow.'

'Yes, I think that would be in order. Sleep well Paul,' said Tony.

'Paul, thank you. You did the right thing,' said Karen.

# 23

# You Are My Sunshine

Tony asked for an appointment with the Chief Superintendent at the front desk. The secretary phoned and the C/Supt placed the phone back on the cradle.

'He does not wish to see you,' she said lowering her glasses to peer over them

Tony huffed. 'Perhaps you can inform him that I know the name of the murderer and who planted the bomb at the crematorium.'

The secretary relayed the additional information with a smile at Tony.

Three minutes later Chief Superintendent Rae arrived downstairs to meet Tony.

'Dr Scriven, pleased to meet you. I am told you have some information to share? Do come this way,' he said going out of his way to shake his hand sincerely and greet him warmly.

Tony did not fall for his antics. He remained serious. 'Indeed I have. You may wish to know that I also know where the Kindjal is.'

'Kindjal? Dr Scriven.'

'Yes, a Kindjal, an Afghan knife, the murder weapon.'

Later that morning the Kindjal was in police possession

as a production. The police then went to the hospital and took a fingerprint and three hours later they returned with a duty solicitor to the ward for Paul Risk to be charged with the murder of Farook Elahi aka Frank Armour and the attempted murder of mourners at the crematorium. The police report was then sent to the Procurator Fiscal who noted the accused was not in custody.

Paul's condition deteriorated overnight. The effort exerted by him in revealing the truth had weakened him. A higher doze of morphine was delivered.

Fiscal Fiona Harvie came to visit Mr Paul Risk in hospital to ascertain his state of mind and psyche. She could not waken him from his deep slumber but she left his statement for him to sign if he was able. She returned to her desk knowing that as he was not in custody, she did not have to expedite the case.

Two days later Paul died. The same day the weekly Standard blazed on its front page:

## MAN ACCUSED OF FAROOK ELAHI's MURDER AND ATTEMPTED MASS MURDER AT THE CREMATORIUM.

Full story on pages 1, 3 and 4.

Tony had a copy of the paper when he called at Karen's home an hour earlier than his usual closing time.

When he entered her house, she turned round after closing the door and smiled. They stood like guilty children for a moment then Tony took a step forward and Karen raised herself up on her tiptoes. They kissed.

Then came the embrace. They were still clung together when Tony waved the paper he held behind her back.

'Have you read the Standard today?'

'No, why should I have?' asked Karen.

'Here, read it and I'll put the kettle on.'

Two weeks later Tony received a letter from the council of the Professional Association of Psychiatrists. It contained one long paragraph. It spoke of the risks in the profession to inappropriate liaisons which the profession would not tolerate but where there was a mutual and developing relationship with honest intentions, and the patient was no longer a client, the profession would not stand in the way of any medical practitioner. It was signed by the Society of Psychiatrists' Chairman.

Karen was delighted to read the letter and Tony felt a silent burden lifted from his shoulders. It was up to him now to make the relationship develop with honest intentions.

Tony began attending church. At first it was to hear Karen play the organ but the more he attended, the more he was drawn into the life of the congregation. In time he joined the membership of St George's Church, and six months later Dr Tony Scriven and Dr Karen Kane married in that church. At the reception at the Cassa Mia restaurant, Alan played electric guitar and Ivan the clarinet with Marty on drums. Karen took to the keyboard and Tony's saxophone was on hand too. But not before Karen and Tony danced their first dance, You Are My Sunshine.

## THE END

# SPOT CHECKS

| | |
|---|---|
| Bible or Koran | Both at times |
| Wafer or Chapatti | Chapatti |
| Prayer or Reflection | Reflection |
| Owl or Lark | Owl |
| Twitter or Newspaper | Newspaper |
| Wine or Water | Water (Teetotal) |
| Kneel or Sit | Sit |
| Bach or Wesley | Both |
| Old or New Testament | Old: The Psalms |
| | New: Gospel of Luke |
| Tran substantial or Spiritual | Spiritual |
| Trombone or Drum | Trombone |
| What disc to take on a Desert Island | The Pearl Fisher's Duet |
| The book at your bedside | Death is a Welcome Guest by Louise Welsh |
| Tell us a secret | I have two international sporting caps. |
| Can't live without | a smile each day. |

# Interview with the Author

**What inspired you to write this novella?**

My father was a Church of Scotland minister and he worked all week except on a Monday morning when he played golf with a sports journalist. I heard of many clerics who had mental health issues. The common risk of ministers or priests is that they are not regular team members and are seen as individuals. This increases the need for them to mix and socialise out with their parish.

**Do you think the novella will upset many who have faith?**

No, I doubt it. It is a story, not a biography. The biography of my religious encounters appears at the front. It only shows I have had insights to many religious beliefs. Anyway, aren't those with faith forgiving?

**Is there a message in the story?**

The message is that it is not only legal but surprisingly common for one individual to change from one denomination to another or to leave all to become either agnostic or atheist. It must be said that there is NO religion which denies any individual to change their religion. Anyone who disagrees does so from a biased view and cannot be authorised by any religious text.

# Reading Group Questions

1 What part does religion play in your life?

2 If your religion or none was one you had to change, which religion would you chose to change to and why.

3 Can you think of any other worker's occupation which could suffer from mental health because of isolation?

4 How difficult or professional is it for a doctor and patient relation to develop or a police officer and an accused perhaps? Think of prisoner Jimmy Boyle and his wife Dr Trevelyan, his psychiatrist.

5 How does this novella compare with Miller's other books?

# Books by Miller Caldwell

## The Novels

### Operation Oboe
A Scottish widow of a Hamburg doctor becomes a Second World War spy in West Africa.

### The Last Shepherd
An arrogant city banker clashes with the rural ways of the Last Shepherd.

### Restless Waves
A writer in residence aboard a cruise ship faces daemons on board and on shore.

### Miss Martha Douglas
A nurse and seamstress, Martha obtains a Royal position but becomes a suffragette and when released from prison serves in the trenches where she finds true love.

### The Parrot's Tale
The comic tale of an escaped parrot in the Scottish countryside sits alongside the tragedy of a missing girl. The search is underway for both but it is the parrot which comes up trumps.

## The Crazy Psychologist

Set on Rousay in the Orkney Islands, the childhood difficulties of Dr Angie Lawrence come to light to explain her bizarre treatment programmes while her fragmented family come to terms with their past and her marriage is secured. To hear the BBC interview go to:

http://www.troubador.co.uk/news.asp?newsID=6514

## The Reluctant Spy

This novel is soon to be a film and traditionally published book. Hilda becomes a double agent. Controlled by Gerhardt Eicke in Germany and Lawrence Thornton in Britain, how could Hilda cope under the strain and how did one handler confront her at the point of his death? The book is based on the life of the author's relative.

## A Lingering Crime

A novella about circumstantial evidence and how it can be used in courts for both the accused and victim. This novella is heading to be an episode in a crime series on TV and possibly on Netflix.

# Biographies

## Untied Laces
The author's autobiography

## Jim's Retiring Collection
The illustrated cartoons and musings of a city and then

rural Church of Scotland minister gathered and set in biblical context.

### Poet's Progeny
A line of decent of Robert Burns maintains his influence over succeeding generations.

### 7 point 7 on the Richter Scale
The diary of the Camp Manger in the NWFP of the Islamic Republic of Pakistan following the 2005 earthquake.

### Take the Lead
The quirks of dogs experienced by the author over his life in Scotland, Pakistan and Ghana, together with canine poetry and recording medical advances in their training.

## Children's Books

### Chaz the Friendly Crocodile
Chaz the Nigerian Crocodile visits a Scottish river to help people keep their towns tidy. Set in poetry, this is a book all parents require to train their growing children.

### Lawrence the Lion Seeks Work
No more animals are in the circuses. So what happened when Lawrence the Lion went in search of a new job?

### Danny the Spotless Dalmatian
All Dalmatian puppies have no spots at birth. They appear after three weeks. But Danny's spots never

appeared. Follow him as he searches for spots to make him a real Dalmatian.

## Self Help

### Have you seen my Ummm...Memory?
A valuable booklet for all whose memories are declining. Student memory tips as well as advice for those more senior moments to get through life.

### Ponderings   IN LARGE PRINT
Poems and short stories, as it says, in large print.

### It's Me Honest It Is
A short book commissioned by the School of Nursing to record the decades of the elderly and to offer them a page for their last requests. It is a valuable aid for family members as well as medical attendants.

### Coming in 2018

### The Reluctant Spy
Earmarked to be a feature film by film agent Mathilda Vuillermoz.

### Love in Flanders Trenches
A suffragette leaves prison to serve in the trenches where she finds love.